MW01118250

Benjamin Bishop

ERINTENDENT
OF
SCHOOLS
PRINCIPAL

Benjamin Bishop

Bernard F. Ryder

VANTAGE PRESS
New York

FIRST EDITION

All rights reserved, including the right of
reproduction in whole or in part in any form.

Copyright © 2002 by Bernard F. Ryder

Published by Vantage Press, Inc.
516 West 34th Street, New York, New York 10001

Manufactured in the United States of America
ISBN: 0-533-13959-7

Library of Congress Catalog Card No.: 01-130523

0 9 8 7 6 5 4 3 2 1

To
Gretchen, Chris, Jeff, Priscilla and Suellen

Contents

Acknowledgments ix
Preface xi
Introduction xiii

Teacher
The First Day 1
Lunch Duty: Eight Switchblades 5
Discipline: The Principal's Son 8
The Open Door 10
Sick Leave 16
Stolen Property 19
Fire 22
The Challenge 25
Horsepower 27
Twenty-Pound Test Monofilament 29
Parents' Night 33
Captain Football Graduates 38
Senior Prom 42
National Honor Society 46
The Tropics 48
A Ball for Christmas 53
Modern Technology 56
Faculty Mischief 59
Names and Nicknames 62
The Wheelchair 64
The General's Son 67
Author's Comment: Entrance Age 71
Principal
Welcome?? 77
Truant 81

Boxing Lessons 84
The Missing Rankbook 86
Adult Education 92
I Am a Teacher 96
That's My Daughter 100
The Music Teacher 103
Bomb Scare 108
Not So 113
Holiday Letters 120
The New Superintendent 123
Study Hall 130
New Job 132
Vietnam 138
Senior Play 147
The Substitute 152
The Hearing 155
Mischief—Happenings 159
Drugs 166
Marriage—Murder 171
Looking Back 173
Author's Comment: Subject Matter Majors 175
Superintendent
The First Month 179
Fire Him 189
Expelled 196
The Budget 202
Payroll Problems 205
The Architect 209
Peephole 221
The Reference 227
Phone Call 232
Coach(es) 236
Ten Percent 243
Political Wrath 248
Retired 255
Author's Comment: Classroom Visits 257

Acknowledgments

THANK YOU

I am deeply indebted to my bride of 42 years, Nancy Anne Partridge, whose quiet strength and support enabled me to act with integrity throughout my life's journey in the most difficult as well as in the best of times.

THANK YOU

To the educators, support staff, students and parents whose paths I shared throughout this odyssey of my life. I feel privileged to have worked with you. Particular thanks go to Winifred (Winnie) Del Ponte for her imaginative drawings as contained in this publication.

THANK YOU

To my five wonderful children (adults now!) for your support and belief in Dad.

THANK YOU

To my special friend "Jo," whose generous encouragement

rekindled my desire to complete this task which I had abandoned a few years ago.

THANK YOU

Dear reader. I hope you enjoy reading these selected pages from Benjamin Bishop's imaginative diary.

Preface

I am Benjamin Bishop. I am an Educator.

As a young child, I disliked school immensely. I had no intention of becoming a teacher. Years later, I realized that I thoroughly enjoyed my career as an educator! The author of this story intends to tell you of his many happy and sometimes frustrating adventures as a teacher, as a principal and as a chief school administrator. The author believed that he had to include a few important points of his life which will help you, the reader, to more fully comprehend his message. He incorporates a few of these anecdotes in each book of his story on my life, i.e. Mr. Bishop—Teacher—Principal—Superintendent.

Most of my elementary school teachers can clearly recall several incidents involving my early academic career which readily illustrate this point. I rarely did my homework and *I refused to read books for book reports.*

Throughout my three years of junior high school English, the teacher frequently assigned a book report for homework. This weekly assignment usually frustrated me because the teacher expected all of us to read a book AND then to write a report on the story we had just read.

Our benevolent instructors always gave us a list of books available in the city library. This meant that they (all of them!) expected me—Ben Bishop—to go to the library, select a book, take it home AND to read it. Then I was to write a report listing the title, the author, and publisher, along with a brief review of the story. Imagine how much time I saved by simply creating a book title, author, publisher as well as a short synopsis of the book's imaginary contents. I was always pleasantly surprised when my report came back with an A or B letter grade.

I refused to memorize poetry—I would not recite poetry in the classroom when requested to do so by the teacher. I frequently explained to her that poetry was for girls—it was not a subject for boys, at least not this boy. I refused to participate in such recitations. Per my favorite teacher's request, I stayed after school every afternoon from early October through to the last week in April because my teacher was determined that I would recite the poem *If* by Rudyard Kipling. Obviously she was just as stubborn as I was. She won the war in late April when I stood up and quickly recited *If* at 3:45 that day so many years ago. My buddies were outside playing baseball AND I wanted to join them.

Finally it must be noted that I was a subject matter major in college. I was not an education major!! Upon graduation, I planned to join the army and advance through the ranks as quickly as I could. Unfortunately I was hospitalized for five weeks and the army refused to accept me as a result of my lung operation. A friend gave me a newspaper ad which identified a local high school searching for a math teacher. Needing a job, I applied for the vacant position AND to my great surprise, I was hired.

Thus the saga of Benjamin Bishop began. Now my friend, the author, will attempt to tell my story. Please turn the page and as you progress through my story feel free to laugh at Ben as he discovers that teaching is the most important profession in our universe.

Introduction

The saga of Benjamin Bishop was written by taking selected passages from his imaginative diary. Benjamin Bishop's Ed-Ventures reflect his 40-year journey as an educator.

As I developed his journal of service as a teacher and as an administrator, I decided that his story would be more interesting if I adopted the media's attitude. It rarely is worthwhile preparing stories for the press which are about positive events in life. Since society's difficulties garner a far larger audience, I didn't include the thousands of days in which Mr. Bishop had a most rewarding teaching and/or administrative experience.

One must ponder the greater picture when he/she thinks about the happenings in America's schoolrooms. Most of the children in our public schools receive a *good* education in spite of what may be happening in their world.

As the author/creator of these unique stories, I have taken the liberty of presenting my personal beliefs on three academic issues. These thoughts are conveniently placed at the end of each unit of this book.

Benjamin Bishop

Teacher

The First Day

Mr. Bishop looked up at the huge wall clock in his new classroom. THREE MINUTES and his teaching career would begin. Ben had completed the paperwork of student registrations, class scheduling, and the other office-mandated activities of homeroom period. The principal's first day paperwork, required of all students, was completed in the allocated fifteen-minute homeroom period which started each school day. Ben's seating plan and the busy paperwork schedule of that fifteen-minute period had kept everyone occupied. Thus no problems occurred during homeroom.

THREE MINUTES to go. Ben stared at the clock as he asked himself the BIG question, "Okay, Mr. Bishop, remember your student days AND your behavior in the classroom!!! What are you going to do NOW?"

As the 37 students entered their first algebra class with the new teacher, not one of them realized that their teacher was more nervous than any student in the entire school building. Benjamin had upchucked his breakfast that morning as he got ready to start his teaching career.

The clock ticked off the last three minutes of Mr. Bishop's non-teaching life. Ben agonizingly recalled the street scene of two weeks ago. He and his bride had finished setting up their first apartment. The young couple decided to drive downtown to check out the stores. The downtown district intrigued Ben's new bride; it appeared to be a great place to shop. As the Bishops were inserting a quarter into the parking meter, a convertible pulled into the vacant spot immediately in front of them. Six tough looking high school aged thugs piled out of the car. Ben turned to his wife and said, "If I have to teach those characters—I'm in BIG trouble."

The bell rang and more than one thousand high school students charged out of their homerooms and down the halls to encounter their first period teachers. Thirty-seven students sat down and stared at their new algebra teacher. On the chalkboard they saw his name in big print: MR. BISHOP. Then they noticed the message on the bulletin board adjacent to the classroom door. Homework assignments for the first week AND test dates for the month of September. WOW!!

Ben passed out sheets of paper to his students, whose names he would learn during this, their first week of school. Mr. Bishop was determined that no student would succeed in putting a fake name on his textbook assignment sheet. The seating chart was not going to become a student-developed-joke: leaving a seat for the Lone Ranger.

He instructed his students to fill out all of the office forms plus his own seating charts, etc. "Once you have completed the office paperwork, I expect you to read the first four pages of the algebra text," announced Ben. He planned to begin his classes as soon as all the first day paperwork had been completed.

Ben hadn't realized that his first day had passed so quickly. The day ended six math classes later—at 2:45 P.M. The new teacher was exhausted. He hadn't noticed the clock hands silently marching around the dial at any time during that first day since his three-minute panic period at the start of his teaching day. Ben went home to analyze what had happened during his first day. He asked himself and his wife Heather, "What did I do to make this first day so successful? What did the students do that made my day successful?" Ben spent the rest of his teaching career using the lessons he learned from his students. In simplest terms he kept them busy in positive, meaningful and mind-challenging activities.

Every class started as soon as all of the students were in their seats. Even if the bell hadn't rung, Ben would begin challenging his students with the mathematical adventures of the new day.

One day in the middle of November, Ben's wife told him that he enjoyed teaching. But during the evening meal Ben disagreed with Heather's comment that he was really enjoying himself as a teacher. After listening to Heather's analysis of their supper time conversations, Ben thought about Heather's reaction(s) to his supper time stories over the past two and one-half months. The next day, Ben was smiling; he had kept his breakfast down for the first time since he had started teaching! He was teaching on a full stomach.

The students and Mr. Bishop learned to enjoy each other's unique behavioral patterns. A majority of Ben's students did quite well on their college board examinations. All of his calculus students scored at the college credit level. Throughout his career, Ben frequently asked Heather, "Why did the principal send all good kids to me?" Even when Ben taught general math and physics to last year's dropouts, he continued to wonder why the principal always assigned the good kids to him.

Mr. Bishop had established a simple behavioral standard for himself and for his students. "We will all act like ladies and gentlemen," said Ben. "And my personal definition of proper behavior will be the standard for all of us."

As a first year teacher, Ben was given several non-teaching duties. He was expected to check all 87 homeroom registers every month. He went over the statistics in each attendance register and reported to the school superintendent as to their accuracy. His additional duties included his serving as the junior class ring selection committee advisor, junior prom advisor and as the lunch room monitor (first lunch).

The class ring selection committee met early in November to interview the five ring company salesmen. One company representative happily informed the ring committee that his company had held the contract for the past six years. He announced that since his company already had the dies cut for this year's ring that he had a greater margin to work with. Mr. Bishop and his student committee members were more than simply astonished to hear that the salesman would pay each student and their teacher ten dollars per ring sold. The students immediately put this unusual story into writing and, with their advisor, handed same to the principal. Ben was extremely proud of his students when they selected a new company to make and to sell the class rings that year.

Lunch Duty: Eight Switchblades

Ben had asked for additional duties in order to make some extra money. He was surprised to discover that his teacher's paycheck wasn't sufficient to pay his living expenses. One additional task he picked up was lunch duty. Ben was expected to eat his lunch in seven minutes. After he had finished eating, he would go outside to patrol the school grounds. Most of the time he walked about the assigned area observing his youthful charges talking, running, playing games, etc.

One warm sunny day Ben's routine changed dramatically. A group of students were huddled at the edge of the schoolyard. As Mr. Bishop strolled over to the area, each step he took brought a hope that the group would disperse. Ben wasn't that lucky. One young man was smoking. Ben assumed that he had encountered a simple problem. He told the other boys to leave the area. They did. Thus Ben was able to confront the single student remaining in the area. Actually the smoker wasn't on school property. Ben asked him if he was a city high school student. Jim C. responded, "What do you care?"

After further questioning Mr. Bishop learned that Jim C. was not only a student caught smoking but that he also was a truant. Jim C. purposefully challenged Mr. Bishop to see what would happen next.

Ben walked Jim across the schoolyard toward the principal's office. He explained to Jim that he, Mr. Bishop, intended to have young Jim suspended. Jim said that he wasn't interested in the opinions of any "chicken teacher." "Besides," he pointed out, "Mr. Hughe had never suspended any student in his twenty years as a principal."

Ben approached Mr. Hughe, the principal, and firmly demanded that he suspend Jim C. immediately because of truancy and smoking on school grounds. (Jim C. had smoked another cigarette as he walked across the school grounds with Mr. Bishop.) Mr. Hughe told Jim to leave the school and to never come back. Ben was shocked by Mr. Hughe's outburst. Jim C. quickly left the building. As Jim left, Ben recalled seeing him jumping out of a convertible, only two weeks before the start of the school year!

As the weeks passed, Ben completely forgot about the incident. On a cool November evening Ben attended his Kiwanis Club meeting, enjoyed having dinner with his Kiwanis friends and the charity preparations for the upcoming holidays. The meeting broke up at 8:30 P.M. as usual. Ben walked through the city's main street shopping district on his Thursday evening stroll to his apartment on the edge of the commercial district.

Ben, true to habit, walked on the east side of Central Street en route to his home. As he approached the city center Ben noticed a group of thugs blocking the sidewalk a hundred feet up ahead. Ben thought to himself, *Do I cross the street to avoid walking past these characters? Why should I? After all there is a policeman watching. He is just across the street on the West sidewalk. Besides, there are people all over the place entering and exiting the stores.* As he completed his mental conversation Ben decided to walk past the gang of eight. He was quickly grabbed and held tightly by three of the tough guys. Obviously Ben had made a mistake that he would remember for the rest of his life. Ben watched in silent horror as the policeman turned and entered a store. Then as if by magic both of the Central Street sidewalks were emptied of pedestrians. Ben was soaking wet with sweat. He wondered when he should yell for help, but realized that no one would hear his call. At this point five switchblades snapped open. The loud clicks unnerved Mr. Bishop. He prayed that the young hoods didn't notice his level of fear. At this point Jim C. stepped into the center of the tight circle, so that he was standing toe to toe with his unwilling guest. Jim introduced each of his friends to Mr. Bishop. All seven of Jim's friends grabbed Ben's right hand and held it for a few seconds. As each young man held Ben's hand in a tight grip, three others continued to hold Ben stiffly in place. Jim then turned to his guest and informed him (Mr. B.) that he was the only teacher at City High School with any "guts." Jim further explained to Mr. B. that his father would not let him quit school. Now he (Jim) was thanking Mr. B for getting him thrown out. Jim told his friends to always be considerate to Mr. B. With the end of this one-sided conversation, the knives were closed and Mr. Bishop was released. Ben was amazed that his rubbery legs carried him home. He was more than a little light-headed. His shirt was soaking wet.

During the last week of school in late June, Ben was at his desk correcting tests and doing report card statistics. A young, well-dressed gentleman entered the empty classroom. He asked the busy teacher how he was doing. Then the young man asked Mr. Bishop if he remembered him, to which Ben responded by saying that he had never seen him before.

At this point Jim C. informed Mr. B., that it was indeed him, Jim C. Jim once again thanked Mr. B. for getting him thrown out of school. Jim informed the surprised teacher that he was employed at a good job and that he planned to work hard, be a good citizen, the epitome of a success story, and that in the future he would run for a school committee seat. Jim said thanks one last time and left.

Discipline: The Principal's Son

At some time during Ben's first year as a teacher he realized that he was having a good year. He had established himself as a just disciplinarian and was convinced that learning was the only thing that would happen in his classroom. An experienced teacher had suggested to Ben that he not smile as a first year teacher until at least the first day of January. Ben accepted this free advice and for him it worked; he never gave away the control of his class to the students. However, no one remembered to warn him about the challenge of having the principal's son in his classroom.

As time marches on every student and teacher discovers the limits of acceptable behavior that will be tolerated in a classroom. Young George Hughe decided to cross this invisible line in all of his classes in this, his last year at City High. Many teachers talked tough in the teacher's room, but no one had actually disciplined George Hughe. Ben suspected that since George was the principal's son he was getting away with a considerable amount of mischievous behavior in his senior year.

George apparently had decided to test Mr. Bishop's mettle. He purposefully crossed Mr. B.'s invisible line. After the appropriate warning(s) Mr. Bishop told George to leave the room and to report to the principal's office. George took the liberty of saying, "My father is the principal. I believe the annual teacher elections happen in April." Since this incident happened in late March, Ben and all of his period four students clearly heard the implied threat. If Mr. Bishop threw George out of his class, then most likely Mr. Hughe would certainly reconsider Mr. Bishop's nomination for a second year at City High School. But Ben said,

"George, go to the office, NOW!" The assistant principal, Mr. K., asked George why he had been sent to the office, and then assigned the same number of detention hours to George as he had for every student sent to him by a teacher.

Ben never heard a word about the incident from Mr. Hughe. George behaved himself that day until he graduated, a few months later. Ben was reelected as a teacher.

The Open Door

Bill Q. was one of Mr. Bishop's better students. Bill always completed all of his math school work; he readily offered unique solutions to challenging math problems. He was indeed an imaginative student who continuously challenged math theories as they were being presented. Ben enjoyed listening to Bill's ideas on another way to solve a problem.

As was his habit, Mr. B. checked the attendance sheet as the advanced math class began. He was surprised to see Bill Q.'s name listed as "absent due to a suspension." None of Bill's classmates knew what Bill had done to be suspended for two weeks. Bill was a good student, and since this was only the second time Mr. Hughe had suspended anyone in his lengthy career, Ben decided to ask the assistant principal what crime Bill had committed. Mr. Kagan (the AP) responded by saying that he had never seen the boss so angry. Further, he said that Mr. Hughe refused to tell him or any one else about the incident. In fact the principal's secretary didn't know what had happened as Hughe wrote the suspension letter himself. The only thing the AP knew was that the incident had happened last Sunday. Ben and the AP agreed that Hughe would have to let the secret out as Bill Q. would be returning to school in two weeks.

On the last day of Bill's suspension, Mr. Hughe called a special faculty meeting. Six teachers were assembled in Mr. H's office after school on that Friday afternoon. The AP had not been invited!! Just Bill's six teachers. Mr. Hughe stated that Bill would be back in school on Monday. Bill was *never* to be out of his assigned teacher's eyesight. The directive, thought Ben, was very specific. Ben asked Mr. Hughe, "When my math class ends, I am to escort Bill to his next class?"

Bill's English teacher also asked what Bill had done to cause such close supervision over him. Mr. Hughe told all six teachers that it was none of their business. Additionally, the principal directed his teachers seated before him to walk into the restroom with Bill if the teacher saw fit to allow Bill to leave the classroom. Before any one of the six teachers present could ask the next question, Hughe announced quite clearly that "yes," this directive did mean that each teacher was to abandon supervision of a classroom full of students and was to accompany Bill to the restroom. "Wow," thought the six teachers, "wonder what Bill did two weeks ago Sunday!"

When Bill entered Ben's math class on Monday morning, escorted by his social studies teacher, Ben had just begun the class discussion as to what is meant by ". . . the angle of steepest slope." A few minutes before the bell rang to end the class, all of the kids were working on their homework assignment. Ben told his students, "Just one problem tonight and I bet that none of you will solve it." At this point Bill asked permission to go to the boys' restroom. Ben said, "Sure, let's go." With a relieved "Thank you," Bill exited the room with his teacher. As they headed down the hall Ben questioned Bill. "What did you do to get suspended for two weeks?"

Bill's story began with several comments to his teacher as to how he (Bill) had always been Mr. M.'s audio-visual helper and how he was frequently in the media room. Bill was usually helping a teacher with the school's electronic equipment during his free time as well as after school for the previous two years. Ben affirmed that he knew about Bill helping a lot of the teachers with the setup and use of school equipment. Bill Q.'s nickname had accidentally been created by his math teacher during the previous school year, when Ben had remarked in response to one of Bill's many questions, "Mr. Quincy, from now on I'm calling you Mr. Q.—the Q will define you as Mr. Questions," Bill had enjoyed that comment during that class. He was surprised when his friends started calling him Mr. Q., or just Q. He enjoyed his new nickname and it had stuck.

Q continued with his story, "You've seen me in the hallway running up to Mr. M. as he threw me his big ring of school keys. Then I'd be off to meet with a teacher to help set up some electronic stuff in their classroom(s). Well, I began making wax impressions of the school master keys. Eventually I was able to make a key in my cellar that opened all of the school doors. Two weeks ago Sunday, Mr. Hughe caught me in the media room sitting on the floor. I had taken a computer apart and had all of the pieces all over the floor. Actually, I had taken quite a few apart as I was trying to make a better machine from several of the older ones. I thought I had solved my problem and was about to assemble my "better idea" machine when Mr. Hughe entered the room. I had been working on this project a little over three months. Since no one had ever entered the school while I was doing my research I guess I got carried away and thought of the media room as my personal electronics lab.

"On the Sunday that Mr. H. caught me, he had come in to work in order to complete a report due to the superintendent the following day. When Mr. Hughe arrived he heard the music playing over the loudspeakers. He became curious as to which custodian was working on a Sunday. I guess I really surprised him.

"I tried to tell him that I would reassemble everything but he was so angry he wouldn't listen to me. He told me to give him my keys, not to tell anyone what I had been doing and to leave the school NOW." Ben told Q. to behave, to study and to continue to be a good student. Ben figured that if the school principal didn't file charges against Bill, he would be able to go to college and succeed in life.

Ben quickly learned that Mr. Hughe didn't want any more people than absolutely necessary to know what Q. had done. No charges were filed. In fact, Mr. Hughe didn't even tell the school superintendent about the incident. The principal just wanted his nightmare student to graduate and to be out of his life forever.

Mr. M., Ben and Bill Q. spent two evenings in the media room reassembling the electronic equipment. No one except for one custodian ever realized that the three men were in the school.

During one of Ben's tours with Q. in the restroom, Bill asked, "Mr. Bishop, do you want to see how the electricity was shut down last October?" With the question hanging out in the air awaiting a quick "NO" from his teacher, Bill jumped up grabbing a heavy pipe close to the ceiling and proceeded to do a few chin-ups. The pipe served as a conduit carrying electrical wires across the restroom ceiling. As Bill dropped back to the floor he pointed out the significance of the one-inch movement of the pipe. Q. informed his teacher that every boy took a swing on the pipe as they were about to exit the boys' room en route back to their classrooms. Q. told Mr. B. he had recently figured out that if two kids jointly hung onto the pipe it moved a little further and as a result would short the wires inside the pipe. Ben realized that Q. had solved the four-month-old puzzle. Q. said that when two boys hung onto the pipe simultaneously it had shorted not only the wires but all of the school clocks. Q. said that he and some friends liked to stop the clocks to get longer math classes and as an additional benefit shorter history classes. Fortunately no member of the boys' Chin-Up Club had ever been hurt. Once the weight of the boys was removed (the pipe)would slowly move part way back toward its proper location—thus canceling the electrical short.

Ben asked the maintenance man to fix the pipe and to check the insulation of the wires inside the pipe.

As the school year was drawing to a close, the principal informed his teachers in a faculty meeting that they were to come up with their recommendations for student awards, scholarships etc., which would be presented at the June 22nd graduation exercise. Hughe firmly ordered his staff NOT to submit Bill Q.'s name for any scholarship or award, even if his almost straight-A average would have earned him one or more.

AP Mr. Kagan and Ben were assigned to the Harvard Book Award committee. The two conspirators placed William Quincy's name into a sealed envelope. Mr. Kagan placed this award envelope with all of the others he was charged to collect and organize for the June 22nd ceremony. Ben and Mr. Kagan had carefully reviewed their boss' instructions and had determined that a book for excellence in science and math had not been specifically included in his instructions regarding scholarships, etc.

June 22nd was a beautiful sunny day, a perfect day to hold a high school graduation ceremony outdoors. Ben was seated in the baseball stadium with the parents, teachers and friends of the graduates. He was merely a spectator. Mr. Kagan was standing at Mr. Hughe's right hand side assisting his boss with the presentations. The graduates were seated on the infield facing the parents and friends in the stadium. The principal and his assistant were at homeplate where a table adjacent to the principal's podium held the diplomas and scholarships, along with other awards and trophies. The podium mounted microphone was connected to a powerful public address system. Every word spoken by Mr. Hughe was easily heard by all attendees.

Mr. Kagan gave the Harvard Book and congratulatory letter to Mr. Hughe. Mr. Hughe began reading the letter, proudly noting the purpose of the award and the significance of winning it. He took a dramatic pause as he loudly announced the winner's name—"WILLIAM P. QUINCY."

It was too late for Hughe to do anything but to proceed. Hughe called "WILLLAM P. QUINCY" a second time.

Bill had been told by the principal a few days earlier that he wasn't going to receive any awards during the graduation activities. As he heard his name called a second time, Bill got up, walked proudly to the podium and accepted the cherished book from his high school principal. The student graduates cheered for their friend's public recognition—his well-earned moment in the sun.

Sick Leave

Mr. Bishop had to take a sick day. His four-year-old son had tonsillitis, and thus Ben Jr. gave his first personal gift to his dad—tonsillitis. Ben went to the school nurse that Thursday afternoon. She looked at his throat and told Ben to visit a doctor on the way home. Ben had a swollen tonsil. The swelling was large enough to cause him to gag on it every time he tried to swallow. The kindly doctor gave Ben a shot which he claimed would solve the teacher's problem within 24 hours. "Take tomorrow off and you will be fit to talk again by 6:00 P.M. tomorrow evening," said Dr. Jones. Ben went home, called the school and reported to the principal's secretary that he would be absent from work the next day due to sickness. Ben had his lesson plans prepared per the required five days-in-advance standard along with a letter addressed to the substitute in order that he/she would be able to cover (teach) his classes.

Most teachers worry when they are absent that their students will say or do something which will embarrass their absent teacher. Ben worried about his classes and his students' behavior during the three day weekend.

Early Monday morning Ben found the sub who had covered his classes on the previous Friday. She quickly told him that his students were well behaved and that they did their math assignments for her. She further stated that she had a little free time to give him a longer report at the end of period three. The two teachers agreed to meet and to talk about Friday's classes later that day.

Ben started his teaching day in his usual style noting with

pleasure that his kids were ready for the day's activities. He did not know what his students had said to the substitute teacher last Friday morning. "We realize that you are an English and history teacher stuck in an advanced math class," stated the mischievous students. The two student spokespersons continued their appeal, "Please let us work on our math problems as a class. We need to be able to solve these problems when Mr. Bishop returns on Monday. We will behave, but we have to work out some of these puzzling word problems in discussion groups." The experienced sub agreed to the students' request. She laughed along with Mr. B.'s students as she realized that they were mimicking Mr. Bishop's every move! Toward the end of the class a group of students told the sub that Mr. B. had a book in his top right hand desk drawer from which he always selected a problem every Friday. After a little additional conversation, the sub readily agreed to their request.

Thus, as Ben was concluding his Monday morning class, a quiet but very polite voice asked, "Mr. Bishop, are you going to make your usual Friday challenge of no homework tonight, *if* we solve one of your special problems in the allotted five minutes today?"

Ben was happy to accept the proposal. He enjoyed the heightened interest his students showed as they spent five minutes to solve a problem which would cancel their weekend homework if they got it right. No previous class had ever won the no homework weekend challenge.

As Mr. B. reached into his desk drawer for his favorite book of unique math problems, the kids held their breath, crossed their fingers and hoped (after all it's illegal to pray in school!!). Ben selected problem #38. It was the one the kids had worked on last Friday. His mischievous students had a difficult time waiting for their teacher to complete the presentation of the weekly challenge problem. As Mr. B. finished they all joyously shouted out the correct answer. The bell rang and the happy students raced out of the room before their teacher could change his mind.

Ben met with the sub at the end of period three and she told him about the planned mischief of his students for his return from sick leave. She told Ben that she was happy to hear of his students' success in their plan to have no math homework on Monday night.

Heather and the children enjoyed listening to Ben's story. All of them told Ben that they were cheering for his students.

Stolen Property

City High Principal Mr. Hughe waddled down the hall in order to catch up with Mr. Bishop. Ben was enroute from his fifth period algebra class to his sixth period study hall when he heard his name called by the principal. Mr. Hughe said that he had been looking at Ben's college transcripts and noted that he had taken a couple of college courses in physics.

Ben said, "Yes I did, but . . . "

Mr. Hughe announced that he was planning to assign Ben one physics class the following September. Ben's "No way" echoed off the walls as he hurried to his study hall.

Two weeks later Mr. Hughe tried once again to tell Ben that he was to teach a physics class in the fall. Finally, when Mr. Hughe invited Ben and his wife Heather out to dinner at a fancy restaurant, Ben knew he had lost the fight and that he would have to teach a physics class in the next school year.

Mr. Hughe explained to Ben that it was necessary for 18 dropouts from the two previous school years to earn their science credit by passing a course in physics before they could graduate. Most of the 18 had attended school less than 20 days each of the past three years. After a lengthy discussion with Heather, Mr. Hughe, ignoring the scowling husband, stated that he needed Ben to take this assignment because no other (science) teacher was capable of handling it.

September

Bishop attempted to begin his physics class as he did his math classes. Ben was telling his 18 charges (aged 18 to 22) that they would be turning in a term paper prior to the Christmas break and . . .

To Ben's dismay he heard 18 voices challenging him. The unhappy students asked, "Mr. Bishop, do you want to end up like Mr. L.,. our teacher of last year? Do you want us to send you out of here with a nervous breakdown? We got to our last science teacher before the end of September. We don't do term papers!"

Ben knew that the "18 team" had tossed pennies at Mr. L. every day and had chanted "Mr. L. stoops for pennies," until the poor man quit after four weeks of school.

Ben told them to be quiet and to listen, "No, I do not want you to give me a nervous breakdown and secondly, I plan to teach this physics course and I expect all of you to do your work and to pass." As he regained the 18 team's attention, Ben started once again to tell them the rules for the term paper due on the last Friday of December before the Christmas break. He continued by telling his class that he had selected three new cars currently advertised by the auto industry as affordable for the young family. The position picked by each student as to which 4-door sedan an underpaid school teacher should buy for his family of five (2 adults, 3 children) was to be defended per the topics they would study from September thru to mid October.

As the weeks passed Ben and his 18 team test-drove the specific cars Mr. B. had named on that first day of class. Eventually, the teacher and his 18 team were asked to leave several car dealer showrooms. The teacher and his 18 team had learned a lot about the laws of physics as they studied these three automobiles. The reports were turned in on schedule. The reports clearly showed the 18 team that they were capable students.

February

The 18 team enjoyed their nickname. Each student was assigned a number from 1 to 18 and they began to refer to each other by number.

Number 17 asked Mr. Bishop if the class could do the experiment on the refraction of light which he had noticed in the lab manual. Ben's response was a simple, "No, I've planned to give you a test on that date."

Number 17 offered to bring in nine precision manufactured prisms, to supervise the experiment and to make certain that all 18 team students completed the lab manual project during the lab period. Number 17 stated that he couldn't find the school's prisms so he would bring in the required items. Mr. B. accepted 17's proposal and scheduled the Thursday double lab period for the light refraction experiment. Number 17 brought in a bag full of precision manufactured prisms and distributed a prism to each team of two students; he instructed each pair of students how to do the experiment, how to look through the prisms and what they were looking to see. He also led his buddies through the lab manual questions. The class went smoothly. A few minutes before the bell Number 17 asked Mr. Bishop for help because two prisms were missing. Just as the bell rang Mr. B. said since the prisms were not school property that he really didn't care about the "lost" prisms. Then Ben said, "Go to your next class. Eventually your friends will return the two missing prisms to you."

At this point Number 17 panicked and cried out that he had to have them back NOW! He then told his classmates (and Mr. B.) that his father had stolen the prisms from the navy yard where he worked assembling submarine periscopes. "If I don't return all nine prisms this afternoon then my dad will end up in a federal prison," Number 17 said with a shaky voice. Number 17's friends returned the missing prisms after hearing his sad story.

Fire

City High School was a handsome building. It stood majestically on a small rise facing the street. The main section of the building faced Main Street. Two wings stretched from its two ends toward the street as if they were protective arms gathering the students into its academic halls. The resulting U-shaped structure embraced an outdoor amphitheater. This grassed-in area was sheltered by the building. Outdoor activities were frequently held on the theater grounds. A narrow drive encircled this well maintained grassy area. It served as a walkway for pedestrian traffic at the musical events held in the outdoor theater area. No cars or school buses were allowed to drive or park on this emergency roadway. The central section of the school consisted of three floors, all of which were regular classrooms. The fourth floor housed just the four science laboratories. The builder of this 1900s facility believed that if a student experiment accidentally caused a fire, then since fires burn UP, the rest of the school and its occupants would be saved. The two wings housed all of the nonclassroom areas which are to be found in all high schools. The gym, showers and locker rooms were on the lower level of one wing. The school cafeteria was on the upper level of that wing. The other wing housed a large auditorium and a small music center.

Each period of every school day four teachers were assigned to the four labs on the fourth floor. The main building was BIG!! It housed more than 2000 students in its academic classrooms, along with the 200+ adults who worked in the school as teachers, administrators, secretaries, cafeteria employees, custodians, teacher aides and several volunteers. The single stairway to the fourth floor was at the back of the building away from the heavy pedestrian traffic areas of the third floor.

Ben was in his fourth floor Physics lab with his 18 team. The teacher and his students were watching a film on the construction of passenger aircraft. This film identified the academic training students needed if they planned to work in the aircraft industry. The film highlighted the math and physics classes high school graduates should take in order to work in this technical field. Unfortunately the filmed demonstration of the safety features built into airplane engines and the actual test procedures had been proven insufficient a month earlier with a disastrous plane crash in Boston, MA. The students were not impressed with the pictured white-coated scientists throwing dead chickens into the running airplane engines as proof that the plane could safely fly through a flight of birds while en route to its destination because that had been the exact cause of the Logan Airport accident.

At this same time someone had reported a fire in the first floor girls' restroom adjacent to the main office. Mr. Hughe viewed the fire and concluded that it was a small fire. First he turned off the fire alarm system so that the students would not be in the way of the firemen or their equipment. Next he immediately phoned the fire station and requested assistance. Within minutes the fire trucks sped into the circular drive and parked in front of the school. At this same time the principal and his assistants hurried from one classroom to the next instructing the teachers not to panic but to evacuate the building via the side and rear doors. As the teachers exited the school with their students, they were directed to assemble everyone on the athletic field in back of the school. In this process the principal felt he was protecting everyone in the building AND was helping the fire fighters get close to the fire. *After all*, Mr. H. thought, *If I had allowed the alarm to go off then hundreds of the kids would have been exiting through the front doors and the fire trucks would have had to wait for the complete emptying of the school.* Hughe believed he was protecting everyone in the school and getting the fire department on the scene faster. Unfortunately, no messenger remembered to run up to the fourth floor!!

One of the teachers on the field in back of the school couldn't find his science teacher friend and asked the principal if he had seen any of the science teachers. At this point Mr. Hughe decided a little belatedly to turn the alarm system back on just in case a student or an adult had been missed by his messengers. "Perhaps someone was in a restroom!" Mr. H. said to himself.

The fire alarm sounded it's shrill call to drop whatever you are doing and to exit the building was heard and obeyed immediately by four science teachers and their students. Ben and his 18, along with three other teachers plus their students thought they were responding to yet another fire drill until they entered the second floor smoke-filled hallway. The four teachers and their students quickly closeted themselves in a second floor classroom. The smoke hadn't gotten into the second floor classrooms yet. With a shout for help from the classroom window, the four teachers and their students awaited their rescue. A few minutes later, a team of fire fighters led them to a stairway which had been cleared of smoke by the department's powerful smoke exhaust fans. A cheer from the teachers and the students greeted the four teachers and their rescued students.

To this day Ben refuses to comment on what he and his science teacher friends said to Mr. Hughe a few minutes after they learned why they had been trapped in a burning building.

The Challenge

As a twelve-year-old grade six student, Ben was quite surprised by what he believed to be a major adult (teacher?) mistake. His sixth grade teacher, Mrs. Beaut, lost her cool toward the end of the English class. The day had been tiring for Mrs. B. The students were not getting her message at all that day. Mary C. wasn't paying much attention to Mrs. B.'s academic presentation. Mrs. B. was frustrated. She had never seen Mary C. lose interest in her teaching. At that moment Mary C. gave her teacher a knowing look which sent a clear message that she knew her teacher didn't have it on that particular day.

Mrs. B., completely upset, turned to one of her better students and shouted, "Mary C., if you think you can do any better then you get up here and try." WOW! Even as a non-interested student, Ben knew that his teacher had just made a huge mistake. Mary C. confidently walked up to the chalkboard and proceeded to teach. Mary easily got everyone's attention. All of the other students thought that Mrs. B was going to kill Mary. To the teacher's dismay, Mary C. pulled it off. She did a great job. Finally, every kid in the class understood that which Mrs. B. had been trying to explain to them.

Many years later, Ben, a classroom teacher vividly remembered Mrs. B.'s humiliating defeat. He had no intention of ever making that type of mistake in his teaching career.

Ben happily finished presenting a challenging trigonometry problem and instructed his students to start on their homework. At this point Bob Majic started to entertain three friends seated nearby his desk. Ben looked at the clock. He remembered Mrs.

B.'s bad day. But, he thought, maybe through a carefully planned situation he could safely challenge his mischievous student. Ben told the class that as soon as they finished the problem they were working on that Mr. Majic would entertain the entire class. Ben instructed Bob to show the entire class what he had been showing his friends. With just ten minutes till the class ending bell, Bob stood up and opened his desktop.

Bob held up a large paper bag and showed everyone that it was empty. He balanced the grocery bag on the palm of his left hand. He reached into his desk and picked up a bottle of Coca-Cola. Bob held the glistening bottle up for all to see. He held it with the fingers of his right hand gripping the bottle cap. After a few seconds everyone understood that Bob was holding a glass bottle of soda. Mr. Majic lowered the bottle into the paper bag. Then he slammed the top of the bag down. He flattened the empty bag and tossed it into the nearby wastebasket. WOW! The entire class sat in wonderment. The bottle was gone. Bob Majic was really Mr. Magic!!

Ben said to himself, "I'm glad the bell is going to ring in thirty seconds—at least I won't be completely embarrassed." Ben immediately reached into the wastebasket to retrieve the crushed bag. Bob asked Mr. B. for his grocery bag. Ben carefully opened the bag and discovered a magician's expensive prop. The fake coke bottle had to be held by the cap. It collapsed vertically once the top was released. The bottle actually had rested on the bottom of the bag as a flat object. Thus crushing the bag downward didn't harm the magician's expensive prop. Bob had just received his new prop and wanted to show it to his classmates. He was scheduled to perform for a children's group later that afternoon. Mr. Bishop told Bob that he would keep Bob's professional secrets secret.

Horsepower

The homework assignment had been assigned to prepare the 18 team for their next lab class on horsepower. The lab manual had a simple formula for horsepower. The three elements of the formula were: *a*. the time (in seconds) it took one person to *b*. climb a measured height based upon that person's, *c*. weight. The 18 team suggested to their teacher that the best place to be used for their climb (height) was the adjacent staircase as it would be easy to measure the distance to be climbed. Mr. Bishop agreed and he sent a team of three students to measure the vertical distance from the first floor up to their fourth floor classroom. Ben described the educational benefits of this experiment to his students. Their comparison of horsepower to the necessary lifting or pulling strength to move weights was sufficient for the teacher and the 18 to think beyond the lab book experiment. Both the teacher and his students recognized that their early 1900s design open stairwell made it possible for one person to visually start and to time each student's run from the first floor up to the fourth. Ben sent the first student down to the bottom floor. He leaned over the fourth floor railing as did the remaining 17 students. All 18 students had weighed themselves in the nurse's office earlier that day, The vertical distance to be climbed had been calculated. The only measurement left to collect was the time, in seconds, to travel from the first floor to the fourth. Everyone was ready to collect their individual running time!! Mr. Bishop called down to his first victim, "GO!" Each student in turn ran as fast as he could in order to get a good horsepower rating. Several times that morning Ben forgot to hit the stop button on his stopwatch. This "accident" forced several students to run the stairwell twice.

A spectator asked Ben if these mental lapses were accidents or was he just trying to use up class time? Actually, Mr. B. was just hitting on a few of his 'favorite' students.

Finally, all members of the 18 team had completed their runs. One student asked Mr. Bishop to take his turn running the stairs. Ben said, "No." The mighty 18 said, "Please."

Ben hesitated. One of Mr. B.'s 'favorite' students of a few minutes earlier offered to hold the stopwatch and to time his physics teacher with this comment, "Mr. B., I will remember to hit the stop button on the stopwatch as soon as you set foot on the fourth floor. I won't accidentally forget as you did a few times this morning."

The 18 Team promised to be quiet while Ben was running the stairs. As Ben walked down the stairs to the first floor, he realized that he weighed exactly the same as the toughest kid of the 18 team. Thus he knew that he would have to . . . well, he couldn't stop now! All the members of the 18 team were watching from the top floor railing. Mr. 'Favorite' shouted, GO!

Ben grabbed the handrail and pulled with his hands while he ran up the stairs. He was running with a greater urgency than he had ever felt before. At each landing Ben grabbed the stair rail post and threw himself into a 180-degree spin around to the first stair of the next flight of stairs. He made it to the top and anxiously awaited his time. As the students returned to their classroom to complete the horsepower chart, Ben walked over to the chart master and reported his weight. Ben reviewed the chart statistics. He finally relaxed when he noted that his time matched the favorite's. Ben never did figure out his horsepower. He didn't have to—he was as strong as the toughest kid in the class! Ben had survived the gauntlet! WHEW!

Twenty-Pound Test Monofilament

Mr. Bishop's physics class was well prepared for their lab experiment on the mechanical advantages of a pulley system. The Thursday morning two period lab had become one of Ben's favorite classes. Mr. B. happily watched his students assemble the pulley system and quietly awaited their subsequent discoveries. The advantages achieved by running string over and around several pulleys quickly illustrated the point that a person (or machine) could pick up a heavy load with little effort,

It was readily apparent to all members of the 18 team that in a real work situation the pulleys would have to be made of metal. The string would necessarily be replaced with strong rope or steel cable. The braces holding the pulleys together for the lab experiment were made of inexpensive plastic. The real work world had pulley systems with steel frames and used heavy duty axles to hold the pulleys in place. It didn't matter that this school demonstration was being performed on a cheap plastic system. It was strong enough to support the class demonstration. The 18 team raised a 14-pound weight using a two-pound lift force. Amazing! A mechanical advantage of seven!

The three groups of six students finished their reports and realized that they had a few minutes left to clean up, to put every thing away—something they usually tried to avoid. They needed a challenge which would attract their inquisitive teacher's attention.

At this point student 12 innocently asked, "Mr. B., what does twenty-pound test monofilament mean?" The class had used twenty-pound monofilament fish line in their pulley system experiment. Their teacher replied that the string was guaranteed to hold a 20-pound fish. Mr. 12 then asked, "At what weight would the 20-pound test line break?"

Although Mr. Bishop knew what his students were up to, he was just as curious as to the breaking strength of the fish line. He told his mischievious friends to develop a serious experiment which they could use to scientifically determine the answer to their ingenious question.

The 20-pound test experiment as designed by the students was quite simple. The students would keep a record of the weight they placed onto the weighted plate they had affixed to the fishline already strung around the pulley system. When the line broke the 18 team and their teacher would know the maximum weight the line could hold. Mr. Bishop added one additional learning condition to the proposed experiment. Their teacher told his students that they would be using metric weights and thus they would have to convert the final metric answer into the English pound system. It was agreed. Everyone was ready. The great experiment began.

The base plate was weighted and suspended via the 20-pound test fish line from the delicate plastic pulley system which had been assembled for the earlier experiment. The students began by placing two 500-gram weights onto the base plate. (500 grams approximates 1.1 pounds.) One of the team members had figured the necessary number of grams needed to register the first twenty pounds. Things proceeded in an organized fashion as everyone was really interested in how much weight would be needed to break the monofilament fish line. As the weights were being added and recorded in their notebooks, one of the group said, "Everybody, please stand clear. Look at how the string is stretching. I don't think anyone wants that weight to land on their feet." Not one member of that assemblage had thought about what would happen when the fish line broke. No one realized that the impending crash would create such havoc. The line broke! The crash generated by the 30-plus pounds of iron weights slamming onto the floor startled everyone.

Crash! The thunderous crash was only half of the reaction when the string broke. The plastic pulley system had bent over due to the attached heavy weights. Once it was released by the swift removal of the weights, the spring loaded system recoiled upward, smashing into the ceiling. The flimsy plastic structure bounced back onto the lab table. It knocked an almost empty (fortunately) bottle of sulfuric acid from its storage shelf to the floor!! The acid storage bottle shattered upon contact with the new tile floor. Ben was shocked, as were the members of his 18 team. He was truly relieved as he realized that no one had been hurt, nor had the spilled acid hit anyone.

The 18 team and their teacher started to clean up what they knew to be their mess! Fortunately, only four tiles would have to be replaced due to the acid spill. The busy students and their teacher were not ready for the next event resulting from their 20-pound fish line experiment.

The classroom door slammed open—three third floor teachers whose classrooms were immediately below Mr. Bishop's physics lab rushed into the room. They stopped in their tracks as they observed the 19 occupants working to clean up the mess. Ben had a difficult time explaining what had happened to his friends without laughing. A minute later Mr. Hughe rushed into the room. Ben had to repeat his story, to his boss, as to how all of his students had been working on an experiment and an accident had happened. Mr. Hughe said that it was difficult to believe as he had been called on the intercom and had been told that three teachers were on their way upstairs to stop an obvious fight in the physics lab. To the third floor teachers, the crash had sounded like the 18 team had knocked their teacher to the floor by smashing a chair or something on him.

Ben rushed home that afternoon. He just had to tell Heather about his exciting day at school. Every adult in the high school thought these 18 kids were thugs. Ben asked his bride of eight years, "Why did the principal give me such a great bunch of kids?"

Parents' Night

Excerpts from Several Parents' Nights

Parents A–E

The typical parent night conversation with a majority of families was a polite and simple comment on the fact that their son/daughter was doing fine. Once in a while the conversation was cheerful and friendly, e.g. "Mr. Bishop, how are you this evening? Our son/daughter enjoys your math class. How is he/she doing?" Ben's happy response was telling the parent(s) that their child was doing very well in class and that if they want to give the kid away he would be happy to take him/her. "After all," stated Ben, "Heather and I have two little ones at home and a built-in baby sitter would be great."

Parent F

Ben recognized Patricia L.'s parents as they entered his classroom. He recalled the unusual note he had received from her mother a few weeks earlier. Mrs. L. had requested that the school excuse Patricia's absence of the previous week as her daughter had been home sick with "A MUMP." Ben had laughed heartily at the unique illness of his student. Patricia gave Mr. Bishop permission to read her mother's note to entertain her classmates. The entire class had chuckled when they heard "A MUMP" as her illness. They obviously knew of her mother's sense of humor. Thus Mr. B. was prepared to begin his visit with his happy line about the parents wanting to give away their daughter noting that he'd be happy to have her as a built-in baby sitter.

Ben was floored; Mrs. L. laughed but Mr. L. stretched himself up to his six-foot height and said in a clear voice, "Hummm, ahhh, Bishop, we are here for serious business, not for your humor. Now, let's talk about Patricia's work and how we can improve it." Ben realized that he was talking to a serious Puritan. Thus Ben informed Patricia's parents that she was doing excellent school work and strongly recommended that her parents compliment her for her success in math.

Parent G

Lisa M.'s parents were quite important and influential people. The principal and his *ad hoc* committee, in an effort to improve the efficiency of the parents' night visitations with their childrens' teachers had decided to limit each family to a fifteen-minute conference per teacher. Mrs. M. arrived at Mr. Bishop's classroom door at 7:15 P.M. and left 15 minutes later. Ben and Mrs. M. discussed how Lisa was doing in Plane Geometry during their visit. At 8:45 P.M., Mr. M. entered Ben's classroom. He had been standing in line for a few minutes awaiting his turn to visit with Lisa's math teacher.

Thus Ben greeted Mr. M. with a polite, "Good evening," and commented further that Mrs. M. had visited earlier and "both Mrs. M. and I had a detailed discussion on Lisa's class work."

Ben suggested that the family could hold a conversation at home on all of the points the two had talked about earlier. Further, Ben suggested, Mr. M. could view Lisa's papers during the family assessment of her work as Ben had given the papers to

Mrs. M. during their 7:15 visit. At this point Ben figured that Mr. M. would leave and let the next set of parents visit their child's math teacher.

Mr. M. emphatically announced that he was a correspondent for *TIME* magazine and that he was entitled to his 15-minute visit. In fact, he said, "My wife and I separated as we entered the school this evening. Each of us expects to visit Lisa's teachers separately. And, yes, we intend to have a family discussion when we get home. We intend to compare notes and for all of Lisa's teachers' sake, they had better be telling the same story to both of us!

"Now, Mr. Bishop, please explain to me why your geometry class is working on page 156 and the geometry teacher across the hall is only on page 127. If you would just slow down, my Lisa would be able to get an A in your class rather than the B she had on her report card."

Ben suggested that Mr. M. feel free to transfer Lisa into his friend's class across the hall. Mr. M. left in a huff. Ben told his friend about his visit with the M's. Old Len (He was two days older than Ben) said that he had lived through a similar challenge last year. Lisa remained in Mr. Bishop's geometry class for the remainder of the school year. It was, as Lisa informed Mr. B., "A family decision."

Parent H

Mr. H. did not show up on parents' night. Ben had been looking forward to meeting Mike's dad. Mike H., a senior, had abruptly stopped studying and his Math classwork had fallen from his usual "B" work to a failing grade of F.

A few days later, as Ben was walking from his cafeteria study hall duties to his second floor math classroom on the opposite side of the building, a hand reached out of the restroom and dragged Ben into that men's room. Ben, although shaken, was prepared to defend himself. At this point Mr. H. introduced himself. Ben shouted for help. He quickly figured that Mr. H. was angry due to the fact that Mike was failing. When another male teacher entered the male teachers' restroom, Ben relaxed a little. Mr. H. assured the two men that he wasn't there to hurt his son's favorite teacher but was there asking for help. Further, Mr. H. didn't want his son to ever find out that his dad had visited Mr. Bishop. After apologizing to Ben for his rough approach for this meeting, he told Ben about his problems with his son Mike, who always passed all of his classes. Mike always did everything that his dad demanded. Now, all of a sudden, Mike was failing everything.

"Now," wailed Mr. H., "Mike won't graduate from high school and he won't be going to college . . . " Ben promised to talk to Mike and would try to change his behavior.

A few weeks later Ben asked Mike, "What's going on? Why am I losing a good student?"

Mike told his math teacher that he was failing on purpose because his dad had decided that he was going to go to college and would have to major in the same program his dad had. After a lengthy visit Ben told Mike that he would talk to his father and get him to drop the college ideas if he, Mike, would pass all of his classes and graduate as the honor student that he was.

Mike said that if Mr. B. could do this that he would keep his end of the bargain.

Ben called Mr. H. and arranged a private meeting with him. Ben asked Mr. H. to tell his son that he would not talk about college ever again unless Mike brought the subject up.

Ben informed Mr. H. that his only job now was to keep his word, never to pressure Mike to go to his alma mater, and, most importantly, to ask his son to forgive him. Ben's parting words were, "Ask your son to please graduate from high school and that you will be one real proud dad."

Mike and his dad reached an agreement which was similar to the one proposed. Mike graduated with honors. In early August Mike decided to apply to college and was accepted as a late candidate into State U.

Parent I

One student who particularly enjoyed Mr. B.'s inquisitive math classes was John I. John was one of the brightest calculus students Ben had ever met. Ben continuously pushed John along—well beyond the text. John scored a perfect "5" on his advanced placement test and had a combined 1598 on his college boards. The evening that Ben and Mr. I. met went along very smoothly. Mr. I. told Ben how much he and his son were learning as a result of his son having a great math teacher. By this point Ben was feeling pretty good and was saying good night to his kind guest. As Mr. I. was leaving he turned and asked Mr. Bishop how old he was. Ben replied, "1024 to the half power; thirty-two." Mr. I. immediately responded that Mr. B. was too young to hold such an important job and that he was heading downtown to see the superintendent, "To get you fired."

Young John apparently learned of his father's comments as he apologized for him the next day.

Captain Football Graduates

The captain of City High's football team had been a decent student through his junior year. He was a favorite of his classmates as well of his coach.

During Ben's first year as a high school teacher, the athletic director visited with Ben as he was the basketball star's algebra teacher. The basketball hero was failing algebra. The AD demanded that Ben pass this student. "Give him a D in algebra on his January report card. The team needs him. We will lose the state championship without Kevin!" Ben politely responded, "Tell Kevin to study. His report card will report the grade that he earned. He can easily do the work. Good luck in the finals."

The unhappy AD immediately went to Mr. Hughe and demanded that he lean on Bishop. The AD suggested that the principal could hint to Bishop that his next contract might depend on his decision in this matter. Hughe visited with Mr. Bishop the next morning with the proposal concerning his next contract. Ben informed his boss that he was a math teacher, a person of integrity and that he proudly would begin looking for a new teaching job for, "Next September."

The basketball star failed algebra that January; the team lost the state championship finals. Mr. Bishop was offered a second-year contract with a salary adjustment to the sixth year level. Ben continued to teach at City High School for another year.

With this known behavioral background we find the football captain entering his senior year. Ronald K. studied hard and played hard through to the end of the first semester of his last year as a high school student. Ron won all sorts of awards as City

High's football hero. The city was proud of their star quarterback. As a reward to himself as a last semester senior Ron decided that he wouldn't do any more schoolwork. He decided to attend every class, to behave and attempt to pass by taking the weekly tests without any studying. Senior activities began three weeks before graduation. Ron knew that he had failed two subjects and as a result was not eligible to graduate. He also needed a passing grade in math to enter the army.

Ron asked Mr. Bishop for a second chance. The AD demanded that Mr. Bishop give Ron another and a much easier final exam. Mr. Hughe directed Mr. Bishop to reconsider his scoring of Ron's final exam. "Perhaps you (Ben) made a mistake when you graded the test," said Hughe.

Ben and Ron had a long visit the next day. Ben told Ron everything that had transpired and asked him if what was being proposed was honest. "It wasn't the right thing for either the AD or the principal to do—but . . . " Ron begged Mr. Bishop for a second chance. He promised to study. Mr. Bishop told Ron that no amount of last minute studying would prepare him for a legitimate final exam. After considerable debate Ben said that Ron could take a simple test to see if he would be eligible to retake the final.

Two days later Ron said he was prepared to take the eligibility test. Mr. Bishop had prepared a very simple (entrance level) test on definitions and formulas used in the original final. Ron scored a 10 out of a possible 100 points. Ron thought, *Why can't Mr. Bishop give ME a gift? All of my other teachers did.* It was all over. Ron had failed and finally realized that he would not graduate.

Ron picked up his school desk and hurled it at his teacher. Ben stepped aside and the desk crashed against the wall. Ron picked up a stack of books and threw them at Ben. Ben ducked. The books missed his head by inches. At this point Ron stood toe to toe with Ben. The athletic powerhouse offered his teacher the right to throw the first punch. "We can settle this like gentlemen," Ron shouted.*

Ben told Ron to leave NOW and said that he was calling the police to report Ron's behavior. The next door teacher heard the ruckus happening in room 207 and, with another teacher, rushed into Mr. B.'s classroom. They physically removed Ronald K. Ben immediately called the office and reported what had happened. Mr. Hughe said that he would call the police and have Ron arrested. He stated that Ron would not graduate from City High. Hughe directed Mr. B. to write up the incident and to have the two witnessing teachers sign the report which was to be turned in before Ben left for the day.

Ben called Heather and told her briefly what had happened and asked her to call the police if Ron, on his way home, "so much as stepped on a blade of grass."

At 6:15 that evening the Bishops' doorbell rang. Heather answered the door. Mr. Hughe stated that he and Ron were coming in to visit with Ben and that Ron was there to apologize to Mr. Bishop. The two pushed their way past Heather and sat down in the Bishops' living room.

"Ron," said Mr. Hughe, "Apologize to Mr. Bishop."

Ron said, "I'm sorry about what I did and I apologize."

Mr. Bishop said, "I do not accept your apology. Now, either the two of you will leave my house immediately or I'll have the police remove you." As they were leaving, Mr. Hughe told Ben to be in his office the next morning at 7:15. Ben's workday usually began at 8:15, and on that next day he reported into the high school at 8:15.

Mr. Hughe was quite upset when he spotted Ben. He yelled across the office at him, "Where were you at 7:15 this morning? I told you to be in my office at that time."

Ben responded in a determined voice, "I don't work for you

*Expletives deleted by author.

at 7:15. You are my boss at 8:15. I am here to teach and I am on time."

With an angry comment Mr. Hughe told Ben that he (Hughe) would see him later—and so the new day began. Mr. Kagan was sent upstairs to tell Ben what was going to happen. He told Ben that Ron would be given another final written by a math teacher from a neighboring school district. Ben asked when he would be given the completed test to grade it. He was told by the AP that the other school would take care of that.

Ben sat down and wrote a letter to the principal noting that Ron had failed senior math and that his report card had been turned into the office with an F on it. He further cited the legal fact that no one is allowed to change a teacher's letter grade on a report card.

Ron spent the next two weeks seated in Mr. Kagan's book storage room studying math. A few days later Ron's name was called during the graduation ceremonies. Ron crossed the stage and was handed his diploma by a proud principal. Ben wrote another letter noting that he had never authorized anyone to change Ron's math final letter grade.

Ron entered the army. He did very well in the math section of his entrance/placement examination.

Ten years later, Ben was teaching days and working nights to support his growing family. Ben stood behind the package store counter ready to serve the next customer. Ben was moonlighting in a liquor store three towns away from where he taught as he didn't want his students to discover him working in a liquor store. Sgt. Ron K. was his next customer. Ben recognized Ron immediately. Ron made his purchase and as he paid his bill said to his old math teacher, "Mr. Bishop, ten years ago you were the only one who was correct and honest. I'm truly sorry for everything that happened. I hope you can forgive me." Ben grabbed his hand and said that he indeed could forgive him, "Because your apology comes from your heart."

Senior Prom

Ben's last year as a City High School math teacher began with the superintendent personally telling him that he would be paid on the maximum pay step due to the unusually high achievement levels his students earned in mathematics. With great personal pride Ben committed himself to leading his students onto continued success in understanding and enjoying the pleasures of mathematics.

Ben's senior math class was filled with many of his students from the three previous school years. This particular group of 37 students included all of the differing personalities that anyone could find in a high school.

Jimy G—Jimy was an habitual after-school guest of Ben's. Jimy was outgoing and a 100% happy character. His humor permeated Mr. Bishop's math class. On many an occasion Jimy frustrated his teacher, who in turn invited him to be Mr. B.'s after-school guest for an hour. During these afternoon sessions Jimy quietly studied and completed his math and English homework. On Thursdays after Ben arrived from school, Heather would go grocery shopping. As Heather and Ben headed toward the check-out aisles, Ben would ask his wife to please find a cashier distant from one that Jimy was working as a bag boy. But Heather usually went directly to Jimy's aisle. Jimy was always extremely polite. His, "Good afternoon Mrs. Bishop, how are you today?" and her responses upset Ben every time*. Heather's

*The author believes that Heather and Jim enjoyed these mischievous moments.

interest in Jimy's schoolwork conversations carried on into the store parking lot. Jimy would place the bags of food into the Bishops' car and thank Mrs. Bishop, telling her that he looked forward to visiting with her the following week.

Patricia L.—The "a mump" girl was in this class.

Bob Majic and a long list of other unique characters were also in this class.

The year was progressing quite well. The kids were absorbing their mathematics. All of the senior prom committee members were in this class. Before and after class, conversation for their last semester was about the senior prom. *The Prom* was the only subject any student talked about if they weren't responding to a math problem. Superior math term papers had been submitted. Ben enjoyed reading a 22-foot-long scrolled History of Mathematics report. He had to spread it out on his living room floor and to crawl down the length of the report to read it. Liz H. had listed every known math fact she had found from the first use of a counting system to present-day advanced math topics.

Kevin Z. had estimated the weight of the high school. His many adding machine tapes stapled to his report as to the method he used to estimate the weight of concrete, bricks, doors, windows etc., etc. clearly illustrated his future interest in engineering. Kevin Z. had received his early acceptance notice as an engineering major at State U. several months earlier. In fact Ben realized that all 37 term papers/projects were outstanding.

The prom committee invited Ben and his wife to attend the prom as special guests. The Bishops declined the considerate invitation as Ben had to work his second job on prom night. Ben didn't know that the kids were going to make a presentation in his honor at the prom. Had Heather known about the presentation honoring her husband, she would have sacrificed the extra monies and made certain that both she and Ben attended.

Ben arrived home from his evening department store job at 11 P.M. The Bishops watched the evening news and went to bed a little after 11:30. The phone rang awakening the Bishop family at 3:00 A.M. One of Ben's math students called to tell his teacher that four of his senior math students had been in a serious auto accident. Two died instantly. The other two had been rushed to the hospital. Ben was stunned. One of his favorite students was crying on the phone as he tried to tell his teacher the story as to what had happened.

Ben was informed that the two couples in the car were Kevin D., Liz H., Patricia L., and Bob Majic. Later that Saturday morning Ben learned that Kevin D. had been driving very properly on the way home from a non-alcoholic after-prom party. His date was Liz H. seated adjacent to him in the front seat. Bob Majic and his prom date were both asleep in the back seat.

A state trooper had been chasing a drunk driver traveling with his lights off at a high rate of speed toward Kevin's car. The drunk driver was trying to elude his pursuer. The chased car careened around a sharp curve on the wrong side of the road and crashed head-on into Kevin's vehicle. The two front seat students were killed instantly. The medical team called to the accident scene that morning saved the lives of Patricia and Bob. Many days later the two hospitalized students were beginning to comprehend what had happened the previous Saturday morning. They finally realized that they had to heal both in mind and body. Once again Ben was at the hospital to visit his friends/students.

The two had renewed their commitment to live.

Bob Majic, whose scalp had been ripped off in the accident greeted his teacher with this comment: "I'm glad I took your final exam before my brains leaked out." With a relieved chuckle the student and his teacher visited as old friends. Both of them knew that Bob was on the road to recovery.

Patricia's back had been broken along with some internal injuries. The doctors expected Patricia to make a complete recovery. Ben arrived shortly after Patricia had finally accepted the fact that life goes marching on. She was quite pleased that her teacher would visit her in the hospital. She didn't remember his earlier visits. The two of them had a pleasant and cheerful visit. Later that day as Mr. L. was visiting his daughter, he observed that she was beginning to be her happy old self. Mr. L. decided that Mr. Bishop had put the positive spirit back in his daughter. Several weeks later Mr. L. spotted Ben in a local store and hurried over to thank him for visiting Patricia and for his work in renewing her positive attitude. Ben responded to his new friend that he had nothing to do with Patricia's recovery as she was always cheerful and a great young lady. The two men parted after Mr. L. (The Puritan) attempted to tell a joke to Mr. B.

National Honor Society

The first meeting of the senior class was held on the second Friday of the new school year. Principal Hughe was pleased to note that his son George was a candidate for president of the senior class. Mr. Hughe instructed the seniors as to the class officer election format. He chuckled and said, "As City High School principal, I will be hard pressed to say NO to any request made by this class if George is elected class president." This simple suggestion worked. George Hughe was elected president of his senior class. The year proceeded without any significant differences from the previous year. George did his job in an uneventful manner.

Principal Hughe had applied to the National Association of Secondary School Principals to open a NASSP National Honor Society chapter in City High School. In late November Mr. Hughe was thrilled to receive written authorization to establish a NASSP sponsored chapter in his high school. This meant that the new chapter could be established in early January. His son's graduating class would be the first from City High to list membership in the National Honor Society on their college applications.

Mr. H. assigned Mrs. Esque to serve as the new club's adviser. Senior honor students met with Mrs. Esque to develop plans for the establishment of the honor society, the election of its charter officers and the necessary inaugural activities. Mr. Hughe wanted his son to be the Charter President. Two weeks later (mid December) Mr. H. was in his office anxiously awaiting the balloting results. Mrs. Esque had promised Hughe that he would be the first one to hear the results.

Ben's classroom was across the hall from Mrs. Esque's English classes. Ben was in his homeroom correcting papers during the last period when he heard Hughe attempting to run down the hall to Mrs. Esque's room. His panicky gasps for breath after struggling up a flight of stairs were evident to everyone on the second floor that day. Although Hughe had closed the door after he entered Mrs. E.'s classroom, Ben clearly heard Mr. H.'s shouted announcement that the election had been erroneously conducted.

"Further," Mr. Hughe in a loud voice stated, "Every student and their advisor will stay in this room until George Hughe is elected charter president of the City High School National Honor Society."

This outburst generated a deadly silence in Mrs. E.'s classroom. Without saying a single word, Mrs. E. passed out a second set of ballots to each member of the new society. *The ballot results were exactly the same as those recorded on the first set of ballots.*

Hughe blew his cork!!! He shouted that there would be one final ballot to select the charter officers of this new Honor Society. "And," he continued, "If George doesn't win the president's role then I, Mr. Hughe, will cancel this new club permanently."

Mrs. Esque quietly passed out a third set of ballots for the honor society's officers. The results were exactly the same as those she had reported after each of the first two ballot counts. Mrs. Esque picked up her classroom phone, called the NASSP headquarters in Arlington, VA and reported to them the results of the three separate votes held that afternoon. Mr. Hughe angrily left Mrs. E.'s room. A few days later George told Mrs. E. that it had taken him two days to talk his father into accepting the Honor Society ballot results. Hughe never talked to Mrs. Esque again.

The Tropics

Heather suggested to Ben that he might want to teach overseas in order to have a family adventure and to enhance his resume. The idea appealed to Ben. He was just as enthusiastic about a two-year trip abroad as was his wife. Further, both of them believed that this unique experience would give Ben a better chance for a promotion when the Bishop family returned to the States a few years later.

Six months later, the Bishops agreed to move to the tropics. Ben had accepted a teaching job at Tropic High School. He was assigned to teach his favorite math classes, algebra and plane geometry, to U.S. dependent students whose families lived in the tropics. A few tuition students also attended Tropic High School. These were the children of international politicians living in the area.

Ben and Heather had never traveled outside of their home state. They had no idea as to what international travel entailed. The two adventurers and their young children were excited and anxiously awaited September and a new school year IN THE TROPICS!! They thought that their hardest task would be telling their parents about their planned adventure.

The great adventure began with the government moving contractor's explanation as to how their furniture and personal belongings would be shipped to the tropics. The young couple watched as the movers wrapped their dishes and other breakables. Everything they owned was packed into the truck. The Bishops took one last walk through their empty apartment. They were off, "On a great adventure."

As they closed the door for the last time, they realized that the movers had packed the garbage and the live plants along with all of their stuff!!!

"Oh well, we will have garbage to throw out on our first day in the tropics," said the happy pair as they headed to the airport for their first flight. (It took six weeks for their household goods to reach their new home in the tropics. Their stuff was shipped on a freighter with a last stop in the tropics.)

The Bishop family was thrilled. "Wow, we are going to fly to Panama!" They flew from Boston to New York. After a two-hour wait, the second half of their journey was about to begin. As the stewardess was closing the door a team of security guards angrily pushed their way onto the plane. In a strong and clear voice the leader demanded, "Whomever it is that has smuggled a baby onto this plane is to hand over that baby to me NOW."

After a few seconds of waiting for someone to stand up with a baby, the guards marched down the aisle of the aircraft checking every passenger's tickets and passports. Within a few minutes they found the baby. The guards took the child and its mother (handcuffed) off the plane. After the security team left the plane, the pilot announced that the plane had been cleared to depart. From New York the plane raced to Cuba. (It was September 1, 1958. Batista was still in power. Castro would take over in December.)

The pilot had circled a hurricane off the coast of Charleston and lightning had struck one of the four engines. The pilot immediately shut down that engine. Fifteen minutes later he restarted the engine without any problems. As the plane landed in Havana, the pilot announced that every passenger had to deplane and report to the airport customs building. Two rows of soldiers holding machine guns at the ready flanked the walkway from the plane to the customs shed. Every passenger was told to sit and wait.

After one hour the passengers were herded onto another

airplane which was scheduled to complete the flight to Panama. The Bishops, inexperienced and weary travelers, deplaned and entered the terminal building, collected their baggage, sweating profusely as a result of the tropical heat and headed for the exit at 1 A.M. Ben hadn't realized that he and his family had to clear customs. He believed that the government had taken care of everything for his family in advance. The guard at the exit door yelled something at the Bishops in Spanish. The guard didn't understand English and Ben didn't understand the guard. As Ben tried to tell the guard that he and his family were traveling per U.S. orders and that a U.S. car was awaiting his family to take them to the hotel for the night, the guard raised his machine gun, stuck it into Ben's stomach and pushed him into a seat and said, "Yellow paper."

Ben turned to his wife and said, "I think we made a mistake. Maybe we should try to go home."

At this point the customs agent yelled, "Bishop!" Ben handed the yellow pass to the guard and the Bishop family passed through the door and thankfully sat in an air-conditioned car.

After the family had been comfortably settled in their new quarters, Ben and his family visited his new high school. The children enjoyed sitting at the teacher's desk. Ben familiarized himself with his third floor classroom, lunchroom, cafeteria, study hall rooms and the textbook storage area. Two days later Ben was starting a new school year as a proud teacher in Tropic High School.

Three weeks passed before Heather and Ben realized that their family would be stuck in a third floor walk-up apartment for the two years of this overseas teaching assignment. The contract he had signed for the job was quite specific. *If a contracted employee (Ben) were to leave before his/her two years were completed, then the employee would have to reimburse the US government the ENTIRE COST of shipping their fam-*

ily goods to and from the tropics.

Ben decided to meet with his principal, the school superintendent and the housing supervisor. Ben requested to be assigned to a more appropriate housing unit. Since all housing was assigned based upon a seniority system, Ben was informed that it would be more than two years before he could win a first floor apartment or more than five years before he would have a chance to get a three bedroom house in a decent location. Ben asked what he could do, since he could not pay to reimburse the governmental costs to move his family back to the States nor could his family continue to live in such a substandard apartment.

The housing officer said, "Tough, you can't do a thing about it. Now leave."

His new principal said, "I told you that you will have to live there so accept it and go home to your family."

Ben determinedly stated, "I'll not report to work until either you fire me, in which case the U.S. government will pay my family's repatriation OR you assign my family to a better house."

The two school administrators convinced the housing director to find a way to get the Bishops a better housing assignment. The director called Ben at his apartment that night with a plan to help the Bishops!!

He offered to post a single family house which was 14 miles from the high school if the Bishops would accept it and live in it for at least two years. The Bishops said that the 14-mile drive wasn't a problem and they toured the proposed house the next day after the end of his teaching stint.

All available houses/housing units were always posted on the housing authority's bulletin board(s) for one week. The winner always was the most senior person to have signed the vacancy notice as posted on the bulletin board. The housing director posted the house that the Bishops had already inspected the day after they agreed to live in it for the next two years.

The house was posted on a clipboard nailed to a tree; the tree was a one-mile walk into the jungle.

The route to the tree was described in detail to Ben. Ben hiked into the jungle with boots on. He was afraid of every jungle noise he heard. He signed his name on the clipboard and hurried back to his parked car. The following Monday all the previous week's postings were listed with the winners names highlighted. The Bishops had won a single house. They moved into their new home that weekend.

A Ball for Christmas

Rebecca R. arrived at Mr. Bishop's classroom door during the last week of October. Her parents had been transferred by the military three times since the first of June. Rebecca informed her new teacher that she and her parents had been shuttled all over the United States before the government had finally decided to place her father at the "A" Airbase in the tropics.

Ben greeted his newest student warmly. He then firmly informed her of his rules for late entrants to his math classes. He gave every late registering student exactly three weeks to catch up with his/her class. In most cases this policy was an easy one for the incoming student to live with as they usually were only about one week behind. But in Rebecca's case, today was her first day of school.

As a result of the late assignment transfer(s) her dad received, she had not attended school until the day she registered in Mr. Bishop's geometry class. Rebecca's new classmates were working on problems found on page 147. Rebecca not only had to pay attention to the daily geometry class work, she also had to do a challenging but abbreviated catch-up program. Rebecca affirmed that she accepted these catch-up rules and that if she had any difficulties she would stay after school and Mr. Bishop would readily assist her. Ben had used this method to help his school year transferred students to catch up with his classes for the two years that he taught at Tropic High School. Rebecca was the only student who never stayed for extra help during her three-week catch-up period.

On the first day of Rebecca's fourth week in Ben's plane

geometry class, he announced that she was required to answer truthfully the question: "You have learned and you thoroughly understand all 147 pages of the text in addition to the class work we have covered during the past three weeks?"

Ben had allowed several students four week catch-up time because they had stayed after school and asked for help during their three week catch-up windows; Rebecca had not asked for help during her three-week opportunity and her, "Yes, Sir!" clearly indicated that she had academically caught up with her classmates.

Ben proceeded to question her on her three weeks of catch-up work. Rebecca answered each question with a perfect response; Ben then continued by asking her questions about the most challenging problems from each chapter in the text up to page 147. Rebecca, in each instance, responded immediately with a perfect answer.

Ben was exceptionally pleased with her preparedness and apologized to Rebecca for his aggressive challenge of her readiness for his geometry class. He then complimented her for doing her school work so accurately.

Shortly afterward, Ben would ask Rebecca to explain unusually hard geometry problems to her classmates. She was always thoroughly prepared. Ben had discovered one of his brightest students.

* * *

Mr. B. had a habit of spending 25 cents each month to purchase the Tropic High literacy magazine, *The Pulse*. He read every story authored by one of his math students and then he would toss the magazine into his desk drawer, He read "A Ball for Christmas" written by Rebecca R. The next morning Mr. B. told Rebecca how much he had enjoyed the article and commented on her vivid imagination. He further complimented

Rebecca on her outstanding writing style. As he continued to praise the young writer, Rebecca quietly said to her favorite math teacher, "That story is about me—when I was a three-year-old."

Mr. Bishop apologized to her and was at a loss for any additional words regarding Rebecca's revelation, but he took his copy of *The Pulse* home in order that Heather could read about Rebecca's belief in Santa Claus.

Rebecca's story was about her life as a three-year-old living with her parents in a World War II concentration camp. One morning Rebecca and her mother were forced to stand and watch as her father was shot and killed. Later that same year Rebecca, a three-year-old who believed in Santa, asked for a ball for Christmas. On that Christmas morning little Rebecca received TWO balls as gifts from Santa. One ball had been given to her by a German guard. It was a real rubber ball. The second ball had been made by the prisoners. They had taken threads from their clothes and had wound them tightly, making a ball for the little one who could believe in Santa!!!!

Modern Technology

Ben rarely departed from his habit of starting his math classes before the bell rang. His students were used to his teaching patterns and always tried to be in their seats before the bell rang. One day as Mr. B. was standing in the hall awaiting his students he noticed a dark-haired young lady seated in his room. He assumed her to be a friend of one of his math students. He decided to wait until the bell rang before he'd enter the room to begin class.

As the bell rang Mr. Bishop told the stranger to leave and go to her period 4 class.

"But Mr. Bishop—" she said.

Ben interrupted firmly and directed the stranger, "Don't BUT me! Now leave my room immediately and go to your next class."

Philip W. quietly reminded him that the girl was one of Mr. B.'s algebra students.

Ben looked at the young lady slouched down in her seat and politely asked if she was indeed one of his students.

Barbara B. replied, "Yes, I am Barbara B."

Mr. Bishop stared. It was a lengthy few seconds before Ben finally recognized his student. Barbara had dyed her hair! Last Friday she had been a blonde; today (Monday) Barbara's hair was dark brown. *Modern technology,* thought Ben, as he apologized to Barbara. Mr. B. quickly began asking heavy thinking math questions in order to get the students' minds off of his embarrassing moment.

* * *

Mary D. sat in the second seat of the second row of students closest to the classroom door. Mary was a quiet student. She had never done anything in the classroom which would have made someone notice her. On the opposite side of the room, everyone knew Billy T. He was seated at the fourth desk adjacent to the windows. Billy T. was a happy character who loved to entertain his classmates by distracting his teachers. After many confrontations with Mr. Bishop, Billy decided to change. He planned to drop his mischievous ways. "Mr. B.," said Billy as he left Tropic High one hour later than his friends as a result of visiting with his teacher as a *house guest.*

"Yes, Billy," responded Mr. Bishop.

"From this day forward, I'm going to be good. You will never have me as your guest again."

Ben's "Great!" ended the conversation that afternoon.

Several weeks went by without a Billy incident. He obviously was keeping his promise. Ben stopped looking in his direction in an attempt to stop trouble before it started. Billy had changed and Mr. Bishop cheered him on. He told Billy, "Keep up the good behavior, your grades are improving as well."

Mary D. entered her math class just as the bell rang. Ben started teaching—he was visually distracted by Mary's tight sweater and her enhanced chest! Ben directed all of his mind-challenging questions to the back of the room. At this point poor Mary's new physicality evidently became a little too uncomfortable. She rested her extended chest on her desk.

With her mind obviously on her new self, she reached through the V-neck of her sweater and started to move things around!

Mr. B immediately started yelling at Billy T, attempting to focus the student's attention on the other side of the classroom to protect Mary from any embarrassment

Fortunately for everyone the bell rang. Billy had angrily shouted that he hadn't done anything. "Mr. Bishop, I didn't do nothin'! I've been good for six weeks now. You're not being fair."

As the students left the room, Ben told Billy that he had used him as a distracter and proceeded to thank him for his help.

Ben did not answer Billy's, "Distracter for what?"

Ben ran downstairs to the nurse's office and asked her to find Mary D. "Please show her how to handle her plastic surgery enhancement—but not in the classroom!" pleaded Ben. *Modern technology*, thought Ben as he raced back upstairs to his next class.

Faculty Mischief

Ben was a member of a team of good teachers. They acted more like a family than a group of non-related faculty members.

Mr. Bishop frequently was the recipient of friendly insults as a result of his name. "Hey, Bishop, do you have to confess to the Pope? Did you tell the Pope about all the erasers you stole from the second floor classrooms?" On other occasions, Ben would be walking down the hall and he'd hear Mr. Montgomery telling a passing student that the Pope really was Mr. Bishop's dad!!

One afternoon immediately after the school buses had left the school yard with most of the student population, Mr. Montgomery entered Ben's classroom. Ben was seated at his desk developing a lesson plan for the next chapter. Mr. M., a friend of Ben's, visited for a moment before he stepped through the open third floor window onto the roof of the gym and auditorium. Ben watched his friend from his desk. Mr. M. walked over to the huge air ducts and leaned into the air ventilation shaft, shouting his brief message into the main ductwork of the building's fresh air exchange system. It was clearly heard in the school gym and in most of the adjacent rooms, including Ben's.

Approximately one-third of the school heard only a ghostly howl. Students and staff in the central section of the school heard his insulting message to one of his fellow teachers. Mr. M. climbed back into the classroom, ran toward the door and disappeared down the hall without being spotted by either student or staff. As Mr. M. passed Ben's desk, he begged Ben to forget what he had seen and heard. Ben was laughing so hard that he could only wave at his friend as he raced to his own classroom.

The words which had vibrated through the airshaft that afternoon were heard by most of the staff and many of the students who had remained on the premises for after-school work.

Mr. M.'s message traveling through the airduct to his friend, "MR. AJAX, YOU ARE A COMPLETE NUT!!" caused quite a stir. Alex Ajax never solved the puzzle as to which "friend," did it; nor did he ever discover how it had been done. The teachers' room conversation for a few weeks after the shaky message had been aired was usually directed toward finding the culprit and conjecturing how to pay him back.

The principal moved Ben's classroom to the center of the third floor, to a new room which was centered between the two stairwells. The principal informed Mr. B. that he needed a strong disciplinarian located in the center of the third floor. Several teachers believed that the move was made to get Mr. B. away from the airshaft. At this point Mr. Montgomery had to confess to Mr. N Heart, the principal, in order that he could assure his staff that Ben was not the ghostly voice. In spite of the fact that the principal was using him, Ben was excited because he now had what he considered to be the best classroom in the entire school. His math classes would be taught in a classroom which physically was between two stairwells. Thus Ben didn't have any noisy students on either side of him, and Ben enjoyed teaching in his new classroom.

One day as Ben concluded a chapter in the math text, he was distracted by the typing class across the hall. Mrs. Remington was playing syncopated music for her students to type in sync with. The students were typing rhythmically to the music speed as selected by their teacher. Mr. Bishop and his students heard the music and the syncopated typing coming from Mrs. Remington's class. Mr. B. asked his trigonometry students if they were interested in visiting the class across the hall. Every math student cheerfully agreed to participate in the impromptu visit to the typing class.

Ben entered the classroom door adjacent to the teacher's desk with a distracting, "Good morning Mrs. Remington" as his organized students quietly passed through the door at the rear of the typing room. The first math kids through the door quickly and silently moved toward the front of the room in order that the last students entering would be able to introduce themselves to the typists at the back of Mrs. Remington's classroom. Ben's entire class were at their planned positions. The silent signal was given. Mr. Bishop asked the teacher while at the same time the math kids asked the typing students for "This dance!!"

Ben and Mrs. Remington twirled about once or twice before she was able to stop him. Each young couple completed at least one rhythmic twirl before the loud command restoring order and directing the crazy math students and their teacher to leave was clearly heard and obeyed. Mr. B.'s students exited immediately and quietly. The math class enjoyed a mischievous laugh in the confines of their classroom. Ben apologized to Mrs. R. at the end of the class period.

Names and Nicknames

Bishop had established a pattern of making certain he pronounced every student's name correctly. Ben readily admitted his native language was that of a New Englander. He wasn't fluent in any language other than his New England-based English. As a high school student, Ben's report cards noted he had taken 4 years of Latin, 2 years of French and of German. In spite of this academic background, Ben's language skills were strictly New England English.

Mr. B. began his first class at Tropic High as he had all of his classes in the States. He asked his students to politely correct him if he mispronounced their names. Ben called Phillip O.'s name. Phillip said, "Mr. Bishop, my last name is O . . . "

After several attempts to pronounce the name correctly, Phillip gave up and stated that his teacher had finally got it. No other student offered any corrections to their teacher's attempts to say their names.

During the May homeroom elections for student representation to serve on the principal's team in the ensuing school year, Ben instructed his homeroom students that all nominees had to be from this room, i.e., "Your homeroom." Yolanda M. stood up and nominated "T. Bur-ee-o." Ben emphatically reminded Yolanda that the nominees had to be members of THIS homeroom, to which Yolanda responded, "Mr. Bishop, T. Bur-ee-o is in this room!"

Then Yolanda pointed at her friend. Ben looked at the student she was pointing to and realized that he had been calling this student "T. Burillo" not only in his homeroom but also in his algebra classes. Mr. B. asked T. why he hadn't corrected the pronunciation of his name on the first day of school. T. reminded his teacher of his many attempts to correctly say Phillip O.'s name; then T. informed his favorite teacher that he had decided at that moment to accept whatever pronunciation of his name Mr. Bishop used. Ben apologized to both students and to their classmates. The kids said it was okay because Mr. B. was an okay teacher. Ben felt badly about his language errors. He visited with the language teacher for a little name pronunciation tutoring. A week later he was pronouncing every student's name correctly,

On his way home from work (school), Ben always stopped to pick up the family mail. Heather and Ben were happy to have received a letter from his history teacher friend, Bill W. The two had taught together at City High School. Bill's epistle highlighted many of Mr. Hughe's escapades during the current school year. The lengthy note concluded with "—OLD TWO TON FELL OFF THE STAGE and broke his ankle."

Ben chuckled over his vision of the related incident. He knew that when he and his family returned to the States he'd visit with his old friend to hear the whole story. Ben's thoughts about his former principal gave birth to an idea. Ben was thinking for the first time, "I could do a better job as a principal." Hmmmm!!

The Wheelchair

Tropic High School Principal N Heart had decided to align his school by academic areas. The first floor housed all science, business and shop classes. Language classes, both domestic and foreign, were on the second floor. Math and social studies classes were to be taught on the third floor. N Heart believed that by using this simple scheduling pattern, he would be able to significantly reduce—if not eliminate—student wandering throughout the school. All of Ben's math classes were to be taught on the third floor.

Eugene H. was accidentally shot and as a result was paralyzed from the waist down to his feet. The accident had occurred in mid-June. His brother had been playing with the family rifle. The unexpected shot had severed Eugene's spinal cord. He had no control or ability to move any part of his body below his waist. But when school reopened that September, Eugene believed that he'd be walking by Christmas.

Principal N Heart called a special staff meeting of all personnel who would be working with Eugene during this new school year. N Heart explained in detail the sad facts of Eugene's accident ten weeks earlier. N Heart gave explicit instructions to all the staff members attending the meeting as to the methods which were to be used to handle Eugene's personal, social, physical and academic needs. After an examination of Eugene's class schedule, N Heart discovered that three of his classes would be on the first floor. The exceptions were English (second floor), social studies (third floor) and math (third floor). N Heart instructed his teachers as to how they were to use student help to get Eugene from one classroom to the next.

The student's first period was a first floor class. Eugene's second period was English. Third period history was followed immediately by fourth period math. Eugene was scheduled to have his lunch in the cafeteria after math. The cafeteria, as well as his last two classrooms, was on the first floor.

N Heart told the first period teacher to have two students carry Eugene in his wheelchair up to his second floor English class. At the end of period two, the English teacher was to have two male students carry the chair with Eugene seated in it to the third floor for his history class. At the end of his math class, Ben was directed to have two students carry Eugene and the chair back down to the first floor so that Eugene could eat his lunch and complete his school day.

Ben asked one of the first floor business teachers if he would swap fourth period classrooms with him. The English and history teachers asked their first floor confreres to make similar classroom swaps. The three teachers were trying to resolve a potentially dangerous problem. N Heart shouted at his staff, "I run this school! No teacher will exchange their assigned classrooms with another teacher. All of you will follow the directions I just gave you. No one is to question my plan in this or any other matter." Ben and his friends tried to reason with the boss, but they didn't get anywhere.

Ben's sophomore class had exactly two weight lifters capable of carrying Eugene and his chair down the stairs to the first floor. The boys proudly volunteered for this assignment. Ben emphatically told them that they were not to be absent this school year.

The first four months of the school year passed without incident. During the second week of January, one of Mr. B.'s Eugene carriers was absent. The other student politely asked Mr. Bishop to help him carry Eugene down the stairs to the first floor. Ben was definitely surprised when he discovered how heavy the load was that his boys had been carrying without complaint every school day. A few days later Mr. B. was concluding his third period math class when he heard a crash and a painful scream. It sounded like Eugene!!! Ben ran out of his class to the stairwell. He was shocked to see Eugene on the stairwell landing with his wheelchair resting on top of him. Ben instructed one of the two carriers to go to the office for help, to call Eugene's family and the school doctor. The other boy assisted Ben in removing the chair from Eugene's face and chest. The two tried to comfort Eugene until the school nurse arrived. Eugene told his teacher he was okay. The doctor and nurse arrived together. They arranged for Eugene to be carried by stretcher to the nurse's office.

Ben returned to his class as the bell rang. He dismissed his fourth period students. He decided to skip lunch and to sit with Eugene until he learned how badly his student had been hurt. The doctor and Eugene's parents said that he would be fine. Eugene was just badly bruised. That afternoon, Ben asked Principal N Heart to schedule all of Eugene's academic classes on the first floor for the remainder of the school year. N Heart's 'NO!" was loud and clear.

Eugene returned to school a few days later. He was carried between classes as before. No additional accidents occurred.

Ben and Eugene talked about Eugene's future on many a school day. Ben made a suggestion which Eugene thought might work for him. Eugene had decided to become a teacher. (*Math teacher*, thought Ben.) The two conspirators figured Eugene could teach on a raised platform built at the front of the classroom to help him to be able to see his students. Eugene was excited about going to college, becoming a teacher and using an overhead projector to make his future classroom presentations.

Mr. Bishop refused to let this author print what he and the entire Tropic High School faculty said to the principal on the day of the accident.

The General's Son

Ben sent two students to the principal's office during his two years at Tropic High School. The first student Ben had sent to the office was a result of a major disruptive act in the classroom. The second case happened about a month after the first. Mr. Bishop had directed the second student to step outside and wait a few minutes so that they could talk while the other students were doing class work. In the first case Ben wanted the principal to strongly discipline the recalcitrant youth. (Actually Ben wanted the boy to be suspended for a day or two.)

The first offender sent to the office by Mr. B. was the General's son. Ten minutes later the young man returned to his math class with a note written by the principal—Mr. N Heart. The note clearly stated that Mr. B. had made a mistake. The General's son had not misbehaved: "It must have been another student." The note instructed Mr. Bishop to let this boy back into his classroom WITHOUT any further disciplinary action.

In the other case, five minutes had barely passed when Ben stepped out of his classroom to talk to student #2. Ben was surprised to discover #2 was nowhere to be seen. Mr. B. checked the boys' restroom, but #2 wasn't there.

Ben used his classroom in-house phone to report the missing boy. The secretary responded by telling Mr. Bishop that #2 was in the office and waiting for his parents to come to take him home; Mr. N Heart had suspended him for a week.

At the end of that class the principal stopped by Ben's classroom to tell him what had happened. Mr. N Heart complimented Mr. Bishop for taking the correct action in this matter. N

Heart had found #2 quietly waiting outside his math classroom, and the student had told Mr. N Heart that he was instructed to wait outside to talk to his teacher.

N Heart took #2 downstairs to his office and informed him that it was essential for him to discover the importance of good behavior in school. N Heart further commented to Mr. B. that he had made the correct decision when he sent, "That Sgt.'s son to the office."

As Ben was completing his last year of teaching at Tropic High he realized that someday he'd be a secondary school principal. He knew he would treat every student via the scout uniform theory. Regardless of what side of town a kid came from, justice would be the same for everyone.

On the flight back to the States, Ben was seated next to the father of a June Tropic High School graduate. The dad told Ben an incredible story about Mr. N Heart. Although Ben had heard many rumors about the incident being discussed, he had never heard the *whole* story. Ben's seatmate on the flight to Boston recounted a most unbelievable story about his son while a student at Tropic High. Two young friends, both high school seniors, had taken the school chaperoned train to the high school football game 40 miles away against West Tropic High. All Tropic High football games were played at night when the temperature dropped below 80 degrees. The two boys were wrong. They deserved to be punished. Mr. N Heart's method was clearly unacceptable. The two friends had left the football game and had walked into the nearby town for a few beers. They were lucky enough to get back to the field before the train left to travel the return 40 miles through the unlit jungle. N Heart had observed the boys return to the field just as the game ended. N Heart stopped the train at marker 8. Marker 8 was exactly 8 miles from the station adjacent to Tropic High, N Heart put Ben's story-telling seatmate's son off the train into a little clearing. N Heart told the frightened kid that he would send his father to get him as soon as the train pulled into the station.

The train arrived at the station. N Heart called the student's story-telling dad. Ben's seatmate and a neighbor rushed to the depot where they were assigned a handcar to travel the 8 miles to find his son. Fortunately he and his friend were strong enough to propel the handcar the eight miles into the jungle. The three exhausted and scared travelers worked hard to get back to the train station. The rescue trip had taken two and one half hours. The dad knew his son had discovered the error of his behavior that evening. He didn't punish him at all. He was relieved that he found his son and that he was okay. The dad, his son and the dad's friend who helped to rescue the stranded kid didn't get home until 3 A.M. the next morning. The dad tried to have the principal arrested for what he had done to his son. He tried to get N Heart fired. Nothing happened. The principal wasn't even reprimanded for placing one of his students in such a dangerous situation. "Imagine how frightened my son was as he sat in the pitch black clearing in the middle of the jungle praying to be rescued? My family grew up in the city; we are afraid of the jungle, bugs, wild animals, and the vegetation itself," the dad continued. "He was scared."

As the dad finished his story, Ben asked him about a few seemingly missing details, "I thought you began your story stating that your son and a friend had left the game for a beer? You mentioned just your son being left in the jungle clearing. What happened to the other beer drinker?"

"Nothing," said the dad. "He was the general's son!"

The plane landed in Boston. Heather, Ben and their children passed through customs and waved goodbye to their fellow traveler. He was a postal clerk in the tropics, NOT A GENERAL!!

* * *

*　*　*

Ben spent the four years following his return to the states teaching math, working a second job as well as working on advanced degrees. He was spending his (extra ??) time preparing himself for the administrative job(s) he dreamed about. Even without the coveted advanced degrees, he knew that he'd be a better principal than either Mr. Hughe or Mr. N Heart.

With Heather's quiet support, Ben earned three additional academic degrees. He also received several certificates for additional academic work. Ben thought, *Now, I'm ready academically, am an experienced teacher and will function with integrity on all occasions in behalf of the students, their families and their teachers.* Then he announced to Heather and their children, "Now I'm ready to step up to the plate and take a good swing at the advertised principal vacancies."

Ben was ecstatic when he received Dr. Haberdasher's call and subsequent contract to serve as the first North Mountain Jr. High Principal. The city had just converted its school district from a K–8, 9–12 program to a K–6, 7–8, 9–12 one.

Author's Comment
Entrance Age

I firmly believe that every child in the United States should have an equal opportunity to enter public school *under the same standards in all 50 states.*

Current state laws vary to the point that children entering first grade in one state must be six years of age on or before December 31; yet in an adjoining state, children will not be accepted unless they have celebrated a sixth birthday on or before October 15.

To further complicate this matter several states have adopted entrance age guidelines for their cities and towns to follow. State law in these states is frequently written so that the individual cities and towns can establish an independent entrance age as long as it is a date between September 1 and December 31, of that year. In these states, neighboring towns can have different entrance age standards.

Prior to WW II the majority of age-defined first grade entrance dates usually was December 31. During this period through to the early 1950s, most families lived in or near their birthplace. With the rapid growth of families and the changes in societal behavior, i.e., families relocating all over the country as they chased their family dreams, school populations grew too rapidly for the harried taxpaying families to handle.

New schools had to be built. At first the communities struggled under the impact of overcrowded school rooms. Eventually that ever growing burden forced the construction of additional classrooms AND the hiring of additional teachers, needed to fill these new schools/classrooms. At this same time the taxpayers were working hard to make a living. The taxes on their first homes were heavy burdens on these young families. They turned their struggle into a political directive to the city's town fathers—SLOW DOWN—the annual increase in our taxes is too much. New ideas were needed to slow this extraordinary and costly growth cycle. One frequently adopted solution to delay the construction of new schools was to move back the first grade entrance date from December 31st to November, or to October. This process was developed to reduce the incoming class size by either 8.3% or 16.7%. Some districts moved their entrance dates in a two-or three-year period back to September 1st. Intellectual arguments were created to make these construction stalling decisions appear to be in the best interest of the students.

A byproduct of these 1950s, 1960s and later decisions of pushing back the first grade entrance dates is the impact it has on individual children.

I wrote to every State Commissioner of Education in the fall of 1978 asking them to work toward establishing a national standard for the entering first-grade student into our nation's public schools. Approximately 30 percent of them responded to my appeal. Their general comment leaned toward agreeing with me as long as the nation adopted the standard currently accepted in *their* state.

The United States is comprised of more than 20,000 cities and towns. It is a nation of frequent family relocation. If one family were to move from just 5,000 of these communities to another having a different first grade entrance policy, then it becomes possible that hundreds of families may be impacted by these varied standards. Since each case generally represents just one child in his/her new school district, no one feels the need to do more than to say "Sorry, but your son/daughter will be accepted next year."

The plight of the child whose family, knowing the local

entrance regulations, and having registered their child for the first grade spent the summer talking encouragingly with the child about starting school in September, suddenly becomes disheartening when the parents decide to move to improve their family life only to be denied acceptance in the new school district.

At this time, I am not arguing the academic points as to how old a child should be upon entering first grade, what behavioral standards he/she should have developed, or the size of the vocabulary needed by the entering student. I am simply pleading that the U.S. Department of Education must establish a national school entrance policy to protect *all* children whether their families move or not.

Should a national debate develop on this subject, then I beg that the decision makers consider the average high school exiting age to be equally important as the school entrance age. Educators on occasion discuss a later entrance age without any consideration to the concomitant impact, resulting in either a high school graduate or a dropout.

SCHOOL BUS

Principal

Welcome??

The superintendent, the school committee and the press greeted the new principal with happy smiles and fanfare. The Bishop family moved into their new house on the second Monday in July. The superintendent met with Ben to go over the details of the school district's conversion from a K–8, 9–12 system to the new plan, K–6, 7–8, 9–12. The new junior high was a district decision. Superintendent Haberdasher told his new junior high principal that he had to design the curriculum, the scheduling, the appropriate staffing etc., etc. Dr. Haberdasher then asked Mr. B. how many weeks he'd need before he would be ready to present his plan to the school committee for approval. Dr. H. also noted a few additional district changes that the committee had made in conjunction with the adoption of a new junior high school program in Mountain City. Ben responded to Dr. H. that he'd have his plan ready for the superintendent's approval on Friday morning and would appreciate presenting Dr. H.'s approved plan to the school committee on the following Monday evening.

The additional district changes which the committee had adopted along with the scheduled September opening of the junior high school included the following:

Transfer all students with an IQ above 120 to the state college K–8 training school located in Mountain City.

Transfer all experienced teachers to district vacancies in the five city elementary schools.

Additional transfers out of the building to each of the five elementary schools were not adopted by vote. Rather, these decisions were made by the five elementary school principals striving to improve their schools in a weakly funded school system. The five principals transferred most of the larger student school desks and chairs. (They needed these desks for their taller students!) These school desks were replaced with "WORN SHOULD BE DISCARDED" school desks and chairs.

Ben spent the next four days developing Mountain City Jr. High School's curriculum, its schedule as well as noting the staff necessary to present such a program. Ben's call(s) to his two assistants and the few staff remaining as assigned jr. high teachers to meet and to assist in the designing of the jr. high program were greatly appreciated. Everyone met with him during the week to highlight their perception of the needs of the new program for the success of their students. Ben inserted most of the staff's ideas into his proposal, and presented his team-developed plan to Dr. Haberdasher on Friday morning as he promised. Dr. H. approved the plan in totality. Dr. H. told Ben that he, Mr. Bishop, would be making the presentation to the school committee on Monday evening.

Ben presented his jr. high plan to the committee at 7:30 on that fateful Monday night. A little before 9 P.M. the committee chairman informed him that the plan was "Too rich for our blood!" Mayor Fred Firmby offered to reconvene the committee in two weeks so that Mr. Bishop could present a less expensive plan. Ben asked the committee to please agree to meet with him on Wednesday evening so that after the committee approved his plan he would have time to put the plan together, interview the necessary staff members to fill the approved vacancies, etc. etc. The committee agreed to meet two days later on Wednesday evening.

Heather had spent Tuesday evening typing Ben's more conservative junior high plan. She finished the project a little after 2 A.M. Wednesday morning. Ben wouldn't have secretarial help until two weeks prior to the opening of school. With Dr. H.'s support, Ben presented his '"watered down plan to the school committee.

Once again the committee chairman, Mayor Fred Firmby, as a result of the committee's vote, informed Mr. Bishop that his plan was a little too generous for Mountain City Junior High.

Mayor Firmby offered to host another special meeting on Friday evening to consider a basic plan for the project. Mayor Firmby was quite surprised and taken aback when Ben said that he would not need a Friday meeting. Ben reached into his coat pocket and pulled out an envelope containing his basic plan!!! Mayor Firmby proudly listened to his newest administrator as he in plain words stated, "Either you adopt this, my final plan, this evening or you can have my resignation as I will not serve as a principal in a school designed to limit its students' chances for success."

Mayor Fred Firmby applauded Principal Bishop's assertive behavior and asked the committee to approve the plan Ben had just finished presenting. The basic plan landed in the convenient wastebasket. Superintendent H. and Mayor Fred let Ben know that they were cheering him on from that day forward. A proud Ben joyously thanked his bride of 14 years for her tremendous help in getting the project approved.

* * *

Two years later Mountain City parents were demanding that their children attend the city junior high rather than the college training school. Ben and his teachers had been offended by the selective student transfers from their school. As a result of that public insult to transfer the students to the training school, Ben and his staff had committed themselves to teach their students so that they would competitively and academically beat the training school kids in high school. Within a year, every marking period at the high school ended with the statistics clearly showing that higher grades had been earned by the junior high students.

* * *

In August of Ben's first year as a junior high principal he discovered that the five elementary principals hadn't borrowed everything they needed from his building. Each time an elementary principal dropped over for some necessary supplies, Ben readily agreed they could take whatever they needed in exchange for a few desks, etc., etc. By September the school was properly equipped and all the principals had become happy and mischievous friends.

Truant

"Harry is truant again, Mr. Bishop." Ben's secretary informed her boss that Harry T. was truant for the seventh consecutive school day. It was early October and Harry was absent again! Ben knew that if he reported the seventh day of truancy to the authorities, Harry would be taken to the juvenile detention center. Harry's mother came to the school in response to Ben's call and informed Mr. Bishop that she didn't care to get involved in this truancy matter. She had awakened Harry each morning and told him to get dressed and to go to school. She had done her job. Now she would go back to work. Harry's mother directed Mr. B. not to call her ever again.

Ben watched in disbelief as she walked to her car to return to work. *She has a thing for yellow,* thought Ben. Her hair was a bright yellow. Her sweater was yellow. Her slacks were yellow, as were her shoes and socks. *Wow, even her fingernails are yellow . . .*

Mr. B. decided to warn Harry T. regarding the consequences of this, his seventh day of truancy. Ben drove over to Harry's Sixth Street duplex-style house. Harry, his brother John, and their mother lived on the left side of the building. Ben rang the doorbell. He watched the curtain move as Harry peeked out to identify his visitor. A moment later Ben heard the back door close and he watched as Harry jumped the fence to escape. Harry ran down the next street and disappeared. Mr. Bishop returned to his office and reported Harry's seven days of truancy to the authorities. Several days later the city police department picked up Harry and took him to the juvenile detention center.

Weeks later Harry dropped in to visit his school principal. Mr. B. told Harry that he would report his escape from the detention center to the police; in fact, Mr. B. had already asked his secretary to call the police station to report Harry's return to Mountain City Junior High. Harry coldly responded noting that he would be long gone before the police arrived. He had just stopped in to say "Hello" and to brag about his escape from the center. The police didn't catch up with the elusive Harry for several more weeks.

On the second Wednesday morning in December, a police cruiser doing traffic control on Main Street spotted a tall young man walking across the Main Street bridge. Harry had re-dyed his blond hair black. He was dressed completely in black from his shirt to his shoes and socks. The two policemen hopped into their cruiser and drove onto the bridge. One officer got out of the car and started to walk toward Harry. The other officer drove up the bridge to where Harry was standing at the middle of the bridge. He rolled the window down and asked Harry to jump into the car for a nice warm ride back to the juvenile center. Harry started to run away. The policeman drove the cruiser to the other end of the bridge. He got out of the car and began to walk toward Harry while his partner was moving in from the other side.

Harry felt trapped. He jumped off the bridge into the frigid water 20 feet below. The policemen watched as Harry struggled to the east side of the river. They rushed to the river bank to rescue and to take Harry into state custody once again. The two officers returned Harry to the center. Then they visited with Mr. B. to explain the delay(s) in arresting Harry. Their search warrants had been for Harry's home, but they never could catch him there. En route to the juvenile home Harry laughed at the policemen and bragged that he was always there when they were searching his home for him. Every time they went to the house looking for him, Harry had climbed through a well hidden hole in the cellar wall which allowed him to be in his neighbor's half of the duplex.

Harry was released in early April and returned to visit his principal. Ben had arranged with a local factory manager to put Harry to work. The manager made special arrangements to keep Harry out of the dangerous equipment areas, to give him a most boring job, and to report his attendance to Ben on a daily basis. Thus Harry began a work program.

Harry returned to his eighth-grade classes in September.

Boxing Lessons

Harry was six feet tall. He towered over most of the seventh grade students in Mountain City Junior High. Harry enjoyed cornering a small seventh grader in the restroom. He then would proceed to terrorize the youngster. This roughing up of seventh-grade boys by the bully, Harry, went on for several weeks before any teacher learned about it. Harry was appropriately punished and continuously watched in order to make certain that he didn't restart his bullying game. One small boy continued to worry about what Harry would do to him when the teachers were not around to protect him.

Ben and one of his mischievous staff members decided to form a boxing club for any interested junior high students. The concerned boy was the first club member. He recruited many of his classmates. At first the club met every night after school. Everyone appeared to be having a great time and they were learning to protect themselves. A few months later the coach informed Mr. B. that his seventh graders were ready to challenge the school bully in a supervised fight. Harry refused to fight, "I don't want to hurt the little kid." After a few days of verbal harassment by many of the seventh graders chanting, "Harry is afraid to fight." Harry agreed to box after school with, "any cheeky seventh grader."

When Harry arrived in the school gym after school on that soon-to-be-historic Tuesday afternoon he knew he had to fight. All of the seventh graders put in an appearance at the event. Harry decided he would show these little kids how tough he was and that they had better watch out. The five-foot-tall seventh grader had been thoroughly trained to dart in under Harry's roundhouse swings and to tap him on the nose. After the nose tap the youngster quickly stepped back out of Harry's reach. As he danced about the fight area, Harry shouted at him to stand still, "So I can hit you!" With three or four taps on Harry's nose and with Harry making no physical contact, Harry's frustration grew. The plan was working, The students and the teachers cheered the underdog on. It had been agreed that the fight would be stopped as soon as Harry's nose was bloodied. Harry had been taught a lesson. Harry was afraid to use any unsupervised restrooms.

Two days later the superintendent told Ben to disband the boxing club. Harry's mother had complained to the school board about her son being beat up by a professional boxer.

During the last week of May, Harry and his 21-year-old brother decided to avenge his embarrassment and to straighten out the little boxer. The two six-foot-tall tough guys trapped the little boxer in the boys' room. They went after him as a single unit. The tough guys were flashing knives as they approached the seventh grader. The little boxer decided that if he had to lose this battle he might as well go down fighting. The seventh grade boxer attacked. Harry and his brother ran out of the restroom and out of the school. The police picked up the pair and charged them with assault (attempted) with dangerous weapons. A year later Harry and his brother were arrested for stealing cars per the orders of a local chop shop.

The Missing Rankbook

Martin Murphy, a seventh grade science teacher, was waiting for the principal to arrive early Monday morning. Martin was always the first teacher to arrive at school every day. Mr. Bishop usually entered the building a few minutes before the majority of his staff arrived. Martin grabbed Ben as he entered his office and asked him to hurry down to Ms. Sharpe's first floor classroom which was a mess. Jim, the custodian, had called the police when he discovered the broken window and the evidence of the break-in that had caused damage to Ms. Sharpe's classroom.

Ben immediately closed the classroom door after viewing the damage. He rescheduled Ms. Sharpe and her students to another room for the day. Detective Jurand arrived and inspected the room with Martin and Mr. Bishop. Their initial reaction was pure disgust. The three men agreed to allow Jim to clean up the insulting message left on Ms. Sharpe's chair before she was invited in to inspect her classroom. Detective Jurand asked Ms. Sharpe to itemize everything which was missing. The three men correctly surmised that the weekend visitor was one of her students. Jim had worked hard to remove the stench which had permeated the area around her desk and chair. Ms. S. was not told about her personal message from one of her unhappy students that morning. She reported to the detective that the only item missing was a small portable radio which she listened to after school while preparing her lesson plans. The broken window was replaced later that morning. No other evidence was discovered during a thorough search of the school building. Thus everyone concluded that the late night tourist hadn't visited any other classrooms. It appeared that someone wasn't too happy with Ms. Sharpe as his/her teacher.

Ms. Sharpe had been Mr. B.'s most frequently called substitute teacher during the previous two years. Ben had hired Ms. S. as a full-time teacher at the start of the new school year. Ben had jokingly told her he didn't want to hire her as a regular teacher because he needed her expertise as a most successful and dependable sub. Ms. Sharpe proved to be an excellent full-time seventh grade English teacher. The break-in had happened on the same weekend which ended the second marking period. Every teacher had this one week to average their students' grades in preparation of the report cards which were to be distributed at the end of the school day on Friday.

Tuesday

On Tuesday morning Martin told Mr. B. that he must have left his rankbook at home. Martin continued his conversation by noting that last evening he hadn't been able to do his grades at home because he believed he had left his rankbook in school. Now that he had just finished searching his classroom for the rankbook he figured it was someplace at home. "Tonight, I'll find it. I'll search the house as I did my classroom this morning." At home Martin realized that his missing rankbook was not in his house.

Wednesday

Martin informed his boss that his rankbook was missing. "I cannot find it at home or in school." By the end of the school day, the teacher had informed all of his classes about his lost rankbook. He told them he would need their help to reconstruct their class records in order that he could issue letter grades to each student on their report cards Friday afternoon. Mr. Murphy asked each student to list on a sheet of paper all the test scores which they had earned during the marking period so that he could average them out for letter grades. Martin told Ben he was convinced that every student had given him exactly the grades they had earned, or lesser scores when they were in doubt. "No one turned in grades which were higher than that which they had earned," said the proud teacher.

Thursday

On this morning a likable but mischievous student asked Mr. Bishop if he wanted to know where Mr. Murphy's rankbook was. Ted was usually in some kind of trouble, and was a frequent guest of the principal "... But never enough to get him suspended; he was just a nuisance," said Mr. Murphy at the end of that most interesting day.

Ted explained to Mr. Bishop that he wasn't a squealer but... and then he offered to take Mr. Bishop to the place where the radio and the rankbook were. Ben, with his passenger, drove to the specified section of town. Ted led his principal to the trash barrel at the back end of the city dump. The destroyed radio was found in the barrel. Then Mr. B. and Ted walked to the center of the street which served as the rear exit of the city refuse center. Ted stopped standing adjacent to the covered manhole and asked Mr. Bishop to help him remove the heavy steel cover.

Ben asked, "Why?"

The response was a simple statement, "This is where the rankbook is."

As the two worked to remove the heavy cover revealing the filthy underground work/sewage passageways, Ben told Ted he didn't plan to go "Down there! I will not drop down into this subterranean slopway to retrieve the stolen rankbook."

Ted offered to go down into the tunnel, "If Mr. Bishop promises to pull me up and out." Ben agreed to help Ted out of the tunnel if—and only if—he would behave in school for the rest of the school year. With this attempt at levity Ted jumped into the hole. Within a few minutes the delinquent student held up the damaged rankbook.

Ben took the rankbook and with a mischievous smile said, "Thanks for your help and goodbye."

Ben dropped to his knees, reached down to grab Ted's hand, and pulled his new friend back to the surface. When Mr. B. asked Ted how he knew where the missing rankbook and the broken radio were, his response was quite direct. "I asked the kid who did it and he told me where they were." Ted had promised his fellow student that he would not squeal on him. He also had told his classmate that he had done something terribly wrong. The rankbook was slimy, smelly and certainly nothing that Ben wanted to touch. He placed the damaged rankbook in the trunk of his car. They returned to the junior high school about an hour after they had left.

Ted suggested that Mr. Bishop either recite the name of every student in the school until there was no response (hence the principal would discover the culprit) or he (Mr. B.) could make a list of all the smart kids who failed science. Mr. Bishop named one student. Ted didn't comment!

Walter admitted he was the boy who had broken into the school over the weekend. Detective Jurand and Ben pieced together the story about the break-in, the stolen radio, the defecation found on Ms. Sharpe's chair and on Mr. Murphy's stolen rankbook. Walter, age 14, admitted he had staged the gross insult to Ms. Sharpe in order to distract the investigators from discovering the real reason for the break-in, which was that he wanted to destroy Mr. Murphy's markbook. Walter, an A student, had failed science and feared having his parents seeing an F on his report card.

The solution to the break-in had been discovered. The resolution of the matter was developed by Detective Jurand and Mr. Bishop. The more difficult task lay ahead for the two men. Mr. Bishop called Walter's parents, and then he and Detective Jurand took Walter to his home. The four adults and Walter visited in the family kitchen. Detective Jurand informed Walter's parents that no charges would be filed for the break-in if Walter paid for the property damage and told his parents the complete story about the incident. The parents also agreed to Mr. Bishop's demand that Walter would transfer from Mountain City's East Junior High to its West Junior High. Ben was principal of Mountain City's Junior High School which was in reality two school buildings approximately one half mile apart It was further agreed that Walter would walk the additional distance to school every day. Neither Ms. Sharpe nor Mr. Murphy would have to see Walter again.

Every detail was agreed to. Ben was worried how the family would resolve their personal feelings for their son after Walter reluctantly told them what he had done. Detective Jurand and Mr. Bishop left the house and returned to the school to inform Ms. Sharpe and Mr. Murphy the sad details of Walter's confession and corrective measures taken in the matter.

Detective Jurand had pointedly directed Walter to tell his parents what he had done.

Walter: I broke a window and entered the school.
(Detective) Jurand: Tell your parents what you did.
W: I stole a radio.
J: Tell your parents what you did.
W: I stole Mr. Murphy's rankbook.
J: Tell your parents what you did.
W: I destroyed the radio.
J: Tell your parents what you did.

W: I destroyed the rankbook.
J: Tell your parents what you did.
W: I broke the window.
J: Tell your parents what you did.
W: I . . . uh . . . uh . . . uh . . . uh . . .
J: Tell your parents what you did.
W: I defecated on a teacher's chair.

The parents were in tears as Ben and the detective quickly exited the house. Walter's parents visited with Ben every week for the remainder of the school year. Ben was certain that the family had healed. Walter was doing well. But Mr. B. knew the scar would always be there.

Adult Education

Donald Mayier was the assistant principal at Eastside. The two units of Mountain City Junior High quickly became known as Eastside and Westside. Don had wanted the principal's job which Mr. B. had won a few months earlier. Don had been working with Ben for three months when he decided to tell his boss how he had tried to get him fired immediately after he had been hired. Don admitted he was a sore loser and had tried to use his political connections to get rid of Mr. Bishop. Now, as a result of all of the positive things that the staff were working on, it became clear to Don that Mountain City had hired the better man. With the apology made both men worked harmoniously together for the next three years. At the end of their second year together Don was appointed to serve as the Adult Education director for the city. Don worked on this task four evenings each week the schools were open.

Don usually finished his junior high duties, went home for supper and then he'd head out to the high school. Most of the time he had no problems with his adult education students. Most of these students were working on their evening school diplomas. Several of these high school dropouts had returned to night school to complete their work to become a high school graduate. They were married, raising children, working and attending school. Between classes these students frequently overheard their instructors talking about their evening classes at the local college where they were studying for an advanced degree. Two teachers had enjoyed a good laugh about their college instructor arriving 12 minutes late only to discover that all of his students had left the building.

Adult Ed Director Don was talking with one of these two teachers the next evening. The teacher had arrived at her classroom 11 minutes late as a result of having visited with her boss. The evening high school class figured that if it was okay for their instructor to walk out if the professor was late then it must be okay for them to leave under the same circumstances. Ms. Huff immediately reported her absent students to Mr. Mayier.

Don spent the rest of the evening calling each student (young adult) at their home and informing them that the college rules did not apply to adult education. He further informed each student that no second chance would be given. Therefore each student had to get to all of his/her remaining classes or they would automatically fail. Everyone said that they were sorry and that it wouldn't happen again. Most of the students continued to delight in telling about their mischievous behavior.

The following morning at Eastside Ben and Don were talking about the Adult Ed incident while standing in the lobby just inside the front door. They immediately rushed to the door as soon as they heard the car screech to a stop. An angry young man jumped out of the car and rushed toward the door which happened to be the same one that the two administrators were trying to exit. He had a gun in his hand!!! Mr. Bishop immediately stated that no guns were allowed on school property. "Either leave right now or we'll have the police take you away," commanded Ben. It was obvious to the two school leaders that the angry man had no idea as to whom Mr. Mayier was. As he left the building, he said a Mr. Mayier had called his wife and that no man was allowed to talk to her.

About an hour later, Mr. B. received a polite phone call from the same person he had confronted earlier that morning. He assured Mr. Bishop he was leaving his gun at home and noted he would be polite during his visit with Mr. Mayier if Mr. B. would let him in the school. Don informed Mr. B. he was willing to visit with the guy; after all he (Don) had only called his good looking wife because she had skipped class the night before. Ben did not know at that time how much Don enjoyed clandestine meetings with married women. The meeting was scheduled for 11 A.M.

Don was certain he could handle the visit. The subdued angry spouse arrived. Mr. B. checked him out—no weapon. Ben led Mr. Mayier's guest upstairs to Don's second floor office. The school had been built in 1894. The windows were made of thin glass which stretched from the floor to the ceiling. As Ben and the angry spouse entered Don's narrow office, Mr. M. walked around his desk and greeted his guest with a handshake. Ben waited until the two men seated themselves, the guest facing the desk and Mr. Mayier who was seated at his usual spot in back of the desk. Don's back faced the windows approximately six feet behind him. The two men began their visit. Ben overheard Mr. M.'s explanation of his phone call of the previous evening as he exited the office.

Ben instructed his 4-foot, 9-inch-tall secretary to walk past Mr. M.'s office every 4 minutes. If anything unusual was happening she was to call Ben and the police immediately. Ten minutes later, Bev ran into Mr. Bishop's office and called to him, "Come quickly, he is punching Mr. Mayier!" Ben reminded Bev to call the police as he rushed into Don's office.

Ben noticed the angry spouse straddling Don's crossed legs while he proceeded to punch him in the chest and face. Don was trapped in his chair. He had great difficulty in attempting to protect himself from the pummeling which the angry spouse was delivering. Ben quickly moved in and wrapped his long arms around Mr. Mayier's attacker. He forcibly pulled him away from his defenseless assistant. As Ben pulled his prisoner back and away from Don, he walked backward toward the second floor windows. Don's frustrated anger was unleashed the moment he was freed from the weight of his attacker. Don's attack pushed both Ben and the angry spouse into the window. Bev's scream, "Mr. Mayier!" made him realize that he had to pull the attacker back into the room in order to save his boss. Ben's back had crashed through the window. He held onto the angry spouse more firmly as he thought that he was about to fall onto the concrete walkway 20 feet below. He hoped as he fell that he could twist the two of them around so that he would land on top of the angry spouse when they hit the ground.

As Bev screamed she grabbed onto Mr. Mayier and, with her 95-pounds of determined strength, began to pull the two men back into Don's office. It had taken the combined efforts of both Bev and Don to rescue the two men. Ben asked Bev if she had called the police. She replied, "I'm going to do that right now." Ben realized that Bev had saved his life by not immediately doing as he had directed.

The angry spouse was arrested. Ben profusely thanked Bev for her help and all Don said was, "Now that he is in jail, I bet I can meet her on Saturday."

I Am a Teacher

Amanda Doruth was an outstanding teacher. Every time Mr. Bishop visited one of Amanda's science classes, he would always leave with a positive feeling. Amanda was a great teacher—and every week Ben told her how successful she was.

Amanda didn't believe her boss' comments. She believed he was just saying good things to her in order to get her to work harder. Actually, all of North Mountain City junior high teachers did a good job. Although the teachers in both the East and West side did a great job, there was still room for improvement. *Perhaps*, thought Mr. B., *they all get their students to learn so well is a direct result of the school committee's insult—transferring all the brightest students to the state college training school.* Whatever caused his staff's high achievement rates didn't matter as long as the staff continually tried to improve itself.

Thus at the next faculty meeting Ben asked his talented teachers to video tape their teaching style in one of their classes during the next month or two. At this point the noise level in his faculty meeting rose to a rebellious chant—"No way!"

Mr. Bishop had been prepared for his teachers' united objection to his proposal. He asked his staff to be patient and to listen to his entire proposal before they said No. "After I have presented my plan in detail, I'll let you decide if and when the video taping of your classes will be done," challenged Ben. Amidst friendly comments of, "You are going to make us do it! You pulled a good one on us during our last meeting when we wanted to vote on a subject to make a team decision. Yeah, you gave each one of us a vote and then said, you had one vote for each member of the faculty plus one for yourself as principal," stated Martin Murphy.

Mr. B.'s mischievous staff laughed uproariously as they recalled the incident and its very successful outcome. "Okay, okay," said their cheerful principal. This time Ben informed his usually cooperative staff that they could vote on the plan AND that he (Ben) would not vote. He asked his teachers to vote their consciences and not to just say NO. The teachers said that they would listen to his plan and then they would consider their decision. The conversation wandered around to, "What type of a challenge does he have in mind which convinces him we will agree to video our classes?" Mr. B.'s smile made a few friendly faculty members more than a little nervous.

Ben presented his plan for teacher self improvement of their own teaching style(s). First point: Each teacher was to schedule to have the video camera in their classroom for at least one full teaching period. The camera would either be manned by the AV director, a fellow teacher, a student from said teacher's class, or the camera could be tripod mounted in the rear of the room.

Second point: After the taped class ended the teacher was to keep the tape and he/she was to watch the entire tape after school on that same day. Each teacher would have the right to watch the video of his/her class in the privacy of their own classroom. After viewing the tape the teacher would have the right to either destroy the tape or to keep it as a souvenir of their Ed-Venture.

Ben told his staff to view their videos with a critical eye toward improving their future classroom presentations. The resultant changes in teaching styles might be simple or major, depending upon the individual faculty member's analysis of his/her video. Mr. B. suggested that each teacher had the right to discuss their respective tapes with their confreres, or, "even with the principal."

The third point was the one the staff knew would trap them into doing this project.

"But how?" they wondered.

At this point Mr. B. reminded his faculty about the fact that some English and history teachers did not like math, Further, he reminded his staff about the academic uproar of a few years earlier when it had been announced that every math teacher would have to instruct their students how to add and to subtract in bases other than ten.

That had been an extremely trying time for many teachers, especially those at the elementary level. Their principal presented his challenge; "I will teach everyone in this room how to add in BASE SEVEN in 15 minutes, or you won't have to video tape one of your classes."

Ben made his proposal in a unique attempt to get his staff to gamble on a yes vote based upon a belief that no one could teach "ME" to add in BASE SEVEN and definitely not in 15 minutes. Ben left the room. A few minutes later an English teacher called him back into the meeting. They happily announced they were accepting his challenge. It was agreed that Mr. B. would be their BASE SEVEN math instructor at the next faculty meeting.

Ben knew that his friendly teachers would definitely harass him if he stood at the chalkboard and attempted to teach the concept to them. Thus he decided to present his math lesson to his faculty via television. He filled the chalkboard with the necessary examples. The district AV director agreed to tape his class for the upcoming faculty meeting. Ben's first attempt didn't quite fit into the fifteen minutes he had gambled on. He realized his main difficulty was his trying to teach to an empty classroom. His second attempt using a few additional props was a success.

As Ben entered the room for the scheduled faculty meeting, he heard comments of acquiescence from his staff. As soon as the teachers realized that Mr. Bishop was making a video presentation they concluded he would win the bet. They appeared to be ready to lose their challenge and to agree to video and to self critique their teaching styles. Mr. B.'s use of a BASE SEVEN odometer model as his teaching tool captured their minds. The BASE SEVEN model used the digits from 0 through 6 as compared to the BASE TEN odometer as found in their cars which used the digits 0 through 9. They all agreed they could add in BASE SEVEN and did the sample problems correctly. The staff assured their favorite principal that he would not win the next contest.

The staff scheduled their video taping dates and times. Within two months every teacher had viewed their respective taped classes. Most of them told Mr. B. what they had learned about their teaching styles and what actions they were taking to improve their instructional techniques.

Two of Ben's teachers said "Yes," he could use their tapes to teach a class at State U on teacher evaluations, to illustrate what to look for to improve instruction and how to work with a staff member to improve his/her teaching.

Amanda D. scheduled her class to be taped on the last day of the taping calendar. As usual Amanda had prepared her class presentation in her habitual thorough manner. Amanda taught at Westside. The school was at the top of a hill almost completely hidden by trees, with no houses nearby. Her classroom was on the second floor. She prepared to view her video in complete privacy. Amanda locked her classroom door. She also pulled down the shades in her room. Once she became convinced of her complete privacy, she turned on the video player. One hour later Mr. Bishop heard Amanda's first recognition of her success as a teacher. She told Ben he had been right all those times he had told her that her classes were great. Amanda's, "Yes, I am a TEACHER," pleased Ben. He was proud of his staff and of their hard work on behalf of the students in their care.

That's My Daughter

Teachers frequently intercept notes being passed from one student to another. Usually the teacher reads the note, then directs the errant students to pay attention to their school work. The teacher asked Jamie to please hand her the note she had just handed to the eighth-grader seated behind her. The young man was visibly upset when his teacher took the note from his hand. Michael was upset because the note was signed MIKE. He didn't know that his teacher had watched Jamie while she was writing the sexy note.

Ms. Textbook read the intercepted note. She was visibly upset. She had never read such trash in her entire life. Ms. Textbook sent Jamie to the principal's office. She sent a second student with a message that she wanted to see Mr. Bishop immediately.

Mr. B. arrived at Ms. Textbook's classroom door a few minutes later. "Mr. Bishop, you have to read this note which I took from Michael. He didn't write it. Jamie wrote that most disgusting note." Ben read the intercepted note and became as upset as his teacher was. The note was a written as if it were a request from a boy (Michael) to Jamie (the author) asking for sexual play after school in the woods behind the school building. Both Ms. T. and Ben surmised that most of their eighth grade boys most likely didn't know what the words meant.

Mr. Bishop returned to his office and with his secretary present asked Jamie about the note which Ms. Textbook had just handed to him. Jamie immediately responded by saying she had written the note. She further explained to her principal that this was her fourth note and she was planning to give one to every eighth grade boy in the school. Mr. B. called Jamie's parents and informed them he was suspending their daughter until they could come to the school to discuss a most serious matter with him and the school psychologist to assess the corrective action to be taken in this affair.

Two days later the family was assembled in the principal's office. Jamie, her parents, the school psychologist, along with Mr. Bishop and his secretary exchanged pleasantries as they seated themselves around the conference table. Mr. B. then announced that he was hosting this meeting in order to discuss Jamie's problem and to work toward discovering the best method to correct her behavior. Ben asked Jamie to step outside and to sit in the outer office for a few minutes while he talked to her parents.

Mr. B. told both of her parents about the note and the most explicit sexual request written therein. Ben continued, "The note embarrassed me when I read it. I am uncomfortable in asking you, Mrs. K., to read such filth. I therefore, am handing the note to Mr. K. and after he reads it he can show it to you."

With that comment, Ben gave the note to Mr. K. Mr. Bishop, Dr. Paul, the school psychologist and the administrative secretary were floored by Mr. K.'s reaction to the note. Mr. K. slapped his knee and exclaimed, "That's my daughter!"

It was obvious that Mr. K. was proud of his daughter, Jamie and what she was trying to do via the note she had passed in the classroom. Ben realized that the K.'s were teaching their daughter to be a prostitute. He asked the family to leave so that he and Dr. Paul could discuss the corrective action which they felt this case demanded.

Dr. Paul and Ben spent the next several days contacting seventeen state and private agencies to find the necessary help for Jamie. One agency said that Jamie was too old for their services, as they worked with children aged 6 to 14 and Jamie was 15.

Another state unit refused to help because she wasn't 16. "We are understaffed and our case workers are overworked," responded several agencies as they refused to help.

The following day was spent with the two men visiting with the local church leaders in their continued effort to rescue Jamie from the life her father had proudly planned for her. During the week Dr. Paul and Mr. B. had spent searching for help, they had clearly been informed that the family *did not want any help*. They were obviously content with their current lifestyle.

The Baptist minister informed his visitors that he could have helped if only Jamie had been a participating member of his church. Their continued conversation resulted in the minister discovering that Jamie's mother did indeed attend his church regularly. The minister eventually discovered the girl was never at church with her mother because she was at home with her father, who was sexually abusing Jamie every Sunday while her mother was at church.

Within a few days, the minister arranged to pick up Jamie at school and transported her to a church camp where she would be educated and counseled in an attempt to change her lifestyle.

Mr. K. was subsequently arrested for child abuse; Paul and Ben with great disgust closed the case with a silent prayer for Jamie.

The Music Teacher

Mr. Bishop visited every classroom on a monthly basis. He worked with his staff to continuously improve the instructional levels in the school. The teachers realized that his support of them and their work was of the highest standard. He believed in each and every one of his professional staff. Ben was convinced his teachers worked harder and as a result more successfully than any other teachers in the school district.

Mr. B. had to admit he also had a teacher or two who wasn't succeeding in his/her classroom(s) and he acted accordingly.

After interviewing two science teacher candidates for the September vacancy, Ben and his assistant Russ concluded that the best candidate was the quiet but bright and personable lady from New York. Miss Onemonth started her teaching career with a bang. Her first two weeks were the best any new teacher could have had. The first day of her third week she sent several students to the office for corrective discipline. Russ and Ben really leaned on these kids in order to help Miss Onemonth to keep her students under firm control. On Wednesday Miss Onemonth had sent half of her period one students to the office. By Friday she was sending half of the students from each of her five science classes to the office.

Russ talked to Miss Onemonth about classroom discipline as a necessity for successful teaching. She continued to retreat from her students. By the middle of her fourth week she told Russ to stop bothering her, "To leave her alone."

Ben took his turn working with his new science teacher. Within a few days Mr. B. realized that he was not going to succeed with her. Ben then asked Martin M. to spend some time with Miss Onemonth. Martin had been a very helpful mentor to new teachers before, and both Russ and Ben hoped that he'd succeed where they hadn't.

Ben wanted her to succeed as a teacher. This plan of assistance also failed. Russ and Ben sat in her classroom every day during her fifth week as a teacher. Their purpose was to establish the disciplinary touch so that she could teach. They hoped this plan would allow her to regain control of her classes as they slowly retreated from direct supervision.

Finally, Mr. Bishop had to ask Miss Onemonth to resign as she was failing to teach the students assigned to her. She angrily told her boss that she would not quit. She said she was teaching those students who were interested in learning. The rest of the kids could do as they pleased.

Mr. B. asked, "How many students are you really teaching each period?"

Her response was, "Five or six per class."

Ben informed Miss Onemonth that he was giving her thirty days notice of her dismissal. Her last day would be Friday of the second week in November.

Miss Onemonth threatened Ben with the statement that her boyfriend would beat him up if he fired her. Her fiance was a high school teacher in the same school system. Ben called his friend, the high school principal, and together the two friends observed Miss Onemonth's fiance's teaching techniques. Ben said to his buddy that her boyfriend was a much better teacher than his girlfriend. The day before the scheduled dismissal hearing Miss Onemonth resigned.

Ben and Russ went to the local research firm and suggested that they might consider hiring Miss Onemonth for scientific research especially if it were an assignment where she could work alone. The firm hired Miss Onemonth and assigned her to a private lab where she would work by herself. She was at a place where she could succeed, and she was never told that Russ and Ben found the new job for her.

Miss Onemonth and her fiance were married a few months later. Ben did not see her again until Dr. Haberdasher's retirement party. When she spotted Mr. B. she looked through him as if her eyes were cold daggers cutting into Ben's. WOW!!!

* * *

The music teacher, Mrs. Mysong, had worked with Ben and his staff in the selection of Sylvia Musica, a young, very much alive and gifted music teacher. Mrs. Mysong was a native of North Mountain City. She was very politically connected. Mrs. Mysong enjoyed working with her new protegee, well at least from September through to January. Sylvia was observed by Mr. B. once each month as were all of the junior high teachers. By mid October, Sylvia's reputation as a great music teacher had spread beyond the junior high buildings. By December the entire school district was talking about the great new music teacher assigned to the jr. high school. The students were enjoying their music classes, a first in any Mountain City school! Ms. Musica didn't have any discipline problems. Her students were mesmerized by their music teacher. Every student was paying attention in her class!!

During the last week of January, a scared seventh grade student came running up to Mr. Bishop crying about the crazy lady who had grabbed him and had pulled him into a closet on the third floor. After a lengthy conversation, Ben realized that Mrs. Mysong had been hiding in a closet adjacent to Sylvia's music room. She had been sneakily (and illegally) observing Sylvia's teaching habits.

As the class ended Mrs. Mysong had opened the closet door while the seventh graders were passing to their next class. She reached out and grabbed the smallest boy passing by her hideaway. She planned to debrief him about Ms. Musica's teaching but he was so frightened she had to let him go. Mrs. Mysong warned the youngster NOT to tell anyone about his visit to the closet

The young seventh grader ran directly to the principal's office. He had to tell Mr. Bishop what had happened to him. Mrs. Mysong immediately left the building. She had not registered when she entered the building. The standard policy was for all visitors to sign in so that the business of the school could be conducted safely. The sign-in policy had been adopted many years earlier. In case of a fire the administrators could thus guarantee everyone had been safely evacuated. The visit by Mrs. Mysong was her first visit that she had not signed into the school.

Mr. Bishop caught up with the district's music supervisor thirty minutes later. He confronted her about not signing in, evaluating a teacher from a closet, grabbing a student and dragging him into a closet with the intent to force him to discredit Sylvia Musica. Ben demanded that Mrs. Mysong apologize to Sylvia, etc., etc., etc. Ben informed Mrs. Mysong of his intent to put this case in writing with a copy to the superintendent, Dr. Haberdasher.

Ben wrote the letter to Dr. Haberdasher stating the facts of the closet evaluation of Ms. Musica. He clearly noted that Mrs. Mysong was no longer welcome in his school. Dr. Haberdasher requested Ben to allow the music director to visit his buildings once each month for the remainder of the school year.

April arrived. Teacher appointments, reappointments and layoffs were always voted upon during the first week of the month. The music director recommended that Sylvia's contract not be renewed. Ben jumped up, interrupted the conversation and with a determined voice cited the illegal teacher evaluation including all the significant details to the superintendent and his school committee. Mr. Bishop strongly recommended the renewal of Ms. Musica's contract. He didn't know that Mrs.

Mysong had used her political connections and had the vote of dismissal agreed to hours before the meeting began.

The story of the unjust teacher dismissal made the local news a few days later. Ben helped Sylvia find a new music teaching position in a neighboring community. He had lost all respect for the jealous music supervisor.

Bomb Scare

The school committee had had it with bomb scares. They were clearly frustrated with the problem. The cost to the city taxpayers was an expensive drain on services, manpower, money and lost class time. The possibility of an accident happening as the police and fire departments raced to the schools to protect the lives of the children and the adults in the schools was just one of the problems created by the called-in threats. The loss of potentially life-saving services in case of a real emergency was another weight on the school committee. The committee had to do something in order to stop the bomb scare epidemic in North Mountain City's schools. The school committee drafted and subsequently passed a resolution which mandated the closing of any school receiving a bomb threat phone call during the school day. The committee members believed that the late June make-up classes caused by the bomb threat closing of the school(s) would stop this dangerous student activity. Most committee members believed the resolution would force the majority of students to become angry enough with the perpetrators to force them to cease and desist.

Every North Mountain City school principal read the bomb threat resolution over their school PA system the following morning. Each principal asked their students to help them stop these dangerous and illegal activities.

The junior high had its phone lines connected to a caller identification system. Every staff member had been alerted as to how to react should they be the one receiving such a call. The plan was designed to catch the bomb threat caller.

The next week began as usual. Mr. Bishop, as per his habit, arrived at the junior high at least one hour before the start of the school day, which actually started at 8:15 A.M. Ben usually entered the building by 7:00 A.M.

At 7:23 A.M. on the fateful Tuesday morning the phone rang. One of the early arriving teachers answered the phone. The caller announced that a bomb had been planted in the school and had a timer set to go off at 10:00 A.M. The alert teacher played her role perfectly. The police and fire departments were notified immediately.

Ben called his friend, Detective Jurand, and asked for his assistance to solve this bomb threat case. The two men agreed not to close the school since the threat had not been received during the school day. They also asked the fire department to wait until 9:30 A.M. before coming to the school. Both the police and the fire depts. agreed not to publicize the bomb threat until later. The two men were convinced that they would solve this case shortly after school opened.

Detective Jurand and a uniformed policeman arrived at the school at 7:31 A.M. Detective Jurand went to the phone company, worked with their engineers and shortly thereafter picked up a written report identifying the specific telephone used to make the threatening call. Detective Jurand called Ben and let him know which phone had been used to make the call earlier that morning. Detective Jurand then headed to court to pick up a search warrant in order to find the specific phone.

When the detective returned to the school, he joined with Mr. Bishop in the questioning of Pamela, an eighth grade student, who was clearly nervous as she answered the questions raised by her two inquisitors

She denied making any phone calls to the school that morning. With a nasty attitude Pamela challenged her principal; "You didn't get a bomb threat phone call this morning or you would have closed school like you announced last week! You said the school committee said you had to close the school if you received a bomb scare call."

Finally, Detective Jurand and Mr. Bishop told Pamela that she was about to be arrested. They informed Pamela that they were taking her home to her mother for the final questioning and subsequently her arrest. At this point Detective Jurand turned to Ben and told him that he, Ben, was Detective Jurand's witness in this matter. Ben readily agreed and told his friend that he in turn would be Mr. B.'s witness.

They arrived at Pamela's house, a desperate-appearing two-family structure in the worst section of Mountain City. Pamela was surprised to see two police cars parked on her street. She also noticed that police personnel were standing on the street facing her house. Neither Pamela nor Mr. Bishop realized that two additional policemen were stationed at the rear of her house as well.

The detective and the principal escorted Pamela through the hallway and up the stairs to the second floor. Detective Jurand knocked on the door, which was answered by Mrs. V., Pamela's mother. She was wearing a see-through nightgown. The two men looked at each other and quietly said one word simultaneously: "witness." Detective Jurand handed the search warrant to Mrs. V. and asked her to show him the telephone. He also stated to her that he was at the house with her daughter as he planned to arrest Pamela for making a threatening call to the junior high school earlier that morning. Mrs. V. pointed to the phone on the kitchen wall. Jurand picked up the phone and began talking. Mrs. V. was surprised—the detective hadn't dialed a number yet he was definitely talking to someone!

Detective Jurand explained to Mrs. V. that he was talking to the policeman at the junior high school. The policeman he was talking to was on the phone that the teacher hadn't hung up after she had answered the bomb threat call earlier that morning. Detective Jurand handed the phone to Mrs. V. and she was informed by the policeman on the line as to his name, the phone he was using, etc.

After the detective had verified the phone connection from home to school, he turned to Pamela in front of her mother and asked if she had made the threatening call at 7:23 that morning. She responded with an emphatic. "*No.*" With that response Detective Jurand turned to Mrs. V. and told her that since no one else was in the house and since Pamela hadn't made the call, it became obvious that she, Mrs. V. had made the call. "Therefore, I am arresting you, Mrs. V. for phoning in a bomb threat to the junior high school this morning!"

Mrs. V. and Pamela asked to be alone with each other for a few minutes. As okayed by Detective Jurand, the two ladies went into the bedroom and talked about their problem. Ten minutes later they returned to the kitchen and Mrs. V. called her lawyer. Detective Jurand and Mrs. V.'s lawyer reached an agreement as to the arrest, etc. Detective Jurand handed the two women over to the policemen waiting outside on the street and directed them to take both Mrs. V. and her daughter to he police station for processing. Ben and his friend returned to the school. The day concluded with Jurand visiting Ben to give him the details of the entire episode.

Yes, Pamela had made the call. No bomb was planted—nor did one exist. She had made the call, had gone to school and awaited the announcement that school would be closed for the day per the new policy. She had planned to spend the day free and clear with her AWOL Marine boy friend. Jurand had called the local U.S. Marine office and repeated Pamela's story about her AWOL friend.

Late that night Jurand awakened Ben with a phone call. Mrs. V. had called the police and told them that her daughter and her boyfriend had stolen the family car and were headed to Canada. Detective Jurand continued his story by telling his bleary-eyed friend that the police and the marines had just arrested the three of them. Mrs. V. had set up the two lovers in their own little apartment in a condemned multiple-family building around the comer from her house, figuring the police would never find the two kids in the condemned building after she had reported them as en route to Canada. All three—Mrs. V., Pamela, and her marine friend—spent time in jail.

Not So

William R. ("Billy") Bright had worked for the city recreation department for a little more than two years. When the city recreation director heard that Billy was applying for the vacant art teacher's job at North Mountain City High, she called Ben and urged him to employ Mr. Bright. "Yes," the rec. dept. had checked his references and "Yes," he was a good worker.

In spite of the rec. dept's strong support of the candidate, Ben waited until the last day of August hoping to find another art teacher candidate. On August 31, at 8:00 A.M., Ben called Mr. Bright and offered the art teacher's job to him. Mr. Bishop was convinced that the only reason Billy wanted the teaching job was the fact that the draft board would give a teacher a military exemption. But he was a certified art teacher, and the junior high needed him.

Russ and Ben were pleased with Billy's teaching style and his success working with the junior high students. Six weeks went by without a single incident. During this period Ben had learned from his conversations with Billy that he was alone in the world. He had no relatives as he had been an only child and his parents had both died in an auto accident while he was in college. Mr. Bishop had no reason to doubt this story or any of the other stories Billy told. Besides, the city personnel director had informed Ben of her reference checks on Mr. Bright's background, character and collegiate degrees. "But?" pondered Ben.

By this time Heather was talking to Ben about inviting Billy to their home for Thanksgiving, as he had no family. Ben kept forgetting to invite Billy for Thanksgiving, although he kept telling Heather that he would remember to do it "tomorrow." As Mr. Bishop stood in the hall between classes talking to a teacher about the upcoming holiday season, his secretary told him that the Vermont State Police Headquarters was on the phone, asking if William R. Bright worked in the junior high.

Ben asked for the commander's phone number and hung up. He then called the number he had been given after his secretary had confirmed the number to be correct via an information call to Detective Jurand.

The state police commander complimented Ben on his cautious approach in sensitive and confidential matters, "Such as this one." The commander asked if Mr. Bright was a teacher in the junior high. He also told Ben as to the reason(s) for his need to "See Mr. Bright." The police commander gave Ben a great deal of information about Billy which contradicted Billy's responses to his questions over the last month and a half. The Vermont Police wanted Billy in court as a result of his many speeding tickets and his failure to appear in court to pay his fines.

Billy owed the state of Vermont $945.00 in fines, plus court costs. He was about to lose his right to drive in Vermont! Further, if Billy didn't show in court the following Tuesday morning, then the Vermont State Police, through the state judicial system would be asking Massachusetts to suspend his driver's license. This action if taken would remove Billy's right to drive in all 50 states. The conversation between the two men continued. Ben gave Billy's address to the police commander and the commander gave Billy's mother's name, address and phone number to Mr. Bishop.

At the next break in the school day, Ben talked to Billy about his phone conversation with the Vermont State Police. Billy was furious. He angrily shouted at his boss when Ben told him that he had given his address to the Vermont Police. "Now, I'll have to move!" echoed off the hall walls as Billy Bright ran down the stairs to his classroom.

Later that day Billy promised Ben he would report to the Vermont Courthouse as requested, pay his fines and do whatever else the Vermont courts demanded of him. He lost his right to drive in the state and he paid his fines. He moved out of his apartment and he moved into a condemned building. The federal highway program had purchased a strip of land to complete the highway through North Mountain City. The condemned buildings were to be torn down in the spring. The condemned buildings had no services; the water & sewer system, along with the gas and electric services, had been disconnected. No one was allowed in these buildings. North Mountain City was known for its cold winters.

By the first of November Billy was no longer arriving at school clean shaven, nor was he wearing clean shirts. The once extremely neat art teacher appeared each day a little dirtier than the day before. The staff and the students began to complain that Mr. Bright "SMELLED." Ben and Russ talked to him about his personal hygiene. A few days later, on a Friday afternoon, the two administrators agreed to tell Billy that he couldn't return to work unless and until he was washed and dressed in clean clothes. Ben waited at the front door of the school for Mr. Bright on that fateful Monday morning. He planned to send Mr. Bright home if he hadn't cleaned up his act. Billy didn't show up for work and he hadn't called in sick. Russ cheered; Russ hoped that he would just never come back. Mr. Bishop said that if Billy didn't contact the school or he failed to show up for work for the next three days then he would officially fire him. At this point Ben was very happy he had never "remembered" to invite Billy to his house for Thanksgiving.

When the staff learned Billy was living in a condemned apartment building they started making jokes using his name, William R. Bright. They questioned him as well as each other if his name was William U. R. Bright? or was it William R. U. Bright?

On Friday morning Ben wrote a letter to Mr. William R. Bright informing Billy that as a result of his unexplained week of absences his employment ceased, effective immediately. As Ben was signing the letter, the phone rang. A nurse, from city hospital, was calling to talk to the principal. She informed Mr. Bishop, after confirming he was the junior high school principal, that Mr. Bright had been in the hospital since Sunday evening. She further stated he was being released from the hospital later that day. Her final comment was to note that Mr. Bright would be able to return to work on Monday. Ben and Russ were disappointed that they couldn't fire Billy, as he now had a good excuse for not having been at work all week.

Billy entered the school on Monday morning dressed in clean clothes, and clean shaven. He also had a clean white bandage covering most of his head. The hospital had arranged to have social services clean his clothes while he had been hospitalized. The nurses had bathed him and had given him several sets of clean bandages for his head when they released him from the hospital.

Billy was warmly and sympathetically greeted by everyone who spotted him as he walked to the principal's office. Ben warmly greeted him and then asked, "What happened to you? Are you going to be okay?"

Billy told his story to his boss. Billy reminded Mr. Bishop that he was living in a condemned apartment building. He further commented that his living quarters had no utilities. His home was cold. He had no electricity or water. He then advised his boss as to his latest art adventures. He was into log sculpting. Billy told Mr. B that he would occasionally cut trees down in the state forest. He would bring six-foot-long logs "home" and into his apartment. He further reported as to how he would do the rough cuts with a chainsaw. Thus he developed the rough outline of his work using a chainsaw. He would then finish his work using wood chisels and a mallet. All of this work was done in his apartment.

"One week ago Saturday," continued Billy, "It was extremely cold in the apartment. I had several new logs standing in my workroom, that is the living room as it had the most sunlight coming through the windows for me to see to do my work. I had several sweaters and a heavy coat on to keep warm. I was using the chainsaw to make the initial cuts. I also had a coat tree holding two additional coats on the other side of my work. I figured that if my coats were hanging in the sunlight that they would be warm when I had to put them on later in the day. Thus I started the chainsaw (inside the apartment) and began to cut the first log. Unfortunately, the chain caught one of my coats hanging in back of the log I was working on. I yanked it free from my coat. But I couldn't stop the backward swing of the saw. It bounced off my head three times. I was lucky I didn't faint as I was alone in the apartment. Also I had no phone to call for help. I had to get to the hospital on my own. I made it to the hospital emergency room door and then I collapsed. The doctors stitched me up and admitted me to the hospital. They (the hospital) decided to keep me in the hospital so that someone could look after me until I was once again capable of taking care of myself. They released me on Saturday and here I am ready to teach."

Ben talked with Billy for a little longer and cautioned him to be careful and to take better care of himself etc. By the end of the week Billy looked like the dirty drummer boy in the Union army during the Civil War. His head bandage was a filthy rag. Ben took Billy aside and asked for his resignation. William R. Bright resigned effective immediately. Ben began thinking of Billy as NOT SO.

Mr. Bishop then told Billy that he had called his mother and she was hoping he'd come home for the winter. Ben phoned Mrs. Bright while Billy was penning his resignation. Mr. Bishop handed the phone to Billy and left the room as the tearful reunion conversation began.

As Billy said good-bye and was about to head home to visit

Mom he suggested that Mr. Bishop might be interested in hiring his friend. His friend was the other Rec. dept. artist. Ben said, "No thanks." Billy sent his friend to see Mr. Bishop as the only applicant for the vacant art teaching job.

Billy's friend Arthur sat across the desk from Mr. Bishop and happily talked about his artistic talents. Arthur was married and lived in a shack in the woods which had all the utilities necessary for family life. He had a photo album with him to show the quality of his work. Arthur came to the junior high with the strong support of North Mountain City's personnel dept.

Arthur opened his album and pointed out the highlights of each photo to his prospective employer. The photos were of his stone sculptured work. Together, they viewed each picture of the polished stones. Finally, Mr. B. asked Arthur to describe each image as represented in the photos. Arthur responded with the following story:

"The first example of my work is a stone sculptured bird with its head tucked under its wing. The second picture is that of a dog seated with its head under its left front leg. The next photo clearly illustrates a man standing with his head under his left armpit. The next is of a fox with its head under its leg. The next is of a seated woman with her head under her left arm. . . . "

Ben interrupted his guest and commented on the apparent quality of his efforts and then asked Arthur what he did or planned to do with his finished work.

Before Arthur replied, Ben let him know that he didn't think he would be employing him for the art teacher vacancy. Arthur then responded to his interviewer's question. He said that when his wife tells him that they are running low on money, he goes to the city and steals a truck. He loads the truck with his finished stonework and drives to New York City.

Arthur further explained as to how he would rent a storefront in Greenwich Village, unload the truck, park it a few streets away, and settle into his studio. He said that the police eventually would find the truck, but meanwhile he would live in the rented store until he sold all of his sculptured work. Arthur completed his story by noting that when he was ready to return home, he simply stole a car, drove home, left the car on a side street in North Mountain City and thumbed a ride to his home. He repeated this cycle every three or four months as the need arose.

Ben hired a long-term sub for the remainder of the school year. Ben and Russ talked about the NOT SO twins for weeks.

* * *

Ben told his friend Detective Jurand the complete NOT SO twins stories.

Holiday Letters

Ben decided to inform the parents of the North Mountain City Junior High students that their children were being educated by a great set of teachers. Mr. B. wrote a letter of commendation to each of his teaching staff. The majority of his professional staff were excellent. Their letters had been easy to write. These letters were brief, personal and definitely complimentary. A few letters were average yet enthusiastic. Although these letters were not as constructive as the first group, they were positive statements of appreciation for the educational services rendered to their seventh and eighth grade students. Two teachers would be receiving letters, each of which, although written with a positive tone, contained a paragraph wishing them well in their next teaching assignment—in another school district.

Mr. Bishop scheduled himself to visit four classrooms per teaching period during the last school week of December. Ben had alerted his staff as to his plans regarding these classroom visits. As he entered each classroom he greeted the teacher with a "Good Morning," and ANOTHER "Good Morning" to the students. Mr. Bishop then explained the purpose of his visit to the class and he handed the envelope to the teacher as he exited the classroom and headed to the next class. Ben repeated his presentation in every classroom of the two junior high facilities.

"Good morning class," said Mr. B. "I am here to ask you to report to your parents about the education you are receiving here in North Mountain City Junior High. All of your teachers are well trained and they work their hearts out for you. Please tell your parents that you witnessed me, the principal, handing your teacher a letter of commendation for his/her hard work. Tell your parents that I am proud of the teachers in this school and of their dedicated teaching services as rendered to all of you students. You are the reason we are here."

Everything was going according to Ben's plan, and all was just fine until Ben handed Mr. Z. his letter. Mr. Z. was one of the two teachers Ben was leaning toward a recommendation for dismissal in April. As Mr. B. exited the classroom, he heard the students shouting, "Mr. Z.! Open the letter and read it to us." Ben prayed that Mr. Z. wasn't dumb enough to do as the kids asked—but unfortunately, the teacher opened the letter and started to read it aloud.

Ben knocked on the door, re-entered the room and interrupted Mr. Z.'s reading of his personal letter to his students. The bell rang, Ben left the area; Mr. Z. quietly finished reading his letter and went to the teacher's washroom where he sat down and cried. He finally accepted what he had known since September but couldn't admit to himself until now. A few days later Mr. Z. and his principal had a long talk about teaching as a career. The meeting ended with Mr. Z.'s submitting his resignation, effective with the end of the school year in June. Mr. Z. eventually got another job in education. This time he would be a success as he had been accepted in a position as a guidance counselor.

Mr. B. had written about the three things necessary to be a great teacher in his holiday letter to Carol Firstyear. Ms. Firstyear clearly had two of these talents as identified by her boss; she was well educated, intelligent and personable. Further, Carol had the unique ability to present the subject matter to her students in a most successful manner. But the third talent which Carol needed in order to succeed as a teacher was discipline. Ms. Firstyear had given away her control of the class and as a result she wasn't achieving the success that she was capable of in the classroom. After a lengthy conversation with Carol, Ben agreed to wait until the end of March to see if Ms. Firstyear could regain control of her classes.

Ben watched as Carol struggled to reestablish the level of discipline necessary to be a really great teacher. Mr. B. recognized that Ms. Firstyear wouldn't achieve her goal by the end of the school year. The teacher and her principal met again in late February. Ben offered to extend her contract for one more year based upon her efforts to date and a promise that she would continue trying to reestablish herself as the teacher/disciplinarian. Carol agreed. Her drive to improve her classroom management skills was clearly noticeable. Ben was convinced that at this time Carol was not enjoying teaching. He also believed that once she completely regained control she would be able to relax and marvel at her success as a teacher.

After school reopened in September, Mr. B. watched Carol as she entered her classes with a personal determination to succeed. Ben conjectured to himself about Carol's thought processes during the summer. The power of positive thinking had clearly changed Carol's teaching style for the better. Ben particularly enjoyed delivering Carol's holiday letter on that December date. He had written, "Three things make a good teacher great. You have succeeded in bringing all three to your classes this year." Ben's letter to Carol concluded with two statements. The first was about Ben's plan to recommend Carol for tenure at the end of her second year based upon her superb teaching. He concluded his letter with this proud statement—

*You **Are** a Teacher!*

The New Superintendent

Teaching had been great, thought Ben. With but a few exceptions, Ben's students had fared well in math. Mr. Bishop's students had always finished the text and had passed their cooperative final exams with decent scores. As a principal, Mr. B. was determined to assist his teachers in whatever way possible to help them be successful as well. During his years as junior high principal, Ben's staff, with two exceptions, succeeded in their work as educators. The report card contest with the State College training school was more than sufficient for him to recognize his teachers were doing an outstanding job as educators. During this happy period of running a first class school, Ben experienced the usual challenges of student behavior as well as the most unusual disciplinary problems.

Friday

The school day had just started on that Friday afternoon in early April. Yvonne, a music teacher, dropped in to visit with her principal just after the last school bus left the property. She informed Mr. B. she had a strange feeling that something most unusual was going on. Yvonne told Mr. Bishop she knew he would get to the bottom of the puzzle. She had been in the library during the last period of the school day when she overheard a strange conversation among four boys seated in a corner of the room. The bits of gossip she had heard were about a game the boys referred to as "RUN HER NYLONS." Yvonne gave the names of these four eighth grade boys to Mr. Bishop with the comment, "I am certain you'll get to the bottom of it."

Monday A.M.

During homeroom period on Monday morning, Mr. B. sent for the four boys. At first, he visited with each student separately. Eventually Bob, Ernie, Malcolm and Cliff all confessed to the sad details of their game—RUN HER NYLONS. Mr. Bishop asked, "How many students are involved in this sleazy game?" Five girls and four additional boys were summoned to the office.

Thirteen students! Mr. B.'s investigation uncovered the following facts: two girls were happy participants. Three were the victims of sexual assault. The eight boys were all involved in The Game, which had been created by Bob, who was the ringleader. The game was always played on the school bus on the trip to school. Ben had many questions about the game. How was the game played? How long had it been going on? Why hadn't the bus driver stopped it? Why hadn't any student and/or parent complained? Why hadn't even *one* of the other 52 bus passengers reported the ugly game to him? Ben spent the remainder of the morning finding the answers to these and other questions about the game.

Run Her Nylons

The game had been played either voluntarily or involuntarily since the second week in January; Ben rationalized that the game had been played every school day for eleven weeks!

The other bus students didn't report the situation to their teachers or their parents because they had been threatened, and thus were afraid. The fifty-two students were invited to play every school day. They promised not to watch or to report what was happening on the bus en route to school. They were clearly afraid to report the crime to anyone.

The bus driver was aware that something was going on but he had made an agreement with the tough kids on his bus. If the tough kids would be responsible for the discipline and behavior on the school bus, then he (the driver) would not have to watch the back of his bus while he was driving.

The game had started out as a game of running a ball-point pen up one leg and down the other in an attempt to ruin a girl's nylons. Within a few days the pen had been replaced by the boy's finger. Two girls purposefully did not wear nylons to school. The three forced participants wore nylons every day in order to protect themselves from the probing fingers.

Ben was disgusted. He was deeply saddened by what he learned during his day long investigation. He was ready and determined to take every action possible to correct the situation; to discipline the perpetrators and to find counseling help for the victims. He arranged to meet with the families to discuss religious, medical and psychological assistance to the children involved in the eleven weeks of emotional torture. He planned to turn the culprits over to the police department for the appropriate legal action.

The New Superintendent

Dr. Haberdasher had retired on February 28th and the school committee had appointed Mr. Smythe to assume the responsibility of running the school district. Dr. Haberdasher bragged about Ben's great work and his many successes as a junior high principal during the two and one-half years they had worked together. Ben and his teachers had been frequently commended for their school's strong academic program and its excellent disciplinary standards. At the time of the discovery of The Game, Mr. Smythe had been on the job for a total of six weeks. Three weeks after Mr. S.'s arrival, Ben had suspended two students for bringing beer into the junior high school premises. Mr. Smythe had sent a very direct letter the next day informing Mr. Bishop that he was not to suspend any more students. HE, Mr. S., was not a man who supported suspensions.

Monday—1 P.M.

Mr. Bishop called *The Boss*. Ben told the disgusting story over the phone to Mr. Smythe. Mr. S. responded by telling Ben that his story couldn't possibly be true. He further commented that he would immediately come over to the junior high and take over the case.

Ben called the thirteen students to his office shortly after the superintendent arrived. The kids were individually introduced to Mr. Smythe by their principal. The thirteen told in explicit detail the entire story to the school superintendent. Mr. Smythe began screaming, "I am suspending all of you kids right now. Get out of here! I am suspending all of you for twenty days!" Ben sent the thirteen to the guidance dept. conference room to wait while he contacted their parents. Mr. S. reiterated his command and instructed Ben to suspend the thirteen for twenty days.

Ben commented to his boss that he appreciated his support in suspending these kids but—Ben quietly suggested to his boss that school committee policy restricted principals to suspensions of up to a max of five days.

Mr. S. said, "I told you to suspend them for twenty days!"

Once again Ben attempted to alert his new boss by quietly noting that school committee policy restricted the superintendent to suspend a student for a maximum of ten days.

At this point, Mr. Smythe shouted at Ben telling him that he, Mr. Smythe, was the superintendent and that he would make the rules—"Not Mr. Bishop and certainly not the school committee!"

With these directives still ringing in his ears, Mr. B. dictated a letter to each family informing the parents as to their son's/daughter's involvement in The Game.

Ben made certain that the twenty-day-suspension letter noted that it was per Superintendent Smythe's personal recommendation, based upon his review of the facts. The letter noted that the superintendent had personally stepped in and had judged their child's actions. Mr. B. further commented that he was extremely pleased to have Mr. Smythe's support in this difficult case.

Each family was called. Ben talked personally to the parent answering the phone. One parent stated she was happy that the problem had finally come to his attention. She had been living in fear for her daughter and had personally been threatened by the gang of four. Mr. B. responded to this parent that he and his staff would watch over everyone involved, and assured the parent that her daughter would be safe on the bus and in school. The parent was surprised to learn from the principal that Mr. S. had directed him to not contact the police on this issue as he, Mr. Smythe, was in charge.

Tuesday A.M.

On Tuesday morning Ben had been scheduled to attend a meeting at the high school to discuss redistricting due to the growing enrollment in the school system. As he drove to the high school Ben spotted Bob's dad's car on the road ahead of him. Mr. B. figured Bob's dad was probably looking for him. Ben caught up with him at the next traffic light.

With a brief toot of the horn, Ben attracted the familiar parent's attention. Both drivers pulled into a nearby parking lot. Mr. Forestier, Bob's dad, after the usual pleasantries told Ben that he thought a two-day suspension was more than enough. He needed to have his son in school. "School is my baby sitter. I don't want you suspending my son. This is the third time this year that you have suspended Bob. I don't care if you use rope and tie him to a chair, but you are to keep him in school. After all, I have things to do and I don't need Bob at home getting in my way!" shouted Mr. Forestier.

Ben reminded Mr. F. that his son, Bob, was the ringleader in the matter and that Bob and his friends' stories were being reported to Detective Jurand by Mr. Smythe. Mr. Bishop assured Mr. Forestier that he had no intention of asking Mr. Smythe to reduce Bob's twenty-day suspension.

Mr. F. immediately drove over to the superintendent's office to complain about his son's lengthy suspension. Ben called his boss on the high school phone. He reached Mr. S. via the phone before Mr. F. arrived. Ben reminded Mr. S. that young Bob was the "RUN HER NYLONS" ringleader. He told his boss about the threats Bob and his gang had made against the girls and their parents. He gently reminded Mr. S. about how proud he was to be working for such a strong superintendent. Mr. Smythe reminded Ben that he had been directed by the super, that he had said twenty days and he would make certain that all thirteen would be out of school for the twenty days. "No," said Mr. S. "I won't need you here to help me straighten out Bob's dad."

Ben exited the redistricting meeting two hours later. Mr. Smythe had called and told Mr. B.'s secretary to tell Mr. Bishop he had agreed with Mr. Forestier's request. The message continued: "Mr. Bishop is to personally call each family and to have those kids back in school tomorrow morning. Further, Mr. Bishop is not to call the police to report this case per the BOSS."

Ben called the parents whose daughters were the victims of the game and suggested that they appeal to the superintendent to reconsider his most recent decision. A few hours later one mother called Mr. B. and reported to him about the mothers' meeting and their appeal for help. Mr. S.'s answer was quite emphatic. Every child was to be back in the junior high by tomorrow or the principal would have to answer to him. Every student and their parent(s) were contacted. The process took four days to complete the calls to the families inviting the thirteen back to the junior high.

Ben arranged through the transportation director to have the bus driver involved in the game to be transferred to another bus route. Mr. Forestier readily accepted Ben's request to have his son, Bob, walk to school for the remainder of that school year. Bob's father got what he wanted—Bob out of the house so he could run his illicit home business without his son being present. Detective Jurand was unable to press charges against Bob and his gang because of the families' great fear of retaliation. Yes, Ben had reported the case in all of its sordid details to his friend Jurand. The only satisfaction these two gentlemen had was that at least they had put a permanent stop to the game.

* * *

That night as Ben told Heather the grisly details of this story, the two of them readily agreed that Ben would not spend another school year working for a superintendent who couldn't or wouldn't set high disciplinary standards for the district schoolchildren. Ben wrote his first letter of application for a high school principalship the next day.

The school committee fired Mr. Smythe the following January.

Study Hall

Martin Murphy's study hall was always quiet. No one talked or fooled around in Martin's study hall. The only sound ever heard was that of the clock slowly counting the seconds until the bell rang and rescued the kids from Mr. Murphy. Martin would correct tests while the students read, studied or just sat praying for the bell to ring,

One day approximately twenty minutes into study hall torture, a girl screamed, causing Mr. Murphy to jump out of his chair and to race to help the eighth grader who had just screamed in pain. The 56 students in Mr. Murphy's study were also shocked and quickly reacted along with their teacher. Rachel had screamed because a deliveryman en route to the school cafeteria had spotted his niece in Martin's study hall. He had quietly snuck up behind her. He had grabbed her ear and pinched it. Rachel screamed. Two girls checked to see that she was okay. Mr. Murphy, realizing that Rachel was not in trouble, took off running down the hall after the deliveryman. With the help of several of his students, Martin captured the intruder.

After a brief visit with Mr. Bishop, the deliveryman agreed to ask his firm for a transfer. Rachel was embarrassed, but not hurt. She apologized for her uncle's actions. He never set foot in the junior high again.

*   *   *

Bob T.'s study hall period was usually quiet. Bob T. was a decent teacher, but he had to walk around to control his charges.

He never had to send students to the office for discipline and most of his students easily passed the district's cooperative finals.

Detective Jurand called Ben just before noon one Thursday morning and asked if Marylue was in school. Ben informed his friend that he would check and call him back in a few minutes. After checking with each of Marylue's teachers from the first period through Mr. T.'s study, Ben phoned Jurand and said, "Yes" she was in school. Jurand laughed and suggested that Marylue must have a twin sister as she was seated in a city jail cell. She had been arrested for walking downtown with just a man's shirt on!

Bob T. confessed to never taking attendance after first period as he believed that everyone was in school per the daily attendance sheet(s) . . . "If the kids were in first period, then I knew they were here for the day." Marylue had figured Mr. T.'s attendance patterns would let her escape to visit her adult boyfriend for two hours every school day, as Mr. T. was her History teacher in period three and her study teacher the following period. She had been visiting with her friend for a few weeks before her mother caught on to what her daughter was doing. Marylue's mother had knocked on the apartment door planning to forcibly remove her daughter from the apartment approximately 20 minutes before Jurand called Ben. Marylue had thrown a shirt on before she answered the door. Her mother yanked her out of the room and yelled at her daughter to get home "Now!" She then entered the room to beat on the man her daughter had been visiting.

The man was arrested; Marylue was released from jail and turned over to her mother. Bob T. was totally embarrassed as he sat in the courtroom witness chair admitting that he hadn't done his job correctly. The mother attempted to blame Mr. T. for her daughter's behavior because she believed that had he taken attendance as be was supposed to then her daughter would not have been able to secretly visit with the older man.

New Job

Heather and Ben felt lucky. Ben had received three job offers to serve as a high school principal. Three offers in the same week!!! They decided to accept the principal's position at Verona High School as it also gave the principal membership on the regional board of the College Entrance Boards. The two firmly believed that a CEEB experience listed on Ben's resume would be helpful in the future,

Ben was proud to be a high school principal. But he was slightly upset as a result of learning how and why he had been selected for the post. The primary reason Ben had been chosen for the job was the fact that neither he nor his family drank, smoked or used vulgar language, along with the knowledge that the Bishops were a good Christian family. Although Heather and Ben were happy with their lifestyle, they were disappointed that it was a more important factor used in the selection process rather than his curriculum expertise, his academic training and his success as an educational leader. Although Mr. Bishop's educational background and his success in North Mountain City Junior High were a part of the decision making, it became quite clear that his integrity and behavioral patterns were the main reasons for his selection for the job.

Ben had been invited by his new boss, Mr. Jakes, to meet with him and the school committee chairman to talk about the high school's problems and to discuss methods to resolve them. The superintendent and the committee chairman were more than just worried about the "high school situation." They told Ben about the principal that they had just fired and how he had been a hero to the entire student body. When they suggested that Mr. Bishop read the transcript of the entire dismissal proceedings, Ben said that he had no intention of reading those documents. The two leaders told Ben about the student candlelight vigil which had been held each evening of the week long hearing. They also told Mr. B. about the sex games the fired principal had played with his students.

Ben responded by telling his new bosses that he wasn't going to waste his valuable time learning about his predecessor's bad habits. Ben declared that he would be spending his time and efforts working to improve the school atmosphere. The school committee chairman asked Ben how much time he would need to change the school atmosphere.

Ben replied, "Six weeks."

The chairman turned to Superintendent Jakes and said, "No one can correct what has been happening in this school in six weeks. I think we made a mistake in hiring him."

Ben responded, "I'll have the problem resolved in six weeks. It will however, be on everyone's mind for the remainder of the school year. But, it will not be a topic of conversation by the end of the six weeks. If no one does anything like what the previous principal did during his tenure at Verona High, then the issue will be dead and forgotten when school reopens a year from now."

The chairman offered to come to the school every day to help Mr. Bishop take control of the high school. Mr. B. told the chairman that he wasn't welcome in the school and he wouldn't be allowed into the school until the problem had been corrected. Mr. Jakes supported Mr. Bishop and told the chairman to please stay away from the school so that the new principal could begin his work. Ben exited the meeting with a cheerful, "See you in six weeks."

Ben learned that the late June dismissal hearings had been a divisive community fight. Many parents and a majority of the high school students had wanted the committee to keep the former principal. He was told many stories about the sex club having been the major activity of the high school. The games had been played during the school day! He quickly discovered that not only had the principal been fired but that three teachers had been asked to resign as well.

Mr. Bishop held a school opening day assembly. He informed the students and staff that Verona High School was entering a new era of academic excellence. He noted his intention to support his teachers in establishing high standards of learning, discipline and sportsmanship. The teachers adopted a "we'll see" attitude. A majority of the students thankfully prayed, "About time." A few students had other plans.

That night as the Bishop family sat down for dinner, a rock crashed through the dining room window. Ben raced to the front door to see who had thrown the rock. At that same moment a second rock crashed through the rear bedroom window. Ben didn't catch the two rock throwers. He inspected the damage to Heather's new dining room table. Heather was more upset about the second rock. It had landed on their daughter's bed. Broken glass had also landed on their daughter's bed. Ben reported the incident to the Verona Police Dept. The investigating officers shrugged their shoulders and said it was just high school kids acting up. The Bishop family wasn't impressed.

Mr. B. told the superintendent about his "welcoming committee's" rock throwing message the next morning. He then asked his assistant principal, Tony Ketchum, to name the toughest boys in the school. Ben also asked for the names of the major players with the former principal. Tony picked three students from the 1600 plus high schoolers and said, "Most likely the two you are looking for are on this short list."

Ben found the three boys, one at a time. He gave the same message to each boy. "If you can, please tell the rock throwers that I had nothing to do with the dismissal of your friend. However, I firmly believe he should have been fired. If you or your friends want to hurt me, then be man enough to attack me. You or your friends damaged some of my family's furniture. It will be fixed. They also threw a rock which landed on my daughter's bed, along with broken glass. If the rock had been thrown through the window one hour later, my daughter would have been cut by the glass and injured by the rock. Now please tell your chicken-livered friends that I am here. If they have any guts they will come to me and tell me they did it. My family is not to be bothered again."

No further rock throwing incidents took place—nor did Mr. B. ever learn the names of his family's two first day greeters.

On Wednesday morning of the second week of school, Mr. B. was standing in the school corridor talking to Steve Joseph, a Social Studies teacher, when a senior class student stepped in between the two men and started talking to Mr. Bishop. Ben immediately and firmly explained to the young man that he had rudely interrupted a conversation and common rules of courteous behavior were the standards expected of everyone in the high school. Ben directed the student to stand a few feet away from Mr. Joseph and himself and to wait until their conversation had been completed. Mr. B. further stated that had he and the student been talking, he would expect the teacher not to interrupt unless it was an emergency. Mr. Joseph finished the original conversation and then he told his new boss that his former principal always allowed students to interrupt as the senior had. Mr. Joseph didn't tell Mr. B. how thrilled he was as a result of his action in the hallway that Wednesday morning. Steve told his fellow teachers that day about Mr. Bishop's behavior in the hallway and of his courteous standards for all. He then asked his fellow teachers to help the new principal regain control of the school.

On Thursday morning Steve asked Mr. B. what his plan(s) were to return the school to a proper and professionally run high school. Ben explained his simple plan and told Mr. Joseph he was going to present the plan to the school staff during next Monday's faculty meeting. Steve secretly asked his fellow faculty members to begin taking the corrective action of Mr. B.'s plan immediately. The teachers knew the school and the old rules better than their new principal. They added a few ideas of their own thereby improving the principal's plan. The teachers made these suggested plan improvements during the faculty meeting. Although Ben had no idea as to Mr. Joseph's help in the project, he recognized the additional ideas would make his plan a better one. Ben had told Mr. Jakes that he would gain control of the students and the staff in six weeks. Mr. Bishop realized that Mr. Joseph had helped him to pull it off in less than three weeks. Months later, Steve Joseph told Ben that the teachers had accepted him on the day he had told the senior not to interrupt people when they were talking to one another.

* * *

On Friday morning, the last day of the first marking period Mr. Bishop found a senior waiting for him. Augustus "OC" Edgecum was upset and had decided to quit school. OC's guidance counselor had told Gus that he had to take and pass French in order to graduate. OC said he wasn't going to learn French in a one-year course. Therefore the guidance counselor had informed him that he was wasting his time. OC told his principal that he could speak Polish and English.

Mr. B. worked hard to convince OC to stay in school and to graduate. After a lengthy conversation, OC accepted Mr. Bishop's challenge to take a home study course in advanced Polish for his language requirement. Ben offered to grant OC credit for third-year Polish if he passed his other four classes with at least two B's and no letter grades below a C. Also, OC had to pass a final exam in Polish. Ben agreed to have a test prepared specifically for him. OC agreed to stay in school. He told his principal that he would graduate with his class. Ben was pleased that OC had accepted his challenge. Ben had checked his report cards of the previous three years and had discovered several D's along with many C's, one A and four B's.

Ben asked Gus what his initials OC stood for. Gus told Mr. Bishop that his dad owned and operated a gas station named *At the Edge of the Roads Service Station.*

Gus worked for his father pumping gas, inspecting cars, changing oil, doing tune-ups etc. Since his fingers were usually stained with grease and oil, someone had called him "Oil Change" and the name had stuck. Gus said he liked being called OC.

Vietnam

The war in Vietnam generated many political problems in the public sector. Many college and high school administrators had to react to the student-generated pressures to stop the regular education programs for a day in November 1969. The demands included special activities which were designed to look like every student in America wanted the United States government to back out of the war in Vietnam. Mr. Bishop had his personal opinion regarding the war and what action the government should take, as did a majority of US citizens. Mr. Bishop also had a responsibility not to use the school as a voice for his personal views. He also was expected to protect the school community from having their tax-supported property used as a political podium for an anti-government rally.

In late October several students asked Mr. Bishop to allow them to schedule assemblies and work seminars for the entire school day on November 15th. Mr. B. asked these students if both sides of the public debate would be discussed. They told him they had arranged to have a group from the local college, a group of outspoken anti-war demonstrators, to speak at the requested assemblies and to lead the workshops as well. Mr. Bishop asked a second time if 50 percent of the time would be dedicated to the opposing viewpoint. Their response was a resounding "No." Ben concluded the meeting with this comment, "If you do not present a package representing both sides of the subject to me for consideration, then I will not allow an assembly for even one class period on the 15th."

At the end of the school day, November 13th, Mr. B.

noticed a group of students sneaking into the auditorium. He knew these students had their own cars and thus didn't need the school bus to get home. Ben hadn't heard from these students since their October meeting. He entered the auditorium and was surprised to see it completely lit up. He observed the group on the stage planning their November 15th assembly. Mr. Bishop walked down the aisle to the stage and asked the group what was happening.

Their leader responded with a polite but firm statement, "We are making the final arrangements for our assembly on Wednesday."

Ben inquired of the students as to "Who approved the use of the auditorium, who is in charge of your proposed assembly, will both sides of the issue be presented, what time is the assembly scheduled to begin?"

The spokesperson answered with a simple comment, "The college students will be in charge on Wednesday. We are getting the measurements and the seating capacities for them."

Mr. B. directed the students to leave immediately and reminded them that they had not met with him about a balanced program, "Thus there will be no assembly on Wednesday." The students left without comment.

That evening the school committee chairman visited with Ben at his home. He let Ben know that his daughter was one of the student leaders involved with the local college group advocating violence if necessary to stop all public school regular education programs for the day. The students were not interested in hosting a public debate with representatives from the opposing viewpoint. The chairman wanted the high school principal to know that if his daughter was suspended as a result of the confrontation planned for Wednesday that he would act as a parent and support her along with the other parents. He further stated that he would not attend any school committee meetings in which committee action on this subject would be taken. The chairman asked Ben if he could handle the challenge of college kids attacking him with ax handles. He then told Ben that he would be at the high school Wednesday morning to take charge of the situation. Ben told the chairman that he was not to enter the high school at any time during the school day in question. Ben then thanked the chairman for his considerate help in alerting him as to the kids' plan for THE DAY. Ben also thanked him for being so forthright with respect to his and his daughter's role(s) in the anticipated confrontation.

Ben arrived early on that fateful Wednesday morning. Mr. Jakes was waiting for him! The superintendent offered to do anything Ben requested to keep a reasonable semblance to a school day. Jakes even offered to do guard duty at any door in order to help keep order during the school day. Ben readily accepted his boss' offer to help. He assigned him the task of taking the chairman to the superintendent's office for the day. Mr. Jakes responded to Ben's challenge with the comment that he had been given the hardest job but he would do it. Ben said, "Thanks."

Ben knew that his staff was divided on the issue but that no one would start a disruption. The staff members were committed to doing their jobs—but everyone knew that once the disruptions began many of the school staff would participate in the assembly program.

Mr. B. and Tony Ketchum visited with selected teachers and guidance counselors. The two men directed each faculty member they approached to watch the fire alarm call box adjacent to their classroom all day. Tony and Ben fully expected someone to pull a false alarm to empty the school around the time the college kids were expected to arrive. A lady guidance counselor said that she intended to spend the day leaning against the wall with her back hiding the fire alarm call box. No one was going to pull the alarm she was protecting. Ben figured that an alarm would be pulled sometime that day. He just wanted to catch the student who pulled the alarm.

The tension in the building was felt by all the students as well as the staff members. In reality very little teaching was being accomplished as everyone was awaiting the student takeover. The school day started and six students entered the office and asked Mr. Bishop to let them lower the flag to half staff to honor the day and the soldiers dying in Vietnam. Mr. Bishop informed the six students the flag was flown at full staff every day. The only exceptions were Memorial Day and days announced by the president, the governor and/or the mayor. After a heavy debate, Mr. B. proposed that these six students get a signed petition from 50 percent of their fellow students requesting the flag to be flown at half staff. The petitioners said they didn't care what the rest of the students wanted but that the flag was going to be lowered to half staff. Ben told them the flag would not be lowered. He repeated his suggestion: "If you can get 50 percent of the high school students to support your petition I will let you appeal my decision to my boss, the superintendent of schools."

The gang of six agreed and asked for passes so they could visit all the classes to get the required signatures. Ben told them that no passes would be issued, The petitioners would be allowed to canvass all the students during the two lunch periods. The gang of six said that they were afraid the pro-government students would not let them complete their task during lunch. Mr. B assured the six Mr. Ketchum would make certain that they would not be interfered with as they walked to every table in the cafeteria asking for signatures. Tony and Ben were happy to have half of the day pass before they would have to worry about the flag boys.

In the meantime at approximately 10:00 A.M. two aluminum paneled delivery trucks pulled up in front of the main entrance to the school. Both trucks had a red cab, an aluminum body and a canvas flap covering the rear opening. Ben had requested the local police chief to help him if and when the college gangs arrived earlier that morning. The chief and two state police cars surrounded the two trucks. The policemen stood with their weapons drawn facing the college students. They did not allow them to exit the trucks. The Verona Police Chief gave them a choice: "Either leave the high school property in exactly one minute or we'll lock you up in the slammer for the rest of the day. The principal is looking forward to signing a complaint against each and every one of you for interfering with the operation of his high school."

At this point everyone awaited the fire alarms to sound the planned building evacuation alarm. The atmosphere was tense. The students, staff and the anti-government college kids wondered why the alarm hadn't been pulled as planned. Finally, the two truckloads of ax handle bearing college demonstrators left, hoping the next school would be an easier target.

Approximately 30 minutes later another truck arrived in the school yard. This truck was identical to the first two. This time there were four state police cars assisting the local chief. One policeman pulled the driver from the red cab and slammed him against the front fender in the same manner that they had used to greet the earlier drivers. As the policeman frisked the driver, two other officers stood with their guns pointed at the canvas flap at the rear of the truck. Two fellow policemen stood ready to yank the flap aside so they could challenge the students inside the truck to leave or . . . The high school students watching from their classroom windows quietly waited for the fire alarm to sound (which never rang) so they could join the anti-government rally. They witnessed the parking lot scene. The canvas flap was flung aside! The shock of discovering produce for the cafeteria turned a potentially serious event into a humorous one. Everyone in the school felt the building tension melt away. The state police radioed headquarters reporting, "The poor driver didn't know what was happening. He almost had a heart attack. I think he deserves the rest of the day off."

The lunch room petitioners gathered signatures during the two lunch periods. They didn't get the required 50 percent. Several members of the six gang scribbled additional names on the papers. They brought the signed petitions to Mr. Bishop. Prior to the beginning of lunch period Mr. Ketchum talked to a few students and had asked for their assistance to make certain the six gang would not get enough signatures. Tony's plan had worked. Ben examined and counted the petition signatures. He commented on the signatures by absent students and of several students having identical penmanship. Mr. Bishop noted that since the petition had fewer than 50 percent of the student body demanding the flag be lowered to half staff that he would support the majority of the students and leave the flag at the top of the flagpole. The six gang angrily left the principal's office.

Tony watched as the six gang met with seven of their friends in the lobby leading to the main entrance. The 13 students looked at the flag waving in the breeze as if it were taunting them. Tony asked Ben to let him handle this challenge. Ben happily agreed with Tony's plan.

As requested by Tony, Mr. B. walked past the 13 crowd and looked at his watch. Ben announced to the 13 that the bell was about to ring. "You have exactly three minutes to get to class, gentlemen. Don't be late."

Mr. Bishop had overheard the group's conversation as he circled them on his way back to his office. The six wanted all 13 students to walk out the front door and to lower the flag themselves. "So what if he (the principal) suspends us. At least we will have won," snarled the leader. Meanwhile Tony had called upstairs to Mr. Sharky's social studies class and asked him to yell at, and then to send, Joe Muscle to the office NOW. Sharky loved Tony's plan and sent J.M. to the office. Joe Muscle walked by the 13 muttering to himself, "I didn't do anything, I didn't do nothing, that teacher can't suspend me, I didn't do nuthing."

Tony took the angry student into his office, closed the door, and told him what he had asked Mr. Sharky to do, as well as why. J.M. was a frequent guest in Mr, Ketchum's office. He was a tough but friendly kid. Mr. K. asked Tony for his help to keep the flag flying at full staff. Tony was thrilled to help Mr. Ketchum. The two, Tony Muscle and Mr. Ketchum walked out of the office area yelling at each other. J.M. shouted that he, "Didn't do NUTHING!"

Mr. K. loudly retorted that he would suspend Tony for the rest of the month if he didn't straighten out "immediately." They walked through the lobby exuding hostile anger. Mr. K. and J.M. appeared to not even notice the 13. The two verbal confrontationalists walked out the front door around the flagpole and back into the school. Their angry debate hadn't subsided. The 13 ran to their classes. The day ended without any major confrontation. Mr. B. invited the anti-government group to an after-school assembly to talk about the issues. They told him that if they couldn't disrupt the school day then they weren't interested.

From that day forward, J.M. considered Mr. K. as his hero.

* * *

The United States bombed Cambodia on a Thursday in May 1970.

Four days later Mr. John Bakely, a high school principal from Great Britain, arrived in Massachusetts to begin his research of the comprehensive high school programs as they existed in the United States. Ben felt honored that he had been selected to host Mr. Bakely's first two days. His task was to explain the American high school curriculum structure as they toured four of the best programs in the state. After visiting the selected high schools and Mr. Bishop's Verona High School, Ben had a clearer vision of John's mission in the States. John was to return to England with a definitive concept of how the U.S.

schools operated, as his country was considering the adoption of a comprehensive program for several of its secondary schools.

Both men, John and Ben, were impressed with their invitations (scheduled two months before Mr. Bakely left home) to speak at a nationally recognized private college on the differences of the two countries' high school programs. On that fateful Tuesday evening, as Ben was driving with his guest to the college, he suggested to John that they would be lucky if twenty college students attended their presentations. The two principals entered the Hall (the auditorium) and were amazed to see every seat taken. The professor in charge of the assembly was pleased with the large turnout. The program began with the Education Dept. Chairman introducing his "Honored Guests." The chairman informed his audience that the two speakers would each make a twenty-minute presentation and then he would open the conference to questions from the audience.

Mr. Bakely and Mr. Bishop made their respective comments as advertised. The two principals made a joint report as well on their personal analysis of the differences of the two systems. This joint presentation lasted about six minutes. At this point the Education Chairman asked the audience if they had any questions to direct to the principals.

The first question was addressed to Ben, "Mr. Bishop: What did you do in your high school to explain the unjust bombing of Cambodia to the student body? Did you cancel classes? Did you tell the students that the United States was wrong to take this action? Did you enjoin your students to demand the U.S. pull out of Vietnam immediately?"

"No," responded Mr. Bishop. Ben started to explain to his attacker that not all of his students wanted classes to stop for a political assembly. Most students would have this type of conversation in their social studies classes. Before Mr. B. was able to give a complete answer he was interrupted by the inquisitive senior as he shouted at Mr. Bishop, "You Fascist Pig!'

Ben responded to his challenger, "Coming from you, I will accept that statement as a compliment."

The Education Chairman, Mr. Bakely and Mr. Bishop were completely surprised when the entire crowd cheered Mr. B.'s response. The remainder of the evening was almost boring but it was definitely tense. The conversation during the trip back to John's hotel was dedicated to the two men wondering if the Education Chairman had any emergency escape plans for "us" had the crowd attacked?

Senior Play

The school district had lost a good school psychologist when it accepted Dr. Ralph's resignation at the end of the school year two years earlier. Dr. Shirlee Simmer arrived in September. Shirlee was very personable. At first everyone admired her work. Many district staff members wondered how the system could have survived so many years without her. Shirlee was a terrific school psychologist. (Well she was until December!) By the middle of December, 90 percent of the staff hoped Ms. Simmer(ing) would leave the district!

Shirlee chased every man in town. By the end of December it was obvious that her only interests were MEN. Shirlee was fired in mid March to the relief of all. Shirlee stayed in the local hotel providing her simmering services until her arrest in late May. The replacement psychologist hired in early April was a young and a compassionate gentleman.

The senior play adviser had posted his call for seniors to take part in the spring presentation of the Senior Class Play. Tryouts began in January. The seniors and their adviser selected The Policeman's Ball for the school's annual event, to be held during the second weekend in May. Rehearsals, advertisements, scheduling, costumes, tickets etc. were all a part of the adviser's job. The play had been advertised through the local press for the two weekend performances. The Friday evening show was usually attended by the high school students. *It was their school play.* Saturday's presentation generally was accepted as townspeople's night.

Ticket sales had been great. Both performances had been sold out two weeks before the big night!!!! Monday morning—five days before the big night—found Thad, the senior play adviser, knocking on Mr. Bishop's office door.

Thad reported to his principal that everything was going just fine. The play would be a financial success. The students had practiced and looked like professional actor/actresses. The play would be the best yet. However there was just one little problem, "Georgio, a senior playing a leading role, might commit suicide on the stage during the show!"

Ben asked if Georgio was seeing the school psychologist and several additional questions about Thad's shocking revelation of a few minutes earlier. After a lengthy exchange Mr. Bishop learned the following.

Georgio had threatened suicide before.
He was being counseled by the psychologist; in fact he had been counseled by both Dr. Simmer and her replacement, Doc Wil D. Cyde.
Thad didn't want to cancel the senior play.
Thad had no understudy to replace Georgio.
Doc Cyde wouldn't be available until Tuesday (tomorrow) afternoon to discuss the problem.

Tuesday Afternoon

Tony and Ben met with Thad and Doc. According to Doc—Georgio must not be removed from the play cast because he then would definitely kill himself. Mr. Bishop wasn't to cancel the play unless he was prepared to take the responsibility for Georgio's death. Mr. B. then asked the two proponents of The Show Must Go On why they hadn't turned Georgio over to a psychiatric team to help him. Ben heard their plan to do that next week after the sacred play was over. The two "Adults" Ben and Tony were working with had known since January about this "problem"? They had purposely waited until the last minute to let the principal in on the difficulty. Doc told his boss that he had consulted with Dr. Simmer on the issue since she had worked with Georgio from September thru to March. Since they met Wil and Shirlee had spent many an hour together discussing Georgio and they both agreed that he should perform in the senior play. Mr. Bishop called a local psychiatrist and asked his advice.

Wednesday Afternoon

The psychiatrist met with Ben, Tony, Thad and Doc Wil D. Cyde in an attempt to see if any other solution could be found for Georgio's difficulty. Dr. Schmidt, the psychiatrist, finally agreed that the play must go on as planned. During the meeting on Thad's school play challenge, Dr. Schmidt had discovered that Thad hadn't cited all of the difficulties involved in his problem! Thad had concealed one additional problem from his boss . . . as part of the plot the girl playing the lead role in the play had to offend Georgio in the play. At first she would agree to go to the policeman's ball with Georgio. And in a few scenes later she had to tell him she had changed her mind—she would be going to the ball with the police chief, not Georgio!

Well, that's the play, thought Ben.

BUT Georgio's real problem was that this girl was the one he dreamed about in real life. Dr. Simmer had tried to help Georgio and his dream girl to become close friends. She had refused to date Georgio for the past two years! Thad and Doc had known this fact as well. Dr. Shirlee, Thad and Doc had all agreed they could help Georgio by putting him in the play. By having him publicly embarrassed by his dream girl they had all agreed thus he would be cured!! Schmidt, Tony and Ben started yelling at Thad and Doc at the same time, "IDIOTS!"

Mr. Ketchum and Mr. Bishop arranged to meet with all of the play participants. On Thursday afternoon the two administrators met with everyone involved except Georgio.

The play was to go on as scheduled and the seniors were to be responsible for the safety of the girl as well as for Georgio. If Georgio pulled a knife or a gun or produced any drugs, etc., which could be used to hurt himself or anyone else, the curtain was to be pulled closed immediately. At the same time two cast members and two adults hidden behind the stage were to attempt to stop Georgio's planned move to hurt himself or anyone else.

Everyone accepted Mr. B.'s plan to have each cast member searched for weapons prior to their entering the dressing rooms and the stage each evening. Many additional ideas were talked about to make certain the play could go on safely. Everyone had an assignment. One member was to call for help. Another was prepared to give a brief speech to calm the audience if the play had to be interrupted.

The kids planned every detail, "Just in case." Mr. Ketchum was scheduled to attend and to be in charge Friday, and Mr. B. would be in charge on Saturday evening. Ben was relieved to learn that no student had been in on Thad's insane plan. The students first learned of Georgio's emotional problem(s) and of the casting challenges during this Thursday afternoon meeting. Thad however, was proud of himself. Mr. B. was doing exactly what he had planned for his principal to do. "Perfect."

Tony called Ben at home Friday night. The play had gone off without any "unique" incidents. The two men agreed that the Saturday performance might be quite exciting. Mr. Bishop reminded his key students of their important roles of the evening. The MC stepped onto the stage and intoned, "Ladies and Gentlemen, thank you for coming to our last performance as high school students. NOW the Verona High School Senior Class presents

The Policemen's Ball.

Ben stood leaning against the wall awaiting disaster.

The play went on. Everything went smoothly. Ben finally sat down with Heather and commented about how nice all the kids looked as they danced the policemen's ball. The play ended. Nothing had happened. Georgio's promise to "perform" during the play hadn't happened! The student actors enjoyed their three encores. Ben rushed backstage to congratulate his students and to thank them for their concern and support. "You did a great job. Your performance was superb. And again thank you for your help this evening."

At this point one of the students told Mr. B. what really had happened during the show. Just before the ball scene, Georgio had cut his dream girl's gown into shreds. His purpose had been to keep her from going to the Ball with the "chief."

"But," said Mr. Bishop, "She looked so nice dressed in her pretty gown."

The student told his unobservant principal that she had on her After Class Play party dress in the Ball scene. *Wow!* thought Ben, *These kids did an amazing job tonight.*

Georgio spent the next 24 hours sitting on the sidewalk in front of his dream girl's home. When the psychiatric team arrived to take him for treatment, he went quietly.

Thad resigned and found a non-teaching job. Doc Wil D. Cyde was fired in June.

The Substitute

Ben told his new friend and assistant, Tony Ketchum, about his experience at the state meeting on leadership and in particular one comment made by a member of his group on student discipline. The experienced high school principal had reported to his team members on Discipline and Leadership that he believed he had heard every conceivable story or excuse from kids trying to avoid being suspended for their transgressions. As a result he had decided to forgive any student who told him a true story which he had never heard before. Ben decided that he would adopt a similar attitude, as long as the case didn't involve drugs, weapons or physical abuse. Thus the two men agreed that if a student excuse was unique the kid would not be suspended.

A few days before Thanksgiving, Mr. Ketchum brought Henry Glitch into the principal's office. Tony asked, "Mr. Bishop, how are you getting along with the Pope?" Ben replied, "Other than his rules on birth control, he's okay." After Tony's abuse of Mr. Bishop's name to start the day off with a little humor, he suggested to his boss that this might be the time when he would be hearing a most unique story. With this intro Tony left Ben's office. Henry told Mr. Bishop that he hadn't been truant for the past three days as Mr. Ketchum claimed.

Henry said that he had worked as a substitute teacher for the three days he had been absent. Mr. Bishop reminded Henry of the fact that he was repeating his junior year because he had failed all five subjects in the previous school year. Henry acknowledged his dereliction. Then Henry handed his first quarter report card to Mr. B. He readily admitted to purposefully failing all five classes. At this point Henry repeated his earlier statement that he had subbed as a third grade teacher at the parochial school a few miles down the road for the last three days.

Mr. Bishop phoned Sister Innocent, while Henry stood in front of him, and asked her if Henry had indeed subbed as a teacher at the Holy Saints Elementary School for three days. He was pleasantly surprised to hear Sister Innocent, the school principal, compliment Henry's teaching success. Ben was amazed to hear Sister claim Henry was the best sub she had ever had. Further, she noted that he would be the first sub she would call on in the future. Ben suggested to Sister Innocent that perhaps the employment of truants as substitute teachers was not the right thing to do before he thanked her as they finished their conversation. Mr. Bishop then turned to Henry and asked him how he gotten involved in subbing.

Henry explained to Mr. Bishop that his aunt was a third grade teacher at Holy Saints. Henry told his principal his mother had sent him over to his aunt's house with a container of chicken soup. He was to give her the soup as she was "deathly" sick with the flu. "My aunt asked me to teach her classes until she got better. She said she was too sick to call anyone and since I was there she asked me. I said I'd teach her third grade classes for her as long as she was sick, and I did. Now you see I wasn't truant?" Mr. B. informed Henry that he definitely had been truant for the past three days. BUT, since his story was a unique one, he would not be suspended nor given a few days of detention.

Mr. B. then asked Henry to explain what he had done as a teacher that so impressed Sister. "It was easy; I told the little kids that if they were good and did their reading, writing, arithmetic and history lessons like good kids every morning, then I would play my guitar and sing with them every afternoon. Actually, I enjoyed teaching them. It was great."

A year later Ben read an article in the national magazine for school principals, *The Academic Leader* about a contest for school administrators to submit their most unusual story in competition for a $50.00 prize. Ben knew he had a winner. He submitted the story of Henry, the truant, teaching third grade. Ben added an additional note in his cover letter, (not to be included in the published article) noting that Henry started studying again and had been promoted to the senior class.

Ben anxiously awaited the next issue of *The Leader* and the publication of his prize winning story. Ben's story didn't get published. He didn't win the $50.00. "The winning story was not worth the cost of the ink to print it!" retorted Ben in his determined phone call to the magazine editor. The editor responded to Ben's harsh comments that "Yes" his was a great story but the staff realized that he (Mr. Bishop) had made it up. The editor apologized after Ben assured him that the story was true.

As of this date Mr. Bishop has not received his $50.00 prize!

The Hearing

Mr. B. was proud of his teachers. All but one of them were good-to-excellent teachers. Ben continued his practice of visiting a classroom every day. [This statement is based upon his visiting 20 classes per every four weeks of school.] He encouraged his staff to give their best in their teaching. The staff reacted positively to their principal egging them on to greater success in their classrooms. Unfortunately one English teacher didn't meet his principal's expectations. Mr. James Encore was a lazy instructor. He usually made his classroom presentations in less than 10 minutes. Then he allowed his students to use the remainder of the class time as a study period.

Mr. B. had talked with Mr. Encore about teaching the entire 11th grade curriculum which required 180 hours of instruction. Encore readily agreed with Mr. Bishop's request to prepare better and more thorough lesson plans. He promised to work harder as a teacher. Ben suspected that Encore was using his extra class time to prepare for his own evening classes. Encore was studying for his Master's degree. He was taking classes two nights a week. Ben asked the English dept. chairman to supervise Mr. Encore more closely. Dennis A. First, English dept. chairman, agreed with Ben's analysis of Encore's work habits. Dennis said he would work with his friend and he would correct the situation.

In late March Ben had a long talk with Dennis A.(ssociation) First about his plan to dismiss Mr. Encore at the end of the school year. Dennis asked Mr. Bishop to give Encore a second chance. "Give him one more year and I will guarantee he will be a better teacher." Ben hesitated. First said, "I realize Jim Encore is a poor teacher. I will make him change because I want to keep him. After all we might not find anyone who is a better teacher as there aren't many good candidates available. You know our pay scale is the lowest in the area. All the good candidates are usually hired by our neighbors." Mr. B. accepted Mr. First's proposal to keep Encore one more year along with his promise to make him the teacher he was capable of being.

As the staff dismissal deadline passed Ben realized that Encore was retreating to his "style." Dennis had talked to Encore and had been successful in pushing him to improve his teaching habits for approximately a five-week period following his conversation with the principal.

Mr. Encore's second year was a duplicate of his first. No amount of positive reinforcement or cajoling could move him to put in a full day's work Ben and Dennis discussed Mr. Encore's teaching habits every week. At the end of January Mr. B. notified Mr. First about his decision to *not* re-employ his friend for the another school year. Mr. First was upset. Ben told him that he, the school principal, would formally inform Mr. Encore in writing that his services would terminate on the last school day in June.

Ben had dedicated his academic career to service with integrity and he expected the same from everyone he worked with. Mr. First and Mr. Bishop had a good working relationship. This was the reason Ben had agreed to Mr. First's appeal on behalf of Mr. Encore during the previous school year.

Encore appealed his principal's decision. Encore's dismissal hearing was scheduled. Superintendent Jakes told Ben that the dismissal hearing might get nasty as the teacher's union was strongly supporting Encore.

The nine-member school committee sat in one long line with the superintendent on one side of the conference table. Mr. Encore sat in the center seat directly opposite the committee chairman. Encore was seated in the center of nine teachers. Mr. First was on Encore's left. The long narrow table had a single seat at one end reserved for the high school principal.

The focus of the hearing appeared to be aimed down the long table at the principal as he attempted to "wrong" the union. The school committee and the union talked to each other as if they were friends. Both sides took turns challenging Mr. B.'s every word. Ben thought to himself, *If they vote now, Encore will stay.* The union's argument was presented by Dennis First. Mr. First complimented Mr. Bishop's skills as a principal and as a math teacher. Then First declared that the distinguished math teacher had no clue about the teaching of English. The committee was about to vote. Mr. B. made his final statement. First's eyes turned to a heated white as he listened. It appeared as if a white hot fire was burning inside First's brain. Ben repeated the appeal story Mr. First had used to retain Encore for this, his second year. When the committee heard Dennis admit as factual what Mr. Bishop had just stated—that, yes he, Mr. First, wanted to keep a less than mediocre teacher—Dennis knew that he had lost. Everyone watched as the committee members changed their individual votes, The verdict was unanimous. Mr. Encore was terminated.

After the meeting had ended, Ben got the feeling that the committee felt they had let a friend down. The last two months of the school year were tough. Every week someone would call and ask the committee to keep Mr. Encore. In late May, Encore began spending more time working with his students. He had them writing letters to the committee members asking them to rehire their English teacher. The once Encore-supportive-committee finally concluded they had made the correct decision in this case. They based their final conclusion(s) on the time his students spent letter writing and their personal investigations into his classroom behavior.

Mr. Jakes teased Ben about the union's near win on the last

day of that school year. As the two administrators watched Mr. Encore leave the building for the last time Mr. Jakes said. "Jim didn't merit an *Encore!*"

Mischief—Happenings

When everything appears to be going smoothly, there is always someone who decides it's time to entertain the troops.

Steve Joseph asked Mary, one of his brightest and style-conscious students, to take a note to Mr. Ketchum for him, and to bring back Mr. Ketchum's response to the problem he had outlined in his note. Steve stapled his note closed to ensure the privacy of his enquiry. Mary cheerfully danced along the hallway to the main office where she was greeted by the vacant stares of the principal and his assistant, Mr. Ketchum. The two men had been standing at the counter talking about the smooth start to another school day as Mary entered the outer office area. After the "Good Morning" pleasantries had been exchanged, Mary told Mr. Ketchum that Mr. Joseph had sent her to the office with a note for him, and informed Mr. Ketchum about her instructions to wait for the reply to Mr. Joseph's question. At this point both men had noticed Mary's unusual style of dress.

Tony pulled the staples from the note, and unfolded it.

The two men read the brief note simultaneously. They fervently hoped (prayed) that they showed no visible reaction to either the note or to Mary's attire of the day. Mr. Ketchum said, "Tell Mr. Joseph my answer is an emphatic NO."

Mary immediately turned and headed back to Mr. Joseph's class. Tony and Ben ran to their respective offices. The two men were hysterical and needed privacy until they could regain their composure and then return to their duties.

The note addressed to Mr. Ketchum read, "Tony, please note: MARY FORGOT HER UPPER UNDIE THIS MORNING."

* * *

Mr. Jakes arrived at the high school with an English teacher candidate. The super asked Mr. B. to interview her for the recently advertised vacancy. Ben invited Ms. Lucinda Evermore into his office in order to discover her teaching capabilities via a formal interview. Ms. Evermore was seated with her back toward the office door, and Ben was seated at his desk facing the teacher candidate. He observed Mr. Jakes and Tony leaning against the office counter. It appeared to Ben as if they were waiting for someone or something.

Ben would shortly learn about Ms. "Young" Evermore's annual visit to the school district and Mr. Jakes. They were old friends. Lucinda had retired after a brief career of 15 years. She had happily married a wealthy businessman. She had been a mischievous, happy and a successful teacher. Lucinda always dropped in to visit her old boss on her annual visit to the area. She had readily agreed to assist Jakes in his plot to see how long it would take Mr. Bishop to get "Shook up." Henry, Lucinda and Tony had each placed a $5.00 bill on the counter against a selected number of minutes each one had bet on before Mr. Bishop would come running out of his office.

The interview began with the usual pleasantries about family, travel, etc., as the conversation moved onto Lucinda's experience as a teacher and the questions of availability and interest in the particular class assignments. Ben concentrated on his task of discovering whether this candidate was the best for his students and the high school, Even though Jakes and Ketchum were still standing in the outer office, Ben was no longer conscious of them.

Finally Ben reviewed Lucinda's college transcripts and began questioning his guest about specific college courses. He was trying to discover the candidate's area of greatest academic interest. At this point Ben commented on Ms. Evermore's double major. Lucinda had majored in English and in Dance.

Mr. B. finally asked the question the *three* had been waiting for. "Is there any connection of these two majors which is transferable to an English class?" asked the unsuspecting principal. "Young" Evermore stood up and said, "Yes, I'll show you." Mr. Bishop's attractive guest started humming "The Stripper" and began dancing to her spirited music.

Lucinda reached up to unbutton the top button of her blouse; Ben rushed out of his office with a quick comment to his secretary, "Get rid of her!" Finally Ben noticed the three miscreants laughing at the success of their prank. He had to admit they had pulled a good one on him.

* * *

The department head meeting had been scheduled to end in time for Ben to meet with a business teacher applicant at 4:00 P.M. The seven department heads actually completed their work by 3:45 P.M. and the principal had a few minutes to swap war stories with his school leadership team. As the department heads and Mr. B. left the guidance area conference room enroute to the main office, several members of this august group said "Good night" or "See you tomorrow" to their confreres and the principal. There were two heads walking with Mr. B. when he arrived at the main office door. The two had been talking earnestly with their boss about the possibility that someday in the future they might become high school principals. As the three men entered the main office they noticed the Business teacher candidate waiting for her 4:00 interview with Mr. Bishop.

The three men walked into the administrative work area to check their mail and say their "Goodnights" to each other. They had all said, "Hello," or "Good afternoon," to the candidate as they passed through the waiting area. Standing a distance from the candidate, as they checked their respective mail slots, the two department heads reiterated their interest in becoming high school principals. They then commented that a principal's job was much easier than their current task demanding jobs.

"All a principal does is visit with beautiful young ladies all day while we teach!" remarked one department leader to the other. They asked, "Mr. B., how long will this interview last? A couple of hours?" Ben responded with a comment about their juvenile behavior and noted that interviews would last about 30 minutes.

Milissa St. Jean was seated on the student discipline bench. The uncomfortable bench had been designed to force its occupants to sit up straight. Milissa had on a form-enhancing dress. She sat there with her pile lined coat opened and thus framing her body. Her legs were crossed and were quite visible due to the short dress she wore.

Bishop went over to introduce himself to his guest. He invited Ms. St. Jean into his office for the scheduled appointment. The two department heads watched as Milissa walked past them and entered the principal's office, accompanied by Mr. Bishop. They continued watching as Ben offered to take her coat to hang it on the coat tree before he began the formal interview.

Ben lifted Milissa's coat at the collar/shoulder area and let it slide down her arms in order to take it off and to hang it on the coat rack in the corner of his office. Unfortunately, the hook at the back top of her dress had caught onto the loops of her pile lined coat. Thus, as Mr. Bishop lowered the coat to help Ms. St. Jean to remove it, DISASTER STRUCK.

The heavy coat attached to the dress hook started to unzip the dress as he lowered the coat. Ben had no place to rest the coat as Milissa's arms were no longer at her side. She was reaching back trying to unhook her dress from her coat. At this point the heavy coat held the unzipped dress half off of her shoulders.

Ben commanded Ms. St. Jean, "Put your hands down now." Ben then was able to place the coat on Milissa's shoulders. Mr. B.

invited his guest to be seated. All of this embarrassing activity happened in less than 30 seconds. Ben would recall this disaster thinking it had lasted "forever." The interview lasted approximately five minutes. Ben then invited the ever observant business department chairman into his office, and after introducing him to Ms. St. Jean, directed him to take the candidate up to the business area to complete the formal candidate interview.

The next morning Ben beat his two dept. head friends to the teachers' room and gave his version of the story to the rest of his wise guy staff.

* * *

Augustus OC Edgecum had adopted Mr. Bishop as his guidance counselor. OC usually asked Mr. B. for advice while he worked on the principal's car at the family garage. One Sunday, approximately six weeks before the senior prom, the Bishop family had stopped to fill the family car's gas tank prior to heading out for a short ride.

OC told his principal that he had asked all the cheerleaders to go to the prom with him, but every one of them had said, "No thank you." OC was upset because he couldn't get a date for the prom. After listening for a few minutes to the names of every girl who had said 'No' because they had a better date for the prom than a grease jockey, Mr. B asked OC if he had asked Kathy?

Kathy was a quiet young lady. Most students were oblivious of her existence. OC admitted that he had never given Kathy a thought, much less of asking her to the prom. Ben suggested that OC and Kathy might really enjoy each other's company at the prom. Ben paid for his tank of gasoline and drove off for the planned picnic with his family.

As the Bishop's car exited the service station, Ben called back to OC, "You and Kathy would make a very nice couple." First thing Monday morning OC asked Kathy to go to the senior prom with him. Kathy's "Yes!" surprised him. OC was speechless. OC ran down the hall to the principal's office. He told Mr. Bishop about the "YES" he had received from Kathy. Ben congratulated OC on his success in finding a date for prom night.

Prom Night

The first couple to arrive at the high school was Kathy and OC. OC parked his father's car in the first parking space available to the prom goers. Most of the senior class arrived during the next 30 minutes. The "in crowd" was busily gossiping about how they had refused to attend the prom with OC and how lucky they were to be with seniors A, B, & C—clean handsome Harry etc. "Poor Kathy, the only boy to ask her was OC. How sad she must be dating poor greasy OC!"

Approximately one hour later, the gossipers asked their principal who had rented the new Rolls Royce for prom night? Mr. Bishop said, "It wasn't rented. OC's father let him use the family car." Very few citizens of Verona knew that OC's family owned a new Rolls Royce. OC's family only used the Rolls on Saturday evenings. The rest of the week OC's father drove around town in a rusted junk box of a car. Mr. B. could feel the anguish as the girls moaned (not quite to themselves), "If only I had said Yes!"

Two years later OC and Kathy were married. OC's family owned two factories as well as a service station and an oil delivery service.

* * *

Weldon Davis was one of the best biology teachers in the business, whom Ben referred to as "Well Done" Mr. Davis. Every school year Weldon would purchase several pairs of black and white mice from a national science supply company to use in his classroom experiments. He used these scientifically bred mice to illustrate the biological principles he enjoyed teaching to his students. By the end of the second semester many of his students thought of these mice as cute little pets.

The annual argument between the students, the custodian and Mr. Davis was usually won by Tom, the custodian. Tom would take the mice at the end of the specified school day toward the end of May and incinerate all of them. Tom did not like "rats" in his school. The year finally arrived when in late May the annual debate resulted in a standoff between the students and the custodian. The students appealed to Mr. Bishop asking him to tell Tom not to incinerate the cute little mice in Mr. Davis' room.

Mr. B. clearly informed his friendly group of science students when he stated, "There is no way that live mice will be kept in the school beyond the last day of school." Mr. Bishop offered to accept the students' proposal to allow each student to take home a mouse or two if and only if their parents agreed to let their kid keep it as a pet. Ben further informed his friendly students that all "pets" remaining in the school as of June 1st would be given to Tom for disposal.

The school bus drivers were not happy when they were told about the additional passengers being transported on "their" buses on the last school day in May.

Tom reported to his boss that every rat had been removed from the school late that afternoon. "Well Done" Davis was quite embarrassed when he learned the news. "Well Done" reported to his boss the contents of his phone call from the local police department. Most of the kids had released their "pets" as they exited the school bus on their way home! Approximately sixty mice had been released along the bus routes from one end of town to the other! Tom and Ben vowed to never let the students have rodents as pets again.

Drugs

Drugs in the high school changed the student disciplinary process. Before drugs became readily available to teenagers the majority of school problems were handled with the miscreant confessing to his/her teacher. A simple "I did it" allowed the school day to continue with the most of the students accepting the fact that the culprit would be justly punished. With the advent of drugs on campus, students no longer confessed. Further, no one would "squeal" on the guilty party due to their fear of being caught and as a result beat up by the drug dealers. The era of "I don't know" permeated the public schools.

Mr. Bishop received a confidential phone call. The caller identified himself to Ben with the admonition that his name was never to be spoken by the principal no matter how challenging the case became. The caller gave his phone number to Mr. B. in order that Ben could confirm the identity of the messenger and of the factual evidence about to be shared with him. The number was listed in the telephone directory under superior court justices.

The secretary answering the phone asked Judge X. if he would accept a call from Mr. Bishop. Judge X. reported to the high school principal about one of his students who was a big drug dealer. The judge was frustrated because a powerful crime-supporting attorney had negotiated with the district attorney to let him use a technicality which had prevented the judge from sending the young man to jail. The judge gave most of the drug dealing details to Ben. As the judge finished his conversation with Mr. B. he reminded him about his promise to never reveal his information source in this matter.

The next school day the student drug dealer returned to school with a note from his parents asking that his absence of the previous two weeks be excused as "DD" had been sick with the flu. Mr. Bishop told DD that the school attorney was visiting with his parents at that very moment. The school appointed lawyer was explaining to his family that their son was being expelled from school as he was a drug pusher.

DD's response as recorded by Tony and Ben was, "You can't expel me! You are not supposed to know. Who told you? I'll be back." A few hours later two attorneys entered the principal's office demanding that Mr. Bishop allow DD to return to school immediately. The lawyers, upon hearing Mr. B.'s "No," asked the date of the next school committee meeting. The regular monthly meeting had been scheduled for 8:00 P.M. the next evening many weeks ago. The lawyers promised that they would be there.

Ben immediately reported all of the essential details of his problem to his boss, the superintendent. Henry Jakes told Ben that he would make certain DD never returned to Verona High School.

The meeting was held in the high school cafeteria as usual. The cafeteria hall wall was mostly glass. People standing in the hallway could see into the cafeteria but they couldn't hear a sound coming from within. Even when the school lunchroom was serving 400 plus noisy students enjoying their break from academic instruction on a bad lunch day, no sound was ever emitted from the cafeteria into the hallway. As the meeting began four lawyers representing DD stood up and demanded the committee immediately hear their appeal of the principal's illegal decision as they were important men with other pressing matters to attend to. The school committee chairman firmly yet politely informed them that DD's hearing would be held in executive session after the regular meeting if it was to be held at all. The angry spokesman said, "The hearing will be held!" and then he sat down. The committee proceeded with its scheduled meeting agenda. They proceeded to drag out every idea on every subject in order to make the meeting last at least until midnight.

Finally, the public session ended. After a fifteen-minute recess, the chairman received a unanimous vote to enter executive session to hear the high school principal's discipline report. Everyone left the room except the committee members, the superintendent, the principal and the four attorneys. The chairman asked the four lawyers to leave the room as he hadn't had a vote to conduct a hearing "Yet." The four left the room after they learned that they would be invited in to participate in a hearing only after the committee voted to host a hearing. The four stood in the hallway watching through the glass wall at the nine committee members conducting business inside.

The chairman asked Ben to report on his reasoning to ask the board to expel DD. After listening to the tragic story, the chairman asked the committee for two votes. The first unanimous vote to expel DD took about ten seconds. The second vote to adjourn the meeting also lasted approximately ten seconds. Ben gasped in surprise at the efficiency of the votes. He was also completely amazed at the committee's behavior in not having the legal four in to speak their piece. Mr. Jakes explained to Ben that since the committee didn't host a hearing then they had no need of hearing from the legal four. The two administrators and the nine committee members walked out of the cafeteria and headed for their cars. The four demanded that they be heard regarding DD's return to school. The chairman commented, "No hearing was on the agenda, the meeting has ended and we are headed for home. You can place a hearing request on next month's agenda if you want." The chairman's comment angered the Four, who were still yelling threatening comments as the last committee member left the school. Neither the school committee nor the two school administrators ever heard from the four or their client again.

* * *

Two FBI agents showed their badges as they walked into the principal's office. One agent closed the door and stood guarding that door. The other agent told Mr. Bishop about a large shipment of pure heroin which had landed in Boston. This load was at that very moment en route to Verona High School via a student middleman. The agent's plan was to follow the shipment of the drugs as transported by the high school kid so they could locate the area headquarters and the local major dealers. Ben clearly wanted to help the FBI in stopping drug shipments from traveling through his school; but he didn't want *this* load of drugs to pass through the school. He was very concerned that some of the drug supply might remain in the building.

The two agents assured Ben that the entire shipment would move through to the area headquarters. The next day Frank received the drug shipment. It had been placed in his car while he was attending class. The two agents arrested Frank on his way home from school. After a lengthy visit with the two FBI agents, Frank reluctantly agreed to point out his connection in the drug shipment system. Frank worked in a local convenience store. The two agents hid in the back room watching for Frank's signal that the transfer was about to take place.

A dirty car pulled up for gas with two men in it. Their car was identical to Frank's. Both cars needed to be washed. The license plates on the two cars were covered with mud. The driver filled the gas tank with regular gas. When he finished refueling his car he parked it next to Frank's car. The second man entered the store and paid for the gas. Neither the customer nor Frank said anything to each other beyond their business needs, "Pump three" and "Thanks."

Frank gave the man his change with his left hand. The two agents knew the use of his left hand meant, "Okay the shipment is in the car."

Handing change to the man with his right hand would have signaled to the customer that a major problem existed. The two men drove away in Frank's car. The two FBI agents radioed their team members down the road to follow Frank's car. The transfer had taken place.

Frank disappeared that night. He never returned to school or his home. Ben never learned if Frank had a new identity and was living in protective custody or if he was dead. The drugs and their owners were collected by the FBI. Their sting had been a success.

Marriage—Murder

John Francis was a handsome and personable high school student who had developed a major need to sleep with girls. John also had money. Many of the junior class girls dreamed of dating him. John Francis didn't know how much his lifestyle would change as he began his senior year on a Wednesday morning that September.

John Francis turned his attention and his fatal charm toward a tall, shy junior. Ramona was a beautiful young lady who had been absent for several lengthy periods during her sophomore year. Ramona had passed all of her sophomore classes because of the help of a home tutor. John Francis saw his opportunity to pick up Ramona as a date by helping her to once again become a part of the high school social scene. Ramona fell in love with John Francis. He paid lavish attention to her and he knew everybody. He made her forget the many days she had spent in the hospital during her sophomore year. She forgot about the pain of her operations. Ramona was happy with her renewed life. Ramona had plastic tubes in her stomach. The doctors had rebuilt her insides with great care. She could expect to live an almost normal life, BUT she had been emphatically told that she wasn't to ever get pregnant. The surgeons had shortened her intestines and had used plastic "plumbing" to complete the restructuring process.

John Francis had only one thought regarding his relationship with Ramona: "How long will it take me to 'bed' her?" By early November Ramona was pregnant. She told her mother that she was expecting in mid January. The medical team performed the necessary abortion to save her life the next day.

A few days later Ramona's mother told John Francis he was going to marry her daughter; John Francis and Ramona were married during February vacation. The cute couple lived with Ramona's mother. By late summer Ramona was expecting once again.

John Francis ran away.

Ramona's mother was furious. Ramona was hospitalized within a few days. The doctors saved Ramona's life via surgery once again. The doctors told John Francis, immediately upon his return to his wife, about his responsibilities as a husband and as a human being. They explained in detail the fact that plastic intestines couldn't be stretched around a growing fetus; they would separate and his wife would die.

His mother-in-law talked to him like the proverbial "Dutch uncle."

Apparently John Francis didn't listen to his advisers. A year later the medical team had to operate to save Ramona's life a third time. Several days later the surgeons assured her mother that Ramona would be okay.

The next day Ramona's mother used her hunting rifle to blow John Francis' brains out.

Looking Back

Ben was packing his personal effects. Heather and Ben had agreed to have Ben apply for the vacant superintendent's position in Hartland, MA. Ben's excitement upon learning of his appointment in Hartland jumped up a notch when he heard that his unanimous election was referred to by the school committee as, "We have hired a diamond in the rough as our next superintendent of schools."

Ben reflected on his successes as a classroom teacher. As he looked back he referred to his teaching days as the period in his life when he was 100 percent an EDUCATOR. Now that he was about to leave his position as a principal he pondered if he would be able to find a little time to again serve as an "Educator."

He had learned his principal's duties could have consumed his every work day. He knew he had worked hard to protect his role as an "Educator" during his years as a secondary school principal. He estimated that he had been able to spend about 20 percent of his time as an "Educator" while he handled his administrative duties.

Mr. Bishop was determined that he would be a successful school superintendent *and* he would attempt to spend at least 5 percent of his time as an "Educator." He knew that the business of running a 7240–student school system could easily turn him into a 100 percent businessman. He had stated in the interview process of his intention to demand integrity of self and of the district as he worked on behalf of the students in his care.

Heather and the children did most of the work preparing to move to Hartland. Although Ben helped as much as possible, the family couldn't afford to have him at home to help. They needed the extra money he earned by not taking any vacation days. Thus Ben left for Hartland on the following Monday.

Author's Comment
Subject Matter Majors

As I look back on my life's journey as an educator, I recall several instances which focused my thinking on this subject.

In the early sixties I enrolled in a state college graduate level math course. Within two weeks the subject matter was reduced to the teaching of elementary educators' differing techniques on how to multiply and to divide fractions! By the end of the semester the class had advanced to the eighth grade math problem solving level. The semester ended with the last two classes devoted to the methodology of extracting square roots. (Obviously, this occurred in the pre-calculator period of civilization.)

News reports in the late seventies highlighted the National Statistics of the then entering Freshman college students clearly noting the education majors had on average the lowest CEEB test scores in many states in our Nation.

Since that time I have advocated the certification and appointment of subject matter majors in our public high schools.

I sincerely believe subject matter majors take more demanding academic courses in the area in which they expect to spend their work life. It is also a fact that high school teachers are subject matter instructors!

With today's demand for higher student achievement it seems reasonable to reconsider this issue.

Another simple solution to improve the academic readiness of secondary school educators could be that colleges and universities schedule education majors to take their academic minors with the subject matter majors. This proposal maintains the current education major program with but a course shift into the student's planned teaching area.

My preference is to have our future high school teachers majoring in the subject area they expect to teach upon graduation and to have either: a. education as his/her minor or, b. education as his/her second major.

Superintendent

DAILY O
BISHOP
CONSTRUCTION
SCHOOL BOARD AGENDA

The First Month

Superintendent Bishop introduced himself to his new office staff on a hot August Monday morning. This was his first day in the Hartland School district. School would open in exactly four weeks. As of this date Mr. B. became responsible for 7200 students, 638 employees, ten schools and a multimillion dollar budget. The office staff had met Mr. Bishop during the interviewing process. They had participated in the public interviews. Ben recalled the chairman's comments as he signed the contract six weeks earlier, "You will work with the retiring superintendent for one week so you can get acquainted with any ongoing problems—strike that—the ongoing business decisions you will become responsible for. The teachers sued the school district one year ago. The judge ruled in their favor on July 2nd, that Hartland will have a public school kindergarten program in place when school reopens in September. Lucky you. All the work has been completed. All you have to do is to welcome the children on the first school day in September."

After the office greetings had been completed, Ben was introduced to Mr. Gray, the retiree. Ben sat down in the visitors' chair and the two men chatted about family affairs and other general background information each man was willing to share in order that the two men would be comfortable working together for the next five days. Fifteen minutes later Gray called the head maintenance man into his office. Gray introduced Everett Coscoe to his new boss. Everett was instructed to take Mr. Bishop on a tour of the district's schools in order to get him acquainted with the schools and his maintenance support staff.

Gray said he had a lot of paperwork to complete as the two men left his office. He closed the office door as Coscoe and Bishop headed out to the parking lot. Ev and Mr. B. eventually became good business friends. Ben spent the remainder of that day traveling around the school district. Ev introduced his new boss to the school principals, their secretaries and the custodial staff in each building. Mr. Gray sat at his desk with the door closed the entire week. Other than the first morning greetings Mr. B. had shared with the retiring superintendent, Mr. Gray never said another word to Ben. The new super became a daily tourist in each of the district schools as he concluded his first week on the job.

Three weeks before the opening of school!! Ben wondered if everything would be ready? As Mr. Bishop entered his office on that Monday morning, he asked his secretary to get all of the documents on the shopping center kindergarten school and to place them on his desk. Ben reminded Mrs. Positive, his personal secretary, that the papers he wanted to review included the certificates of occupancy from the state board of education, the state fire marshal, the state board of health as well as the contract with the shopping center owner.

Mrs. Positive said that she would have the requested papers on his desk late that afternoon as she had to retrieve them from the town solicitor.

Mr. B called Ev and asked him to stop by to discuss the construction progress on the kindergarten school as well as the work progress on the four elementary schools under construction. The four new elementary schools were scheduled to open a year from September. Two of the new elementary schools were being built to replace two old wooden buildings which the state and the city had reluctantly okayed for one more school year before they were to be torn down. The other two new buildings were being built to house the ever growing student population in Hartland.

Ev and Mr. B. talked about the layout of classroom space for the 640-student kindergarten building. The two men decided that by dividing the twelve stores into two classrooms apiece, the Desert Heights School could be used as a 24-room school. The two center stores (four rooms) would become a business office and a nurse's station, a teacher's room, a supply room and a staff lunch room. The remaining ten stores (twenty rooms) would be used as classrooms. Each small store divided into two small classrooms would house approximately 16 students per kindergarten session. The Desert Heights School had to be completed prior to the opening of school in three weeks. The new Desert Heights school principal had been hired by Mr. Gray. She added to the plans developed by Mr. Coscoe and the superintendent. Late Monday afternoon Ev introduced his boss to the vacant mall's owner, the EG Construction Co.'s owner, Eric Goode.

Mr. Goode informed Mr. Bishop that Mr. Gray had never signed an agreement to lease the 12-store strip mall with him. Ben was aghast!! Ben and Ev worked with Eric and reached an agreement as to the one year lease and the school department's permission to put up temporary partitions to divide each store into two classrooms. Mr. Goode's agreement with Ben was more than reasonable. Eric was happily helping the school district in a time of crisis and he could delay his hunt for twelve store tenants for another year. Ben didn't find the requested papers on his desk when he stopped in to pick them up on his way home after a very long day.

As Ben entered his office early Tuesday morning, Mrs. Positive told her new boss that Nathan D. Honor, the town solicitor, promised to bring the appropriate papers in on Thursday afternoon. Mr. B. accepted her comment as stated. He didn't question the delay but he wondered. Meanwhile, Ev and his maintenance team ordered the necessary building supplies and began to fabricate the kindergarten classrooms, the teacher's workroom, an office, area for the principal and her secretary, etc.

First thing Friday morning, Mr. Bishop called Mrs. Positive

into his office and directed her to, "Get those papers NOW!" She left his office, sat at her desk and immediately made several phone calls. Within a minute or two an emergency call was transferred to the superintendent's private line. Mr. Bishop was asked to come over to the high school to resolve a major problem. Mr. B. observed Mrs. Positive on the phone as he hurried off to the high school. She appeared to be talking to Mr. Honor about the requested certificates.

Ben didn't get back to his office until mid-afternoon. The requested papers were not on his desk! AND Mrs. Positive had gone home for the day. . . .

Ben called her at home and clearly stated, "Either the papers are in my hands by 6 P.M. today or you won't have to come to work on Monday morning." At this point she confessed to Mr. Bishop that the papers *never existed.*

"Mr. Gray had never filed the appropriate applications." She further said that for some unknown reason neither Gray nor Honor wanted him to know this. Ben was furious.

Two weeks until school opens! Ben called the state dept. of education and asked for the appropriate OK to use the Desert Heights Mall as an elementary school for one school year. Ben knew that he'd be out of the rental business once the new schools were finished. The Commissioner Of Education informed Ben that the state would not issue Hartland a permit to use the mall as a kindergarten school—but Hartland could use it and the state wouldn't complain nor would it file any negative complaints against the town or its school superintendent. The Commissioner agreed that it was too late to find another solution to the court-mandated kindergarten program for the ensuing school year. *Wow!* thought Ben. *"Two weeks to get this court-ordered school opened!"*

Mr, Bishop asked Ev and Mrs. L. Childs, The Desert Heights Mall School principal, to work together and to complete the remodeling project by the end of the month. Ev and his team were doing excellent work. Six stores had already been converted into two classrooms apiece. As the maintenance crew began work on the second half of the conversion project, a contractor began the installation of the sprinkler system. Once the installation of the sprinkler system was complete, the fire alarm people were scheduled to install a school-approved alarm system. Every project had been carefully thought out and scheduled during the second week of August. Fortunately for Ben, Ev Coscoe had developed plans for the conversion shortly after the judgment was issued against the town. Ev was extremely pleased to be working on this project with his new boss! Every project had been calendared to be completed by the end of the month. The plan mandated that the cleanup crew had to work Labor Day weekend in order to have the school open Tuesday morning, the day after Labor Day.

Recognizing that the project was in good hands, Mr. B. told Mrs. Positive to get the fire marshal on the phone immediately. Ben hadn't fired Mrs. Positive because he needed her local knowledge and she had claimed she was only doing that which she had been told to do by Mr. Nathan D. Honor. She had readily agreed to her new boss's condition of her continued employment, "The next incident of a like nature would be accepted as her act of resignation." The local fire marshal said he'd be at the super's office in 30 minutes. He said he was looking forward to meeting the new super and wanted Mr. Bishop to know that be was there to help.

The local fire marshall (LFM) told Ben that he had given approval and "Yes," the school could be occupied on September first—assuming the approved work projects were completed by that date. Mr. B. thanked the LFM and asked him to file a written copy of his approval in the school building. The LFM said that his word was sufficient and he, Mr. Bishop, had better learn to live with it. Ben asked him what record of approval would the school system have if a fire broke out in the Mall School and a few children were hurt. The LFM said, "If a fire destroys the Mall School then that becomes your problem."

While the LFM sat in the guest chair in the chief school administrator's office, Ben picked up the phone and directed Mrs. Positive to "Get the State Fire Marshal on the phone immediately!"

Ben proceeded to ask the SFM for written approval to use the converted mall as an elementary school as of September 1st. The SFM said that he would meet with Mr. B. and the LFM at the strip mall building on Wednesday morning at 10 A.M. As Ben repeated the SFM's comments to the LFM he noticed a man in panic. The LFM demanded that the new superintendent "NOT" tell the SFM of his verbal OK.

The Wednesday morning meeting included a tour of the entire Mall School project. The SFM approved the safe design of the classrooms. He noted the two exit doors for each classroom. He complimented the superintendent on his willingness to spend enough money to have a good fire alarm system installed in a temporary school. The SFM said that he could not approve occupancy of the building as a school because the twelve stores did not have school rated boiler rooms. The SFM informed Supt. Bishop that school building boiler rooms had to have two hour fire-rated boiler rooms and inward opening solid core doors, whereas a store only needed a one-hour rated wall and hollow core doors were acceptable.

The SFM told Mr. Bishop that he was going to put padlocks on each of the twelve gas meters so that the school dept. couldn't heat the school until the boiler rooms were brought up to code. All of this time the LFM walked around in strained silence praying that Mr. Bishop didn't accidentally say that he had OKed the school. Ben asked the SFM if he would provide the school district with a written certificate of occupancy once the boiler rooms were upgraded to the mandated school standards. The SFM's answer gave Ben the cue he needed to open the school in less than ten days. The SFM said, "Yes, as soon as the twelve boiler rooms meet the two-hour standards, I'll give you the required papers."

At this point Ben stated, "With padlocks on the gas lines the boilers cannot be ignited to heat the classrooms. Therefore there are no boiler rooms. Therefore may I have a certificate to operate a boiler-less school in September?" The SFM agreed to Ben's unique request. He did note that the weather does get a bit chilly in late September. Mr. B. profusely thanked the State Fire Marshall for his considerate assistance. The two men ignored the LFM.

Ben called and asked Ev Coscoe to join him in a meeting with the Mall owner and to help negotiate the cost to convert the twelve boiler rooms. The EG Co. owner was most sympathetic to his new tenant. Eric Goode, Ev Coscoe and Mr. Bishop agreed to work together in order to complete the twelve boiler room reconstruction work by mid September. EG Construction Co. and the school maintenance team agreed to share the work load. All of the work would be done after school between the hours of 4 P.M. and midnight five days a week until it was completed. The work teams were to be comprised of three school laborers and three EG Co. workmen. The school dept. would pay the contractor's costs for the necessary materials. The plan was to complete at least one boiler room per work day. The EG Co. was very generous in its efforts to help Ben open the mall school.

Mrs. Positive called the state board of health and asked for the director. At 11 A.M. Thursday he returned Ben's urgent call. Director Abe Candid told Ben that the Mall School would not be getting approval to open as a kindergarten school for 640 students. Abe informed the new superintendent that he had personally inspected the property in early July, and unless someone had added to the leach field there was no way he would be willing to create such a massive health hazard. Mr. Candid further noted as to how he had given this same message to Mr. Gray shortly after his inspection of the proposed school. The mall leaching field and septic system had been designed for twelve stores and their several employees—not for 640 students and 27 adults. Abe suggested that Ben might want to confer with a contractor about the cost and time it would take to make the sewerage system adequate for the school.

Ben called EG about this final hurdle. EG reluctantly told Ben that the leach field could not be extended due to its location. He also said that the cost of constructing a new, larger septic system on the other side of the building would be extremely expensive and couldn't be completed until mid October at the earliest. Eric Goode gave Mr. B. the exact figures to build an adequate septic system on Friday afternoon. Mr. Bishop called the school committee chairman and told him that the school would not be opening in September as planned due to the inadequate sewerage system. The chairman was quite impressed when he learned that Ben had conquered the boiler room problem. The chairman told Ben that he would enlist the Governor's help to solve the septic system problem.

Abe Candid called Ben on Tuesday afternoon. There were only three work days remaining before the new school year began. Abe reported to Ben that the Governor had told him to OK the septic system or be fired as of Labor Day. Neither Abe nor Ben could believe they were being forced to do something illegal. The two men agreed to meet on Friday afternoon to review their options.

Ev and Mr. B. spent the next day walking around the Desert Heights Mall Elementary School. The twelve stores had been converted into 20 classrooms, one office, a teachers' lunch/workroom, a storage room, and a small special education class. Chalkboards were being installed as they watched. The furniture was scheduled to be delivered the next day. Fresh paint was everywhere. The fire alarm system was being tested. The boiler room work was expected to start on Tuesday afternoon. All they needed was a solution to the sewerage problem. . . .

Ev explained the history of the mall site to his boss. Desert Heights was facetiously named because the area looked like a desert to the locals. The mall was located on 223 acres of sand. Neither grass nor trees had ever grown on the site. In fact, the mall had been built two years earlier. No small store owners wanted to open a new business in the strip mall as a result of the bleakness of the area.

Abe met Ben at the Desert Heights Mall Elementary School on Friday afternoon. Labor Day was just three days away. The school was scheduled to open in four days! Ben had a court order to have the kindergarteners in school as of Tuesday morning. Abe was an honest and competent state health director who was about to lose his job. Both men seemed to be in an impossible situation.

At four o'clock that afternoon the two men found a way to resolve their problem. They immediately drove over to Ben's office, arriving shortly after it closed for the day. The staff had gone home. Abe sat at one typewriter and Ben sat at another typewriter. Abe typed a letter addressed to the school district approving the use of the mall as an elementary school effective September first. The aforementioned approval was valid until either the end of the school year or until the effluent surfaced on the ground above or around the septic tank. The certificate of approved use would automatically terminate on the earlier date as mentioned in the letter. Ben typed a similar letter. He thanked the Health Dept. Director for his understanding and compassion as he recognized the city's dilemma. Ben's letter continued with the statement that the school would be closed immediately on the first day sewerage surfaced on the school property. As the two men exchanged letters they both wondered if the Mall School would be open in October?

Mrs. Childs sent a letter home with each student explaining the fact that the school was actually a leased twelve-store strip mall and as such had a sewerage system which wasn't designed to be flushed 600 times each day. She politely asked each parent to help and when possible to have their youngsters use their home facilities just before the school bus picked up the children for a new school day. Ev and Ben were pleased to discover that the Desert Heights Mall Elementary School successfully operated the entire school year without a leach field problem. Ben didn't have to close the school at any time during the entire school year. The desert sands had thirstily absorbed the liquid effluent of the happy children all 180 school days that year. "Politics!?!" said Ben to himself as he walked to his car for the short ride home on the last school day of the year.

Fire Him

Ben had enjoyed his years as a teacher and he had been very successful as a secondary school principal. During his years as a teacher and as a principal he had observed several incidents of political interference in the decision-making process. When he began his career as a superintendent he firmly believed that as long as he maintained his positive work ethic politics would not interfere nor influence his decision making. Mr. Bishop was determined to complete his career as an educator with the same high standard of integrity as he had when he entered public school administration. Heather had warned her husband of 15 years that he might be too honest to survive in the super's job.

Ben began his chief school administrator's job in Hartland in August. The city's fiscal year ran from January 1st to December 31st. He had been introduced to his business manager, Harvey Literature, during his first week on the job. During the course of his work in the school district and in particular during the monthly school committee meetings Ben observed the committee member's lack of trust with the performance of Mr. Literature.

Thus as the Thanksgiving holiday was being celebrated by most people, Mr. Bishop was in his office hard at work. This was his first year of being completely responsible for the millions of tax-raised dollars . . . and the year would end in six weeks.

As Ben studied the monthly financial statements from the beginning of the current fiscal year (Jan. 1st) to date he reflected on Mrs. Goodnotes' meticulous recording of every transaction via shorthand into her notebooks. Mrs. Goodnotes frequently asked her fellow committee members why they had changed their opinion on an issue: "Why are you voting against this item tonight? You argued for its passage two months ago!"

Friday, Saturday and Sunday, Ben spent the entire holiday weekend in his office reviewing the school committee approved financial records and payroll warrants. Ben projected his bi-weekly payroll expenses through to the end of the year. He carefully added to these figures an amount equal to the district's weekly expenses multiplied by six. These numbers gave him his best estimate as to the monies needed to complete the fiscal year in the black under the assumption that he would be spending at the current rate.

As Ben subtracted this projected total from the remaining budgeted fiscal year monies, he realized that he would have to stop all nonessential expenditures. Ben intended to close the books in the black. He clearly had enough money for the last three payrolls and just enough to cover the routine monthly vouchers for utilities, insurance bills, etc.

Ben began to relax. He knew he could make it to the new fiscal year without too many money problems. Yes, he would have to curtail all overtime work. He prayed that the schools would not be closed due to a snowstorm. Each day the schools were storm closed, the district had increased expenses of approximately $6000.00! BUT, as Ben was putting his final figures together a nagging issue captured his mind! It took a few minutes. He knew something was wrong! He reflected on his mental message. *It looked like the November school committee meeting warrant for October's expenditures had a different gross figure than the dollar amount he remembered from the vote taken a week earlier.*

Ben sighed. Instead of packing up and heading home for Sunday dinner with his family, he took out the meeting minutes and reread them. He immediately noticed that the warrant total as voted by the committee was almost $40,000.00 less than the bill sheet totals Mr. Literature had given him to study over the holiday weekend!!!

Ben frantically ran to the meeting files, and took out copies of the committee's warrant votes for the entire fiscal year. This included the warrants of the meetings hosted by his predecessor.

An hour later Ben was definitely upset. The office billsheets showed an expenditure of $85,000.00 *above* that which had been voted by the school committee and recorded in its legally adopted minutes!

Ben called Harvey for an explanation. Mr. Literature informed his boss that that was the way the books had been kept for years and that was how he was doing his work as well. Further, he said, "Don't bother me on a Sunday. I only work for you Monday through Friday." Then Harvey hung up.

Mr. B. called his committee chairman. He reported his findings of the money differences to the chairman. Ben carefully noted that no monies had been stolen—rather the monies had been used to pay the district's health insurance bills but had never been authorized by the school committee. Ben told his chairman that he was asking for an emergency meeting on the following Wednesday evening to bring these unauthorized expenditures to the committee in order the legalize them via a public vote. The chairman angrily shouted, "Fire the B—d!"

Ben as he listened to his boss realized that he was thrilled to have found a way to get rid of Mr. Literature.

The chairman immediately called the news reporter, giving him every detail about the mismanaged monies (including his command quote to Mr. Bishop). The Monday morning headlines FIRE THE B—D told the story. The reporter incorporated the chairman's untimely death into his article as if it was the result of his learning about the business manager's illegal financial methods. Wednesday's meeting was brief.

The committee immediately moved into executive session to discuss Mr. Literature's malfeasance in office. Seated at the table were six school committee members and the two administrators, Mr. Bishop and Mr. Literature. The meeting began with a thorough review of the monthly warrant votes as recorded in the minutes of the ten financial meetings from January through to October. Ben continued his presentation by submitting the office records of the actual monthly expenditures for the same ten-month period. The dollar differences were easily understood by everyone. Mr. Literature's staff had typed the word *sub* in front of the word *total* on the warrant sheet a few days after the committee meeting each month. They then added the additional bills for employee health insurance beneath the *subtotal* and entered the new total as was the business office standard. In front of the new total the staff had typed the words *grand total.*

Then Mr. B. informed the committee that he planned to place a correction warrant on the next meeting agenda. He knew the committee would vote to retroactively approve the payment of these additional bills which would also correct the records of that fiscal year.

At this point Mrs. Goodnotes, acting chairperson, asked Mr. Literature how much he was being paid as business manager. Ben was amazed when he heard Harvey's response: "It's none of your business!"

As the shock of his answer hit the committee members, Ben directed Harvey to answer the question. "Our salaries are approved by the committee and are a matter of public record," Mr. Literature answered the salary question.

The committee apparently had talked among themselves about their problem. It seemed to Ben that the acting chair's action plan was being accepted without debate. The committee agreed to approve the corrective action warrant by unanimous vote during the December meeting. Then the acting chairperson informed Harvey Literature that by a unanimous decision the committee had agreed to fire him effective immediately.

Ben emphatically told the committee that Harvey hadn't done anything different than that which his predecessor had done during the previous 16 years. "Actually," said Ben, "Harvey didn't do it. He doesn't know anything about bookkeeping. His business department employees do all of the work. Mr. Literature only makes managerial decisions whenever a problem comes up. The office staff has been using this bookkeeping pattern for years. The former superintendent and his business manager made the decision to use this improper accounting practice at least 16 years ago. They are the guilty parties. Not Harvey. You can't fire him for an action he not only didn't create, he didn't know it was being used. After all you just promoted him to this position last February."

The acting chair thanked Mr. Bishop for his background report and for his "corrections" of the committee. However, by a six to zero vote Mr. Literature, "Is fired." Mrs. Goodnotes asked the committee for a motion to conclude the executive session and to return to public session. The six committee members silently watched as Mr. Bishop opened the conference room doors inviting the press and the public to return to the meeting room for the remainder of the special meeting. All were anxious to hear the committee's executive session conclusions. Mrs. Goodnotes announced Mr. Literature had just been fired as a result of "Improper management of the school district's financial records." Immediately upon pronouncement of Harvey's termination a member quietly said, "Move to adjourn. Second." Mrs. Goodnotes banged the gavel on the table and said, "This emergency meeting of the Hartland School Committee is adjourned."

The press crowded around Mr. Literature for a statement. Ben asked Mrs. Goodnotes to stay so that he might visit with her in an attempt to understand the committee's actions during the meeting.

"You didn't give Harvey a fair decision this evening," said Ben.

"Mr. Bishop. May I call you Ben? Our vote this evening was long overdue."

The acting chairperson gave Ben the background on the committee's action earlier that evening. She told him the committee had asked her to chair this one meeting because she was the least controversial of the six remaining committee members. The other five members were convinced their new superintendent trusted her more readily than any of the others.

Mrs. Goodnotes told Ben that Harvey had been an outstanding English teacher for 26 years. Harvey had been asked to serve as the high school principal five years ago. When the previous principal had died during the school year the entire town believed that as the best teacher, Mr. Literature should be promoted to serve as the next high school principal.

Harvey accepted the assignment. His family had played background politics to create the ground swell movement, forcing the committee to appoint him as principal. Within two years it became evident that he wasn't cut out to be a principal. Thus when the business manager retired last January the committee promoted him out of the high school principal's job into a less visible position. Since that date the committee had been looking for an excuse to fire him.

"Yes, the school committee members knew that the business office work was the work of the office staff. No, the committee didn't know that the records had been fudged for 16 years." She continued to explain the committee's thinking. Once the committee members had been told by their new superintendent about the illegal procedures and of his immediate actions to correct the erroneous financial practices, they had agreed among themselves to use the information to their advantage—to fire Harvey. At this point Mrs. Goodnotes complimented Ben on his outstanding services to Hartland—and then she left to go home.

Wow! thought Ben. *An English teacher is promoted into a*

position where he hasn't a chance in the world to survive. The committee patiently waits for the break it needs. Then ruthlessly takes it and fires the guy. Harvey didn't have a chance!

Expelled

Joseph Scisille was a tough kid. As a Junior at Hartland High he had beat up two teachers. The principal had not disciplined Joseph because he also was afraid of him. Mr. Bishop met Joseph in October of his first year in Hartland. The high school principal called his new boss and asked Mr. B. how he wanted to take care of the "Joseph problem."

Ben asked, "What Joseph problem?"

High School Principal Tom S. decided that he had better visit with his new boss in person. The meeting was held thirty minutes later. Ben listened to Tom's story of putting up with Joseph for the past three years. As Ben listened, he realized that his predecessor had agreed with Tom that the best plan was to put up with Joseph and to wait for him to graduate. Tom stated that he was happy that Joseph was a senior and would graduate in June. Finally, Mr. B. asked Tom why he was telling him this story "Now, in a requested emergency meeting?" "Because Joseph just beat up another teacher," responded Tom.

"Expel him!" shouted Mr. B. Ben repeated his command, "Expel Joseph. How is the teacher? Is he okay?" Tom assured Mr. Bishop that the teacher was "Just badly bruised." Tom started to ask Mr. B. if he really wanted to expel Joseph when Ben interrupted the principal and called Mrs. Positive into the room. Ben instructed her to call the high school and to tell the AP to take the injured teacher to the hospital immediately.

He then dictated a letter to Joseph's parents informing them that their son was being expelled from school at noon as of today's date. Included in the letter was a paragraph alerting the family as to their right to request a hearing regarding the proposed expulsion. Mr. Bishop told Tom to take the letter and to personally hand it to Joseph and to call the family, invite them to drop in at their earliest convenience to talk about the events that had generated Joseph's expulsion.

Tom's, "Are you certain you want to expel him?" upset Ben. Ben's "YES" was emphatic enough for Tom to get the message. Ben's next comment clearly confirmed his decision. "No one touches one of my teachers and remains in a Hartland School!"

The union president stopped by the next day to thank the superintendent for his concern and support of the injured teacher. He then told Mr. Bishop that this was the first time "in years" that an administrator had worried about a city teacher.

Ben and Tom commented as to their surprise during a meeting in mid November as they realized that they had not heard from Joseph or his family since the incident.

On January 17th, a high school teacher called the super and asked to meet with him at the high school as soon as possible. The meeting with the teacher, the union president and Mr. B. took place 45 minutes after the frantic phone call. *The teacher had been severely beaten by Joseph!* Questions jumped out of Mr. B's mouth faster than the teacher could answer them. "How did he get into the school to do this? Are you all right? Do you want me to take you to the doctor? To the hospital? Where is Joseph now? Did this happen in school?"

At this point the UP told the superintendent Joseph had been back in school since December 8th. Before the UP could answer Ben's other questions he heard an anguished cry escape from his boss, "Joseph was expelled. He can't be in school!"

The UP was convinced that every teacher in the building heard Mr. Bishop's shouted remarks. The UP finished his story by explaining that the teacher was going to his family doctor immediately after this meeting.

"Yes," Joseph had been back in school for almost five weeks

now. Principal Tom had been threatened by Joseph during the first week of December and he allowed him to return on the 8th.

Mr. Bishop instructed Tom, the high school principal, to prepare two letters for his signature. The first letter was to be addressed to Joseph's parents informing them that their son was being expelled and that they had the right to ask for a hearing before the school committee. The second letter was to be addressed to the union president informing him and all of the system's teachers that Hartland High School would never again allow any student to be in the school if he/she attacks a teacher. This second letter was to include an apology to the injured teacher for his personal error (i.e., allowing Joseph Scisille to return to school on December 8th).

The next morning Ben visited with Tom S. to gather all of the facts as to why he had allowed Joseph to return to school after the first incident, and in particular why Tom had hidden the fact of Joseph's return to school from his superintendent? At the end of their conversation, Mr. B. suggested to the principal that he might want to look for a new job as there would be a new principal in the high school next September.

When Ben returned to his office that afternoon he found Joseph waiting for him. Joseph informed Mr. Bishop that he intended to return to the high school in a day or two. Ben asked him to have his parents contact his office to discuss a possible hearing if they were interested in what their rights were in this matter.

Joseph roughly told Mr. Bishop that he wanted to have his "official" hearing. He directed the superintendent to "Schedule it!"

Mr. B. scheduled the hearing for Thursday of the following week. As Joseph left the meeting room he repeated his earlier statement that he would be in school 'tomorrow morning'! Ben and a local policeman waited for Joseph's arrival at the high school early the next morning. Joseph was given a choice, "Either leave the school grounds immediately or be arrested for interfering with the operation of a public school." As Joseph turned to leave the school yard he informed the two men that this issue would be corrected at the upcoming hearing.

Thursday—The Hearing

Attendees: Joseph, his attorney, the six school committee members, the union president, the teacher, the high school principal, Mr. Bishop, the administrator's lawyer and a court rated stenographer.

The school committee sat at the head table serving as judge and jury. Mrs. Goodnotes served as the temporary committee chairperson. The two attorneys sat with their clients at two adjacent tables which faced the head table. Presentations were made by both attorneys.

Ben and his supportive committee members began to panic with respect to their chances of winning the case when Joseph's lawyer asked the six-foot-two 30-year-old physical education teacher to "Please point out to the court the student you claim a) beat you up, and b) you are afraid of." As the PE teacher pointed at Joseph, Ben's heart sank. Joseph was a five-foot-six 17-year-old. No muscles were visible under the lacy satin blouse Joseph was wearing for the hearing, He also had his hair curled in ringlets. If the case hadn't been so serious, everyone would have been laughing. BUT the teacher was clearly sweating as he identified the hoodlum who had severely bruised him two weeks earlier.

The testimony was to be transcribed by the stenographer with a copy sent to the two attorneys by Tuesday afternoon. The two lawyers agreed to continue Joseph's suspension until the school committee had time to go over the transcript with their attorney. It was quickly estimated that the committee would be ready to make its decision during their next meeting, scheduled for the second Tuesday in February.

Joseph and his attorney left the room laughing at their vision of the hearing. The committee members and the three educators carefully listened as their lawyer told them not to worry. "The transcript will not show Joseph's unique dress style nor his stature. The teacher was a good witness. We will win this case on the merits if it is appealed." Upon the conclusion of this simple conversation everyone left the school and headed home. Ben was the last person to leave the building.

Ben turned off the administration building's lights and walked to his car as the parade of automobiles drove out of the school yard. Mrs. Goodnote's car was immediately in front of Ben's. Mrs. Goodnotes turned left onto Main Street.

As Ben began his right turn onto Main St., he flicked his headlights as his goodnight signal to the acting chairperson and headed home!

The phone rang as Heather and Ben sat at home watching the 11:00 o'clock news. Mrs. Goodnotes was at the police station!

She told Ben she had just finished making her report to the cops, Joseph had been hiding on the floor in the back of her car waiting for her to leave the school yard. She hadn't noticed him as she entered her car and began her drive home. After she had waved goodnight to Ben and turned left onto Main St., Joseph had gotten up and had placed a knife against her throat. He instructed her to "Pull over." Joseph then announced that if she voted to expel him he would stick his knife into her daughter's stomach.

Mrs. Goodnotes' final comment to Ben that evening was, "I will never vote to allow *'That Thing'* back into Hartland High School."

One week later Joseph was hitch-hiking on a country road when a car "accidentally" went off the road; up and across the front lawn of a house and "accidentally" ran over Joseph. The auto sped on its way.

No one saw the accident!

Joseph's death removed a major embarrassment from the Scisille name.

The Budget

As Ben drove into the city auditorium parking lot he mused, "Gee, the lot is practically empty. Usually when I arrive the lot is filled with cars. I wonder what's happening?" The meeting began as scheduled at 8 P.M. The 157 voters who had signed in for the annual budget adoption were quite a contrast from the participants of the two previous years.

* * *

Superintendent Bishop's first budget adoption meeting had been a unique learning experience for him. Ben clearly remembered his emotional roller coaster ride of that night. First, he remembered the crowd. When he arrived after parking his car in the reserved parking spot 30 minutes before the scheduled start of the annual meeting, he was surprised to discover the hall was completely filled with voters. The fireman posted at the entrance admitted Mr. Bishop, as he was as a registered participant and had been included in the room totals. The doors had been opened at 6:30 P.M.

By 7:30 the occupant limit had been reached and the fireman posted at the door turned away all of the additional voters desiring to enter the hall to vote on the school department budget.

The meeting began promptly at 8:00. The city finance committee chairman was in charge of the meeting. He was the controlling political force in Hartland.

After a lengthy debate on the "need" for the monies listed in the school department budget for the ensuing year, the Finance Chairman (FC) called for a vote to adopt the school department budget.

The FC told the voters to adopt his limited school dept. budget. "I ask you to cut Mr. Bishop's grandiose budget by $875,000.00. He has to learn to run the school dept. on a tight budget. We can't let him raise our taxes. Let's give him a clear message. Continue to run the schools with your positive approach. But do it without raising our taxes!"

Ben argued for his budget. He identified every item which would be lost if the voters adopted the "Cut" resolution of the Finance Chair.

The FC called for the vote. The school budget was cut by $875,000.00 as had been demanded by the FC. The FC asked the voters to stand as a group to show the new superintendent what they thought of his budget. Two-thirds of the voters stood up on that fateful evening. Ben knew he had been beaten by an experienced politician.

One year later Ben talked to the PTA president of each school in the Hartland system. They readily agreed with his proposal. Their plan was a simple one. Every PTA president was to talk to their respective parents' groups and to encourage everyone to be at the city auditorium parking lot BEFORE 6:30 P.M. on the night of the school budget adoption meeting.

Shortly after the doors were opened by the fireman door guard, the 800-plus seats were filled. The fireman began turning away potential voters a few minutes later. On that evening as the FC called for a school department budget reduction he was verbally challenged by the school supporting taxpayers (the definite majority in the hall). Their spokesperson loudly called out to the FC Chairman, "Either you, Mr. Finance Chair, personally vote with us and support the school department as submitted by superintendent Bishop or we will vote to increase his budget by $875,000.00!"

The audience cheered.

The FC realized he had lost his control of the annual school dept. budget adoption procedures. The FC Chairman asked the voters to adopt the school dept. budget as submitted by Mr. Bishop. With a loud cheer the unanimous vote echoed beyond the city auditorium walls. The PTA had finally won the annual budget battle.

* * *

The Finance Committee Chairman asked the 157 voters to make a decision regarding the proposed school dept. budget. The voters adopted the budget with 98 votes recorded *for* and 59 against. As Mr. B. was leaving the meeting both he and the FCC agreed that the small crowd of voters was a result of the annual turnaway of voters due to the early arrival of biased voters determined to control the budget meeting. The voters of the two previous years must have decided it wasn't worth the effort anymore. If the hall was going to be closed to them by the EARLY registrants then the majority of taxpayers obviously had decided to stay home. The two men agreed that the evening's vote was probably the first nonpolitical vote in Hartland's history.

Payroll Problems

During Ben's first two years as a school superintendent he subconsciously wondered as to why everyone made a point of telling him that Debra Quickhands was THE BEST! Deb was always happy. It seemed that everyone admired her. Deb was the payroll clerk. She always had the multi-million dollar payroll ready on time. (It was her job!) Ms. Quickhands was never out sick. She came to work even when she had the flu BECAUSE the payroll had to be ready on time! Although the business manager had to verify and authorize each pay warrant, Mr. B. would compare the totals with the previous warrants. Ben always asked about any changes in the totals. Custodial overtime and substitute teacher expenses were usually the reasons for increases in the totals. The business manager frequently told Mr. Bishop how dedicated Debra was to her job. He complimented Deb every time she turned in her completed bi-weekly payroll warrant for his signature. He always thanked her whenever she came to work when she wasn't feeling well.

Mr. B. arrived at his office, as was his habit, at 8:00 A.M. on that fateful Wednesday morning. His business manager was waiting for him. The BM said, "Sir, Debra Quickhands is in the hospital. She was in a terrible automobile accident last night. Yes, she will eventually be okay—but she will be out of work for at least six weeks. That's three pay periods. What will I do?"

Ben told him that he was sorry about Debra's accident. He also commented on the voiced fact she would be okay in about six weeks. Then he instructed the BM to assign the payroll task to one of his other business office staff members.

When the BM responded with the statement that no other staff member could do payroll, Ben strongly asked "Aren't all eight of your staff cross trained? Can't everyone do payroll, accounts receivable, billing, etc.? Can't you do it?"

The BM's "No" wasn't indicative of a well managed department. The BM finally told Mr. Bishop that he planned to take the payroll time cards, etc., to the hospital so that Deb and he could work on them for the next three pay periods.

Ben's response, noting that the pay records were not to leave the office EVER upset the BM more than Mr. B. realized at that moment. Mr. B. asked the office staff for a volunteer to help. He was looking for someone who might be interested in learning how to do payroll! He then directed the BM to cross train all of his staff (including himself) on how to perform all of the office tasks so there would always be a backup worker to handle the job whenever anyone was absent.

Maria Integrity offered to try to do the payroll while Debra was in the hospital. Maria informed her boss that although she was good with numbers she didn't know how to do payroll. But she would be happy to try and help to get the pay warrant(s) ready. Maria's regular assignment was in accounts payable.

Ben directed his BM to have Maria go over the last payroll and the resulting warrant as a study guide He asked them to try to replicate the process in order to create the payroll. He further instructed the BM to work with Maria and noted that if neither of them could resolve an issue then he was to send Maria to the hospital to ask Debra for help.

Maria seated herself at Debra's desk. The BM gave her all of the previous pay period records. At 5:30 that evening Maria called Mr. Bishop at home. Maria informed her boss that she had figured out how to do payroll and noted she would have it completed on schedule. . . . But she had a problem. Maria told her boss that she was afraid to tell anyone but him about this one problem.

The next morning Ben went into the payroll clerk's office to see how Maria was doing. Maria closed her office door. She then showed Mr. Bishop her "little problem."

There were seven names on the payroll records who were getting a paycheck but did not work in the school system!!! Maria said that the payroll system was well organized, easy to follow and she noted that she could complete the job in two or three days. Ben thanked Maria for her research and asked her to do the next week's payroll minus the extra seven.

Mr. B photo-copied the old warrant containing the additional seven names.

The non employed seven were:

1. Debra's sister
2. Debra's mother
3. The Finance Committee Chairman 's wife
4. Mrs. Positive's husband
5., 6., & 7 'Friends'—People who had learned of Debra Quickhands' payroll gifts and thus blackmailed her into giving them an equivalent gift.

Ben was convinced that the BM had no clue as to what was happening over his signature. As Mr. B. walked back toward his office Mrs. Positive caught up with him. She had correctly surmised that Maria had solved the payroll puzzle. She quickly informed her boss that he would not be dismissing anybody. "The school committee will protect them and if you (Mr. Bishop) don't continue the practice then *you* will be fired!"

Mr. B. entered his personal office, closed the door and called his personal attorney. Actually he didn't have a lawyer. He called a friend who was a member of his service club, a lawyer, and asked for help. Harry Legalfiles agreed to represent Ben. Ben then called the seven committee members and the school attorney. He scheduled an emergency executive session meeting for 6:00 that evening. Everyone showed up for the special meeting. Mrs. Positive had called Debra and the Finance Committee Chairman. She told them about the emergency meeting as well as the fact she believed Mr. Bishop was about to fire Debra and herself. She also noted that she was certain Mr. B. would stop the extra paychecks.

The seven extras arrived just before the meeting began at 6:00 o'clock. Debra's attorney was there to represent his hospitalized client. All involved banked on Mr. Bishop using the school dept. attorney to help him wade through the meeting. But Mr. B. had his own lawyer with him!!! When the dust had settled, the seven accepted Ben's offer: "Either reimburse the school dept. in full or arrest warrants will be issued in 24 hours."

They all agreed to have all of the stolen money on the BM's desk before 5:00 P.M. the next day. Further: Debra, Mrs. Positive and the city Finance Chairman were allowed to resign effective at midnight that evening.

One month later Ben hired his third business manager in as many years.

The Architect

In addition to his countless business tasks which kept the education machine in high gear Ben found himself working many extra hours with the district architect during his first year on the job. One year prior to his employment, the Hartland School District had taken land by eminent domain, hired an architect, approved the educational specifications as well as the final plans for two additional elementary schools. Ben's appointment as superintendent resulted with his being on the job for the ground breaking exercises during his first month in Hartland. Thus Mr. B. got to know this particular architect quite well during his first year as they worked together watching the construction of the two new schools.

During this period Ben felt a premonition that the architect was not the most honest man he had ever met. In fact, Ben thought of him as a sleazeball. As Ben, the school committee, the building committee, the architect and the other stage guests participated in the dedication of the completed building project at the end of his first year Ben quietly thanked his lucky stars knowing he no longer had to work with Moen E. Design, the architect.

Two years later the high school was so overcrowded that an immediate solution of running it on double sessions was necessary. The 9th and 10th graders were assigned to the afternoon session while the 11th and 12th graders attended high school classes in the morning from 6:45 A.M. till noon.

Mr. Bishop asked his school committee to approve his proposal to file the appropriate state papers to begin the task of building a new high school. The committee readily agreed to the timeline and to all of the steps necessary to gain state approval for the proposed school.

Gaining state approval had been easy, a lot of paperwork which resulted in a "well done" note scribbled on the official papers which included 72 percent funding from the state. Ben attended a city council meeting seeking their approval of the school construction project. The city by-laws noted that the city owned the schools. Once the school was built it would be turned over to the school department for occupancy. The school committee's acceptance of a school building always included the entire cost resulting therefrom. Whenever the school committee concluded its use of a school building then and only then did the responsibility for its future use or disposal become the city's responsibility. The city council asked Mr. Bishop if he planned to take the necessary land on which to build the proposed high school by eminent domain.

Everyone in the council chambers heard Ben's quiet "No." All present clearly recalled the grand opening of the new elementary school just a year ago. That school had been built on land taken by eminent domain. It's true, the owner had been paid appropriately for his land. But he had plans to use the land for a more profitable operation at a later date. His dreams of a luxurious future had been politically taken from him. On that September morning a year ago he had blocked the school buses from entering *my property*. He had stood in the parking lot with his shotgun aimed at the school bus driver. A call to the police had removed the estranged former land owner and as a result school opened a few minutes late.

The city council unanimously approved the superintendent's request with one condition—i.e., the school had to be built on the 150 acre Oversight Heights land in the north end of Hartland. Everyone in the hall knew the voters ultimately had to vote during a special election to authorize the bond to pay for the new high school. Although Ben didn't know all of the political obstacles the council was placing in his way, he was conscious of a few of their underground plans. Ben thanked the council for their positive vote and headed home.

Heather could read these politicians and thus alerted her husband to the roadblocks they had put in his path. Ben referred to the roadblocks as challenges. With Heather's quiet help at home advising her husband, Ben succeeded in getting the job done honorably.

Mr. B. drew up the educational specifications with the help of his teachers and administrators. The academic needs of the students and staff were carefully designed into the proposal. At this point in the project Ben was contacted by Moen E. Design. The city council president and two school committee members informed Mr. Bishop that they "expected" Moen E. to be the architect for the new high school.

Ben invited Moen E. to travel with him to New Jersey where an architectural display of the latest high school designs from the entire country were being exhibited. Ben figured a three-day trip with Moen E. would most likely expose Moen E.'s bad side. Ben had no intention of letting this unscrupulous man do any additional work for the Hartland school district while he served as the city's chief school administrator.

During the three-day Architects and High School design conference Ben and Moen E. discussed the educational specifications which Ben and his team had developed for Hartland's new high school. Moen E.'s constant attempts to force Ben to drop the design ideas of his academic team and to replace them with his simpler plans became a visible thorn in the superintendent's side. Moen E., thinking that he had finally convinced Ben to accept his lesser ideas due to his political connections whispered to his conference companion, "You can't get the high school built without me and the city solicitor, Mr. Meilaur."

During the long drive back to Hartland Ben asked Moen E. how he could be so confident about his ability to get the school built. He also asked Moen E. why he thought he (Ben) couldn't do it without him and the solicitor.

Moen E.'s response was exactly what Ben had suspected and was the reason he had just spent three days with him. Moen E. revealed that he had paid $20,000.00 in bribes to be appointed architect for the two elementary schools which had opened a year ago September.

"And . . ." he continued, "I have already paid out $50,000.00 of an agreed-upon $80,000.00 to the *Right People*. They have assured me that I'll be appointed architect for the new high school."

Ben's smile upon hearing this revelation hid his thoughts on the subject, "Over my dead body." Moen E. concluded his comments on the subject by noting that if another architect was hired, "He had the votes to stop the project!"

The next day while Ben sat at his desk disposing of routine matters he received a strange phone call. "Mr. Bishop, I hear that you want to build a new high school on the Oversight Heights land in Hartland. Is that correct?

Ben's "Yes" resulted in his being invited to a business luncheon in a hotel restaurant approximately 50 miles from Hartland. After Ben had heard several "facts" about the proposed building site, he readily agreed to have lunch with Noah Research of Research Properties, Limited, on the following Tuesday at noon.

During the three days Ben had been out of town with Moen E., the school committee had held an illegal meeting with the city attorney, Mr. Meilaur. Mrs. Goodnotes had informed her fellow committee members that the meeting was not a legal meeting as it hadn't been posted per the requisite seven days' notice rules for a public meeting, nor had the agenda for same been published. In spite of her protest the committee agreed to pay Meilaur at his usual hourly rate for up to 200 hours of work. He had been illegally employed to research and to resolve the property title(s) on the Oversight Heights land. The Oversight land had been agreed to (per the city council's directive) as the site for the new high school.

Mrs. Goodnotes complained about the legality of the meeting. Meilaur assured the committee that he was rushing to assist the committee in order to get the land free and clear so the new school could be built on it in the immediate future. Mrs. Goodnotes informed Benjamin about the meeting on the Monday prior to his luncheon meeting with Mr. Research. She had assumed the committee chairman had told Ben about the non press reported meeting immediately upon his return from Atlantic City.

Mr. Bishop and Noah Research had a most enjoyable lunch meeting! Their conversation lasted thru the entire afternoon. Ben called his office and asked his secretary to reschedule his late afternoon appointments for another day as he had a lot of work to do with Noah Research.

Later that day as Ben was driving home he thought about the many details of his enlightening meeting with Mr. Research. Noah had told Ben about the "quiet" schemes of Meilaur, the city attorney, two city councilors and one school committee member. The Slippery Four planned to get the deed to the Oversight Heights land for themselves. They hoped eventually to sell the land, dividing the anticipated $2,000,000.00 profit among the four of them. No taxes had ever been paid to the city in over one hundred years. Every time the assessors' office tried to take the land for non payment of taxes, Mr. Meilaur would declare that the many owners were almost impossible to track down. He always said that he would resolve the issue when he had "more time." Noah had translated this statement to mean that after Meilaur was out of public life for a year or two, he then would do the work and get the land for himself and his friends.

Noah assisted Ben in the development of a plan to get the land "free and clear" in order that the city could build its new high school on it. Although the city council had unanimously voted to build the high school on the Oversight Heights land, most of the councilors were convinced that it would never happen. Their vote was a sham! They had no intention of building a high school. Their vote had been "buying good faith" with the public. They clearly believed that the land could not be legally used.

It was six months until the public referendum on the new high school. Noah and Ben realized that timing was everything. Superintendent Bishop requested two simultaneous public meetings to be held at the Research Properties, Limited offices as a majority of the two committees worked in the area. The Slippery Four as well as the other committee members readily agreed to the requested joint council/school committee meeting(s) in Noah's office. The meeting thus was scheduled to take place at lunch time a week from Thursday. The press had been notified of the unique meeting and looked forward to the event.

On Thursday morning Ben personally called the seven school committee members and the nine city councilors to confirm their attendance at the noon meeting. Everyone said they would be there. Attorney Meilaur said that he also planned to be at the meeting. The table had been set! Noah looked like a 98-year-old man who should have retired 30 years ago. But Ben thought, *Whatever his age, his mind is as sharp as a tack.*

The city council meeting and the school committee meetings were called to order by their respective chairpersons. The meeting(s) were then turned over to Mr. Bishop. Mr. B. explained his needs to the two Hartland legislative bodies. The press was keenly alert as they "knew" something important was about to unfold.

Mr. Bishop detailed his "needs" to his audience.

"I have scheduled 22 architectural firms for interviews in order to find the best talent to build Hartland's new high school. These interviews will begin next week. I expect to have the building committee meet with the final four firms, to select the finalist and to appoint same by the end of this month. Further, we must be ready to ask the taxpayers to vote approval of this project in less than 23 weeks."

Ben turned his body ever so slightly toward his fellow conspirator, Noah Research and continued, "It would be insane on my part to ask the taxpayers for their support if I can't possibly get the Oversight Heights land *free and clear* to build the school on."

At this point Ben reminded his audience that the land had had no taxes paid on it for over 100 years.

"At best it will be difficult to find and to notify all of the owners and/or their heirs of these 150 acres. All had to be notified of the city's intent to buy their land. In some cases the heirs may not be able to be traced."

Ben asked Mr. Research if his firm could help resolve this pending issue before the two Hartland city governing bodies assembled in his office. As Noah began to respond to Mr. B.'s inquiry he was interrupted by Attorney Meilaur, who announced that the school committee had already contracted *him* to do the research that Mr. Bishop had just referred to.

He noted he had already spent 200 hours on the project and that he had hardly scratched the surface of identifying the original owners and their heirs. He projected he needed a year dedicated to just this project in order to trace the original purchaser(s) through to their current heirs. Meilaur concluded by saying, "It's an impossible task. In fact, I just sent my bill to Mr. Bishop's office for the first 200 hours of research along with a request for an additional 500 hours in an attempt to complete this most challenging task."

Meilaur began to inform the assembled group that it would probably take him two years to finish when Mr. Research insultingly asked, "Hey, My Law, show me the work you did to date."

Mr. Meilaur had hoped to kill the clock. He had expected

his friends to say that they had to return to work and as a result to close the meetings.

Meilaur reached into his briefcase, pulled out a stack of index cards and handed them to Noah Research. Due to the fact that press members were in attendance, Attorney Meilaur felt compelled to show his work product to Noah. After all he had just announced that he had completed 200 hours of research on the project and had billed the school dept. for the aforementioned work.

Noah's comment as he looked at the cards which Meilaur had just handed to him brought gasps of surprise and of outrage from almost everyone in the room.

"Why, Mr. My Law, you really haven't done even one hour of work! Have you? These work records are in *my* handwriting. They are just as they were when I gave them to you months ago. You didn't even scribble one note on them. You didn't even look at these cards. If you had, you would have at least turned them around and returned them to the original sequenced order, and then you would have recognized that most of the work is already completed."

As the crowd began to loudly argue with each other Ben shouted, "Mr. Research, can you finish this project in four months? Can you get the land free and clear and provide me with an insurance policy protecting Hartland in case one or more heirs isn't found? Can such a policy protect the city if the courts reclaim the land for a particular heir?"

Noah's "Yes" quieted the group. Noah announced that he would have the land free and clear and that he would provide the city with an insurance policy equal to the value of the land plus the cost of the new high school, so that Hartland could replace the school if said situation should occur.

Mr. Bishop asked the two public bodies to vote as per the agenda to approve the contract with Research Properties Limited, to affirm their earlier vote(s) approving the construction of the high school and to request the public to vote supporting the project upon the research firms completion of its work. The press reported two unanimous votes on the issues as listed on the meeting's agenda. Ben's final request of the school committee was, "To not pay Mr. Meilaur's bill for the 200 hours of work as submitted."

The committee voted to support Mr. B.'s request not to pay the Meilaur bill. The Mielaur vote as recorded was six "yes" and one "abstain." The meeting had lasted 90 minutes. To Ben it felt like six hours. Ben had discovered the true definition of hate!

The Slippery Four met that evening with Moen E. and graphically detailed the events of the luncheon meeting with the superintendent. Anticipating a "go" for the new high school, the FIVE plotted to make certain Moen E. became the project architect. After the group completed their first planning session on how to "milk" the construction project they headed home. They had lived through a very long and trying day. Yet they were convinced that Moen E. would be their answer.

Moen E. left the meeting a happy man. Moen E. knew how to add a few "inconsequential" bills into the $18 million project. He and his friends would enjoy a few "gifts" from the unsuspecting taxpayers and that brutally honest school superintendent. The five were convinced Mr. Bishop would never discover the inflated accounts.

The FIVE team met with the appropriate political leaders to "carefully" select the nine-member building committee and to make certain the building committee would have the power to appoint the architect.

One month later the city council appointed the building committee. The council, as advised by the city solicitor, Mr. Meilaur, unanimously voted giving the building committee the right and responsibility to appoint the project architect. The nine appointees met the following evening and elected Richard Sullivan, Hartland's Chamber of Commerce's president, as the building committee chairman.

The new committee proceeded to establish its operating procedures. Their rules were simple. The chairman could only vote to break a tie vote, a simple majority vote would be sufficient to appoint the architect and all nine members had to be present for the appointment. With these plans completed, the Team Five met and assessed their strength on the building Committee. The Slippery Four had been named to the committee. The nine committee members had elected Sullivan chairman because he was honest and as chair he could vote only to break a tie. They felt confident about their chances of controlling the meeting votes. Their immediate task was to find "one" of the other four building committee members to "join us" in their project of deceit.

Richard met with Ben to schedule the interviews. The two men were in agreement that Moen E. would not be the new high school architect. Ben's determined manner of doing everything legally and with integrity for the taxpayers, students and staff left no doubt in Richard's mind as to what would happen if Moen E. won the appointment.

Ben presented the four finalists to meet with the building committee as agreed. The committee voted in an attempt to make the appointment. Per the secret ballot process adopted by the committee, Ben passed out the paper ballots—one to each committee member.

Mr. B. instructed the nine voters to write the name of one architect of choice on the ballot. Ben proceeded to recommend the firm he believed would design the most academic and cost-efficient high school for the city. His recommended firm had won many honors for its designs at the Architecture and High School Designs conference.

Ben had numbered the four firms as 1, 2, 3, and 4. (His personal choice was #1; Moen E.'s firm was #4.)

Ben collected the ballots. He set Richard's aside as it was

only to be opened if the chair's vote was necessary to break a tie vote!

"Four votes for #1, four votes for #4," announced Ben.

As he started to open the chairman's ballot, Attorney Meilaur jumped up and shouted, "The first ballot reduced the field from four firms to two." Chairman Sullivan quickly agreed with Meilaur's demand. He then stated that the meeting was adjourned. The committee agreed to meet the following evening to select the architect to design and oversee the construction of the new high school.

When Ben arrived home after such a brief meeting, Heather knew he was clearly upset. She suggested to him that Richard probably had a good reason to delay the final decision. Ben phoned Richard shortly after Heather had calmed him, telling him to "Relax!"

Richard's, "I've been waiting for your call" response to Ben's "Good evening, Richard" was a pleasant surprise for Mr. B. Richard told his anxious friend to relax, to get a good night's sleep, etc. and he then said, "Good night, Ben. I'll see you tomorrow night."

The first vote, the next evening, was recorded as "four for #1, four for #4." The lead voice of the Slippery Four immediately announced that the first vote had simply been an affirmation of the two finalists. He then asked for a fifteen-minute recess.

During the declared recess Ben asked Richard about the new committee member. She was a woman whose family name had never been involved in city politics. One member had resigned from the committee a few minutes after the previous night's meeting due to the unique "pressures" of his job. He had confided in Richard as to what would happen to his day job if he didn't vote for Moen E. Richard had immediately accepted his resignation. Richard's first action of this day had been to ask the city council president to name a replacement committee member and to have same at this evening's meeting; thus, the new member. She had been introduced at the beginning of the meeting.

As Ben and Richard talked they were quite observant of the Slippery Four. The lead member felt that he, a "ladies man," should talk to the new team member. He knew he could talk her into voting for Moen E.

The meeting resumed 35 minutes later. Ben passed out a third set of ballots. He recommended that the committee members vote for #1. He collected the ballots and opened them one at a time. and announced the results: "Four votes for #1 and four votes for #4."

Ben opened the tie breaking ballot. and happily announced, "Five votes for #1."

The team Five were furious. Moen E. yelled from the spectators' seating area demanding a "Show of hands vote." At this point Ben realized that the Slippery Four's lead man firmly believed his visit with the new (woman) committee member had been successful. He "knew" she had voted with him for Moen E. The show of hands vote was demanded to discover the 'traitor' on the Slippery Four team. After all the money Moen E. had given the Slippery Four, he was determined to know who voted against him.

Finally Ben realized that Richard was enjoying himself. The public vote had the new member voting for #1 and all of the Slippery Four voting for #4. Ben congratulated the Western Mass. design team as the appointed architectural firm assigned to build the new high school. Ben had collected a few more political enemies. He laughed when later learned that Moen E. had spent the additional $30,000.00 to "win" his appointment as architect of record for the new high school. Not one of the recipients of Moen E.'s $80,000.00 ever returned one cent to him. The new Hartland High School opened two years later. The teachers and the public were thoroughly satisfied.

Peephole

Mr. Bishop was visiting with the Hartland High School principal in his office at the end of another school day. The two men were sharing war stories. After the exodus of the students and teachers, the two administrators decided to take a tour of the high school. Their intentions were to assess the needed repairs to be funded in the upcoming budget and to talk about an additional Art teacher. Cliff was keeping notes on the items the two agreed needed to be "rehab-ed" during the summer.

They completed their "walk around" and stopped in the teachers' room for a cold soda. Their plan was to take a quiet moment of relaxation before heading back to the central office for their 4:00 P.M. negotiations meeting.

Cliff, the compulsive neatnik, noticed the picture on the wall above the sofa was slanted at an angle to the ceiling. As he got up from his seat at the table and walked toward the wall, he commented quietly (almost to himself), "that picture has to be parallel to the floor/ceiling."

He tried to straighten the heavy framed painting three times, and each time he thought he had straightened it, "The Pride of Hartland" slipped down just enough to upset him.

Ben decided to help his friend. He had just reached the spot where he thought he could help when the painting came free from the wall. Fortunately the two men had a good grip on it. They gently lowered the heavy piece to the floor. Cliff started to say he'd get the maintenance staff to re-hang, it when he spotted the hole in the wall. The two men looked at the hole and asked each other, "How'd that happen?"

They were about to leave the teachers' room when a light suddenly shined through the hole. Both men stood on the couch and looked through the small hole. They hurried from the room and rushed into the boys' restroom adjacent to the teachers' room. The night custodian had just entered the restroom to clean it when he had noticed light coming from a small crack between two cement blocks on the wall back to back with the teachers' room. It had been his investigative flashlight which had caught the eyes of the two administrators. The three men rehung the painting and agreed to keep their discovery to themselves.

Cliff spent much of the next few days observing the teachers' room. On each occasion when only a single teacher was in the professional staff's lunch room he would step into the boys' restroom. On the third day just as everyone was headed back to class immediately after lunch, he noticed the light shining through the hole in the wall. A second later the lighted hole was darkened again. Cliff returned to the teacher's room and discovered Mr. Harvey "Know It All" Smith standing on the sofa squinting at the hole in the wall viewing the restroom. Cliff's incredulous, "What are you doing?" was enough to cause an embarrassed Mr. Smith to jump to the floor and to hastily declare that he was trying to catch the smokers in the restroom.

Harvey Smith's story did not convince his principal, Cliff. Harvey "Know It All" Smith stuck to his story of trying to catch the boys smoking by watching them light up via his peephole and then racing into the boys' room catching the kids "in the act." Via Cliff's gentle questioning Harvey's responses created a picture of a sick person. "Yes, I drilled the small hole in the teacher's room wall. Yes, it was carefully hidden by the painting. Yes, it was so located that the painting had to be moved (just slightly) to make the viewing hole accessible if the viewer stood on the couch. Yes, the hole in the boys' room looked like a crack." Harvey admitted that he had disguised the crack so that the hole wasn't really noticeable. Cliff called Mr. Bishop and together the two administrators assessed the situation. Cliff's research the next day produced the following conclusions. Firstly; No other adult, teacher or custodian knew about the existence of the hole. Secondly;

"Know It All" had never in his sixteen years as a teacher ever caught and turned in a smoker for disciplinary action.

The superintendent and the high school principal scheduled a meeting with the union president and Harvey Smith to discuss the situation and the decision of the two administrators.

The meeting began with Cliff presenting the facts as he had discovered them. The Peephole was shown to the union president as well as its method of use which was also clearly demonstrated. Mr. Bishop concluded the meeting by handing a letter to Mr. Smith and gave a copy to the union president informing Mr. Smith that he was being fired effective immediately. Harvey and the union president demanded a hearing be scheduled ASAP in order that Mr. Smith could be returned to work and not suffer the loss of a paycheck. The hearing was planned for the following Wednesday evening—four work days away.

The next morning (Friday) Cliff received two phone calls telling him that if he continued with his attempt to dismiss that *good teacher* both he and the superintendent would lose their jobs. The calls were not threats but merely statements of fact. The two callers had been the state senator and the state representative from the neighboring town. Ben called the chairman of his school committee and was told to drop the case against Mr. Smith. Ben's emphatic, "The hearing will not be canceled" didn't sit well with the chairman.

That evening, as Ben was telling Heather about the case and the pressure to keep Harvey as a teacher, the phone rang. The Governor wanted to see Mr. Bishop at 9:00 A.M. tomorrow (Saturday). Ben agreed to meet with the Governor for breakfast at a well known diner about an hour's drive from his home. Heather said, "Ben, fire that teacher, he doesn't belong in a school. I'd rather you lose your job than to know you would let that kind of a person work in a school district you are responsible for."

As Ben was driving to his breakfast meeting with the Governor, he kept saying to himself, "Wow, Heather says do the right thing even though we have five children and a large mortgage on our house." She had assured her husband that somehow they would survive. Ben entered the diner and was greeted by the Governor. His step was light as he proudly walked to his impending crisis because he carried the strength of his bride of 17 years in his heart.

The breakfast would have tasted better under other circumstances. The breakfast dishes were cleared from the table and the second cup of coffee had just been served when the Governor asked Ben for the details in the Harvey Smith case. Ben provided the Governor with most of the details of his case against Smith. The meeting concluded with the Governor clearly instructing Ben to, "Drop the case; Harvey was just trying to catch student smokers and if for some reason the hearing is held, then Harvey will continue as a teacher and *you*, Mr. Bishop, will be out looking for a job." Ben's farewell remarks to the Governor as the two men parted was an invitation to attend the hearing.

Right up to the night of the hearing, Ben and Cliff continued to receive threatening phone messages demanding the charges against Mr. Smith were to be dropped. The state department of education even called "suggesting" that Mr. Bishop reconsider his position in this matter.

The hearing began as scheduled. In attendance at the hearing were the seven school committee members, the superintendent, the high school principal, the union president, Harvey "Know It All" Smith, the union attorney, the governor's representative and three character witnesses for Mr. Smith. Cliff presented his findings from the accidental discovery of the hole in the wall through to his conclusion based upon the completion of his research. The union lawyer then asked Harvey to tell his story. When Mr. Smith finished his presentation the union lawyer asked the school committee to drop "these false charges" against his client. The committee chairman asked his committee for such a motion.

Ben shouted to the committee, "You will unanimously vote to fire Mr. Smith! No high school can knowingly support the continued employment of anyone who regularly sneaks looks at boys lined up at the urinals! Any questions?"

The union attorney immediately demanded that the school committee "gag" the superintendent. Mr. Meilaur readily agreed with the union's position to "gag" Mr. Bishop. The school committee chairman instructed the superintendent to either remain silent for the remainder of the hearing or be forcibly removed from the room. Ben's, "Fine, I'm on my way to the television studio to tell the public the facts in this case. The facts will include your vote to retain Smith! The television report will be live from the boys' restroom. I will be on the 11:00 o'clock news telling my story. I will ask the reporter to call each of you for your vote during the live broadcast."

Ben had just exited the meeting, slamming the door, when Mrs. Goodnotes yelled at her fellow committee members demanding them to stand up for the children and to unanimously vote to fire Mr. Smith. At this point the governor's representative hurried from the room and caught up with Ben as he started to back his car out of its parking spot. The Guv's rep asked Mr. Bishop to return to the meeting. After a 15-minute shouting match against Mrs. Goodnotes, Mr. Bishop and Principal Cliff by Mr. Meilaur and the committee chairman the call for the vote was made. The final vote was 7 "Yes" votes to fire Mr. Smith. Ben and Cliff left the meeting wondering when the ax of political wrath would fall.

Heather told her shaking husband that she was proud of him. However, Ben didn't sleep well that evening. On Friday morning the Commissioner of Education called Ben and asked him to testify against Harvey Smith in order that the state could recall Smith's teaching certificate. "After all, a man of this low behavior shouldn't teach anywhere." Ben reminded the Commish of his call two days earlier and hung up on him. It was eight months later when the political wrath of the losers would be played out against Ben and his supporters.

The Reference

Mr. Bishop was in his glory. His family knew he was enjoying himself. He talked about his math class every night at the supper table. Mr. B. had asked the math dept. chairperson to schedule him to teach a first period math class. She, with her principal's support had assigned him to teach the worst general math class in the building. The union president and the math chair had purposely selected the "poorest excuses" as students and had placed all of them into the class assigned to their boss. The union's plan was to sit back and watch as their superintendent failed as a teacher. The union knew that few teachers had succeeded with any of these kids. They enjoyed their mischievous scheduling of all the "happy kids" in one class. The principal had always split up these students to protect his teachers from having a major headache. Now he had them "all" assigned to Mr. Bishop. The math teachers were thrilled; they were looking forward to teaching an entire year with "good" students. The union expected the students to drive their new teacher out of the building, to make it obvious that he was a failure and to let him do it to himself publicly.

Every school day Ben looked forward to teaching his first period class. After he taught his math class he hastened to his office to work his regular administrative day, as well as the two or three evenings per week his job demanded.

Ben didn't learn of the plot to destroy him as a teacher until late March. By this time everyone realized that he was a most capable instructor. Several of the teacher conspirators encouraged a few kids in his class to act up and to take control of the class from their teacher. Two students attempted to "entertain" their teacher as well as their classmates. They quickly lost the contest of wills and minds to their teacher and apologized. In early April the union president demanded that the school committee instruct the superintendent to not teach the following September. The union told the school committee chairman that Mr. B. was teaching just to have an excuse to "watch" the teachers. Ben's gracious acceptance of the committee's request to not teach in the fall was reported in the local press. The story began with: LOCAL TEACHERS' UNION ASKS SCHOOL COMMITTEE TO TELL SUPERINTENDENT TO STOP TEACHING AS HE WAS DOING A BETTER JOB THAN THEY WERE.

Ben missed teaching that next school year. However, the union had lost face with many of the staff as a result of its failed plan. Ben's negotiating strength had markedly improved via the union's failure.

* * *

One day in late February of the next school year a student entered Mr. Bishop's office. Linda Swift had made an appointment thru Mr. B.'s secretary and had asked for at least an hour with him. Mr. Bishop had never met Linda before nor had she been in his class the previous year.

Linda told her strange story. Linda was an "A" student in most of her classes. She had a "B" in social studies at the end of the first semester. Linda had asked her social studies teacher to write a letter of reference for her as she planned to be a history major in college. Ms. Challenge had instructed Linda to stop by the next day to pick up a copy of the letter Ms. Challenge would be mailing to the college on her behalf. The next afternoon Ms. Challenge handed a copy of her reference letter to Linda. Linda read the letter and profusely thanked Ms. Challenge for the 'very nice' recommendation. A few days later her mother received a phone call from an old college friend. The friend had been her mother's roommate for the four years the two women had been students at State. The old roommate just *happened* to be the registrar at University and had just read Linda's reference letter from Ms. Challenge. After several minutes of reminiscing the former roommate suggested that Linda might want to major in another subject but definitely not in History.

Linda's mother read the copy of Ms. Challenge's letter to the registrar. After a lengthy silence the friend thought out loud suggesting that Linda and her mother might want to visit with her high school guidance counselor.

Linda and her mother innocently asked to see her college application file. Her counselor showed them Linda's file and suggested that Linda might want to reconsider the schools she was applying to. "Perhaps a state college would be easier for you."

At this moment Linda's shocked comment, "This is not my letter of reference. You made a mistake and placed another student's letter in my file" was heard.

Linda showed her counselor the letter Ms.. Challenge had given to her and made this comment, "Here, you may copy my reference letter and mail same to the university or I will do it for you."

After the counselor compared the two letters, she declared that although the two were about Linda, the one supporting her candidacy was not the one given to her by Ms. Challenge. "It is clear the letter Ms. Challenge has filed with your application strongly states you will not succeed at the university due to your 'extremely poor' study skills." Linda asked the guidance counselor to help her to resolve the situation and to have Ms. Challenge correct the problem she had created. The counselor said, "I cannot interfere in this situation. I have only one letter from Ms. Challenge and per her directions I sent it to the university. That letter is the reason you were denied acceptance at the university for next September."

Linda and her mother met with Ms. Challenge and asked her about the two differing letters. Ms. Challenge stated unequivocally that the two letters were, "The same." She steadfastly refused to do anything about the letters.

The high school principal, as requested by Linda and her mother, held a formal hearing on the issue. He conducted the meeting after informally trying to talk Ms. Challenge into selecting one of the two letters as her single reference letter. Ms. Challenge determinently stated the two letters were exactly the same. "True, I phrased the sentences using different words but the message contained in the two letters is exactly the same." The union grievance counselor and the union attorney caucused with their client for 30 minutes. When they returned to the conference room the union lawyer reported that Ms. Challenge was not going to change either letter as the two letters carried the same message.

The hearing was appealed by both the Swift family and the high school principal to the superintendent. Mr. Bishop hosted a hearing in his office in an attempt to resolve the matter. He listened to the presentations of Linda Swift and of Ms. Challenge. Ben read the two letters and concluded that the teacher had made a mistake. One letter supported Linda as a college student while the other letter recommended the college *not* accept Linda as a student in September. Ben's proposal to Ms. Challenge to pick one letter and to destroy the other to end this 'absurdity' was met with an angry cry, "The two letters are identical."

At this point Mr. Bishop declared that the two letters were significantly different and that he would no longer allow Ms. Challenge to teach classes of college-bound students. His reasoning was simple: "As long as you, Ms. Challenge cannot see the differences in the two letters which everyone else does, then I can no longer place you in a position where this type of a problem can reoccur."

The union appealed Mr. Bishop's ruling to the school committee. The committee ruled to reaffirm the superintendent's decision. Ms. Challenge filed suit against the school committee and the superintendent of schools. The union grievance chairperson stopped by to tell Mr. Bishop that their lawyer refused to carry this case to court as the two letters were clearly different.

Ms. Challenge had to pay out of her own pocket to cover the costs of the court case. Her new lawyer told Ben that he was charging her by the hour as she really had no case. When the judge opened the pretrial conference, he asked to see the two letters. Ms. Challenge handed copies of the two letters to the judge. He then asked Ms. Challenge for her views on the debated letters. After listening for 20 minutes he declared that any eighth grader could easily see that the two letters were entirely different. As Ms. Challenge began to argue with him, the judge instructed her to be silent. Then he closed the meeting with this comment, "The two letters are significantly different. There will be no court case. You, Ms. Challenge, should thank your lucky stars on the fact that Mr. Bishop was so kind to you. I think he should have fired you. No school can afford to have teachers that can't read!"

Phone Call

Ben arrived at his office with a cheerful "Good Morning" to his administrative staff. Naomi, his personal secretary asked him how he could arrive at work every day in such a happy frame of mind, "The pressure on you is horrific. Yet almost every day you greet all of us with a horrible joke or a pleasant comment about your family. How do you keep your sanity with all of that weight on your shoulders?"

After reading the day's headlines Ben understood Naomi's concern. The state newspaper had carried another front page story on the firing of Mr. Smith more than a week ago. This was the fourth story on the dismissal of Harvey "Know It All" Smith.

Ben's response to Naomi as to how he maintained his sanity was based upon his optimistic outlook on life. Mr. B. noted that there were over 200 million citizens in the United States and that none of the people in Chicago or in New York read these stories about Hartland politics. In fact he had concluded a long time ago that the 60 thousand copies of the newspaper carrying these half truths were available to less than three one-hundredths of one percent of the nation. Thus Ben concluded that if his problems didn't keep the remaining 99.97 percent in a tither then he figured he could keep his sanity as well.

As Ben completed his joke of the day the phone rang. Naomi's happy voice told her boss that a gentleman on the phone had a personal message for him. "No, he didn't give his name," responded Naomi.

Mr. Bishop picked up the phone at his secretary's desk and said, "Good morning." The voice on the phone stated that Mr.

Bishop would never know who was talking to him but that the superintendent might want to wander over to the high school and to drop in on the computerized payroll office. The suggestion was from a voice that Mr. Bishop recognized. As Ben continued to listen to the confidential "Never received" phone call he scribbled a note to Naomi asking her to please reschedule his morning as he would be out of the office until after lunch. Naomi hadn't heard her boss utter more than a few words during the five minutes he had been on the phone while standing next to her desk.

Ben drove over to the high school wondering what he was supposed to discover. He hoped it would be obvious as he wasn't a person accustomed to searching for wrongdoing. He reflected upon the city installing a new computer system in a vacant room in the high school. From the date of installation until now, thought Ben, the computer expert had been a problem. He did the school system's report cards four times a year. He also was responsible for the school dept. bi-weekly payroll as well as the city employee payroll. When he had been told to add the city employee payroll he asked for additional help. It seemed that every time the city or the school dept. asked for any extra reports he always said he couldn't get it done without extra help.

Ben entered the computer room. He immediately noticed eight men and two women seated in the classroom area of the computer center/payroll office. It appeared as if Joseph "I Need Additional Help" Base-two was teaching a class of adults. Mr. Base-two said "Good morning" to his boss. Ben responded by stating that he didn't plan to interfere with the class and Mr. Base-two was to continue with his work. During the awkward moment of silence that followed, Mr. Bishop noticed the computer printer spewing out pages of information. Ben stepped over to the printer and removed the last two pages along the perforated line. Base-two immediately snatched the printout from his boss' hands. The tension in the room was felt by everyone.

The ten business men and women realized that something was terribly wrong. Ben demanded Joseph return the papers he had just grabbed from his boss. He then told Mr. Base-two to carry on and to drop in for a visit at the end of the day.

Ben left the room with the two pages of the printout and returned to his office. After he read the incriminating pages he realized that the ten adult students were being trained by Mr. Base-two to program bank computers.

Mr. Bishop called a bank president friend, who was happy to note that two of his employees were students in Joe Base-two's class. Ben reluctantly but calmly learned that Base-two was training bank experts in the use of the computer in the financial world. Actually Joseph was "upgrading their computer skills."

"The seminar as conducted by Mr. Base-two was well worth the $3000.00 fee per person charged," reported the president to his friend. Ben then informed his service club friend, the bank president, that the class was being canceled at the end of this business day.

By the time Joseph arrived at Mr. B.'s office at 2:30 P.M. Ben had the entire story and the evidence illustrating Base-two was using school equipment and his school district paid time to do private work. Joseph was earning $30,000.00 four times a year teaching computer classes during school time! Ben handed Base-two a letter of dismissal effective immediately after he, Ben, had informed him of everything he had learned about his "computer seminars." Ben also told his former employee that he had canceled the remaining classes as of that afternoon. Joseph angrily left Mr. Bishop's office with a parting comment that he was a friend of Mr. Meilaur's and that Mr. Bishop had not heard the last on this subject. Ben's "Oh, by the way. I suggested to all of the bank presidents that they might want to contact you for a refund of the bank's monies," echoed in the room as Mr. Base-two slammed the door closed while uttering a four-letter word comment.

Naomi entered her boss' office and asked if today was just another day in the life of a superintendent of schools. Mr. B. calmed himself by telling his secretary his latest "in poor taste" joke.

Ben asked, "Naomi, what does a cannibal husband give his wife on Valentine's Day?" Naomi's, "I don't know. What?" received Ben's farewell comment of that day. "A box of Farmer's Fannies." With a good chuckle the hard day ended.

Coach(es)

Hartland's head football coach was loved by all. During Ben's first three years in Hartland all he ever heard was praise for Coach Football. One week prior to the annual turkey day classic, Heather answered a late night knock at the Bishops' front door. Ten varsity football team members asked to speak with Superintendent Bishop. Heather's, "Come right in boys" concerned her timid husband as all ten were bigger than he was. Heather seated the team in her spacious dining room and called her husband.

"Ben, you have guests in the . . . " Ben interrupted his wife and whispered, "Why did you let them in? They are bigger than I am!"

Heather knew her Ben was teasing her and that his whisper had been sufficiently loud enough for the boys to hear. Heather closed the door with a knowing smile that her Ben would do all he could to help his late night visitors.

The co-captain recited the team's story to the superintendent. All ten said they agreed with the co-captains' presentation of their problem. It seemed that Coach was about to let a junior bench warmer bump the Senior halfback for the entire Thanksgiving Day game. The junior had never played more than five minutes in any football season because he was not athletically coordinated. Ben's "I'll look in your problem on Friday morning," received a unanimous, "Coach is reacting to pressure. You've got to help him," response. The boys thanked Mrs. Bishop for the delicious cookies and milk. They happily reported to her that they "didn't hurt him."

Ben's visit with Coach Football on Friday morning caused

Coach to ask his boss if the halfback had cried foul to him. Ben replied that he hadn't talked to the halfback since the annual banquet of last June. At this point Coach closed his office door and proceeded to explain his problem to Mr. Bishop. The junior bench warmer was only on the team because his mother had threatened him (Coach) two years ago. She had informed him that her son *would* be on the varsity team!

Coach continued his story, explaining that the only game the Junior bench sitter had ever played in was during the last five minutes of a game Hartland was winning by four touchdowns. Coach finished his story by telling Mr. B. that Bench-Sitter's mother and father paid him a visit a few days earlier. They had told Coach their son would play the entire offensive game on Thanksgiving Day or . . .

Ben's "Or What?" received a startling response from Coach.

"They said that they would put a gun to my head immediately after the game if I failed to cooperate. I didn't tell you or the police as they had warned me not to do so—or else."

That afternoon, Ben held a meeting with the police chief, Coach, the high school principal, the school committee chairman, the city attorney, Bench-Sitter and his parents. The point was made quite clearly that Bench-Sitter would not only not play on Thanksgiving but that he was to turn in his uniform, etc., within the hour. Further, any accidents involving Coach, the principal or the superintendent would result in the arrest of Bench-Sitter and his parents for attempted murder.

On Saturday morning while Ben was waiting for Heather to finish her grocery shopping, a man standing behind Mr. Bishop quietly stated, "Don't turn around, I await Mrs.—'s orders." Ben turned around a moment later but couldn't guess which man of the five walking away had threatened him. His call to the police station resulted in a team of policemen and detectives being sent to Bench-Sitter's house. No one was home.

The Turkey Classic was played on Thursday morning as

scheduled. Hartland won the big game. Coach and Mr. Bishop were nervous wrecks. The family was eventually arrested and charged. Their lawyer apologized for the family with a "No harm was done" statement. The judge dropped the charges with a threat to Bench-Sitter's family to "Not bother Coach again."

Coach gave up coaching sports in early December. He moved to California after the close of the school year in early July. Three years later Coach called Mr. B. on the phone and asked if he (Mr. Bishop) would rehire him as a PE Teacher and as a JV coach. Ben's "Yes," was happily received.

* * *

Two years later Mr. Bishop informed his athletic director that he was suspending the varsity basketball coach for two weeks as a result of his three recent technical fouls. The refs, on each occasion had to ask security to remove Coach BB from the gym in three consecutive games. The next season Ben had to suspend Coach BB again. Ben attended most of the varsity home games every school year. During the period while Coach BB was suspended, people who Ben knew by name would sit behind him at every game he attended. Whenever Hartland was behind they would loudly ask, "Who's the idiot who put that character in to coach? We need Coach BB and we need him now."

Ben always turned around and responded to his critics and clearly, stated, "I did." Ben knew that Coach BB was using his friends to get *his* coaching job back. As the next school year began, the athletic director asked Mr. Bishop to give Coach BB one more chance to serve as head basketball coach for the upcoming season. The AD promised that Coach BB would never embarrass the team or the school again. Coach BB kept his word with respect to boys' basketball. The AD subsequently appointed Coach BB as the high school golf team's coach as a reward for his exemplary services as basketball coach.

Four years later the parents of a student athlete called and made an appointment to visit Mr. Bishop. The family had been in Hartland for two years. Their daughter, Shayla, was about to begin her senior year at Hartland High School. This last Tuesday in August meeting began with the usual pleasantries. After a brief but relaxed review of Shayla's successes in the high school the conversation took on an accusatory tone.

According to Shayla and her parents she had signed up for the golf team in late spring. After one week of summer practice (last week) Coach had wrapped his arms around Shayla in an attempt to adjust her golf swing. Shayla decided that Coach was getting too personal. Coach then informed her that either she would have sex with him or she could forget about ever being on the golf team. He also told her that he would deny asking for favors should the question ever come up.

Mr. Bishop's "Have you filed your complaint with the police?" received an immediate response, "Yes."

Shayla continued her story. The local police emphatically told her she was lying and had made up the story in order to get on the elite golf team. The offended family left the local police station and headed directly to the state police headquarters eleven miles out of town.

They then filed their complaint with the state police department. The family had been assured that their complaint would be turned over to the district attorney for prosecution.

Ben interrupted the one-sided conversation and said if the family was telling the truth that he would follow the case through to the bitter end. He asked his guests to stay and to "please listen to my conversation as he made a few calls."

Ben picked up his office phone and asked Naomi to get Attorney Hugh Practical on the line immediately. Hugh called back twenty minutes later. Ben instructed Hugh to call the state police unit and to assess if charges had been filed against the school dept. and its golf coach. He also asked Hugh to get a progress report on the case to date. Hugh was to inform the state police detectives that he and the Hartland School Superintendent would be involved in researching this matter, and if the details were as he had just been told, then they would be supporting Shayla and her family through to the conclusion.

Another twenty minutes before Attorney Practical called back to report on his research. Yes, the complaint had been filed and the case looked bad for the golf coach. It seemed that there had been many complaints about Coach over the years; at least six families had dropped their complaints over the past few years, but maybe Shayla and her family would actually go through the process? The state police detective had given Hugh most of the facts on the previous cases, as well as confirming Shayla's story. Hugh reported that the state police hoped Shayla would stand and fight.

Shayla and her parents said they would not retreat. "After all, I have a right to compete on a school team without having to buy team membership with my body!" Mr. Practical recited the other cases which had been filed and subsequently dropped by other high school students. These cases included teenage female virginity smashing by Coach, midnight pool parties, nude swimming and coed team showers (which of course included Coach).

Shayla and her parents left the superintendent's office knowing he had already scheduled a meeting with Coach and that he would act immediately to protect the Hartland High students. The family prayed that their request to have Coach removed from his golf team duties would happen before school reopened the following week.

Naomi typed a letter as dictated by Mr. Bishop, directing Coach to report to the superintendent's office for a meeting regarding allegations of his sexual misconduct as a golf coach. The letter was hand delivered to Coach.

Coach phoned Naomi and asked if the meeting could be held immediately. Ben readily agreed to host the meeting at 2:00

P.M. Ben had Naomi suggest to Coach that he might want to exercise his right to bring a union representative with him as the meeting might conclude with his being fired.

Coach arrived at exactly 2:00 o'clock. He assured his boss he didn't need union protection as he hadn't done anything wrong. The conversation between the two men lasted 30 minutes. Coach freely admitted to every accusation recited to Ben by Attorney Hugh Practical over the phone earlier that day. Coach blatantly informed his boss he couldn't do a thing about the complaint(s) as every accuser had always dropped her charges against him, and "Shayla will drop her charges against me in the next couple of days!"

The meeting ended with Mr. Bishop suspending Coach for 30 days with the intent to fire him pending the outcome of a hearing on the merits of the case. The hearing was to be scheduled within the 30-day suspension period. Coach's angry retort was heard as he was leaving the school dept. administration building, "You will lose this hearing and I will see to it that the school committee fires you!"

The hearing was held three weeks later. Ben and his attorney Hugh Practical presented their findings to the school committee. The committee chairperson asked Coach what the committee could do to help him, which brought an angry response from Mr. Bishop, "Your job is to protect the students—not a scumbag like Coach!"

The four "Yes" votes were sufficient to dismiss Coach. Later that evening Ben learned that the three "No" votes were from friends of Coach. The three "No" voters had known for several years that Coach had been "educating female athletes." Many teachers also knew about Coach's extracurricular activities, and most of the varsity basketball players were members of Coach BB's private club, The annual club meeting was always held immediately after graduation. A special award was always given to the male athlete who best emulated Coach

BB's high scores with the female athletes.

Six months later, the district attorney presented his case against Coach before the County Court. The judge's shocked comment to the school committee members' statement while seated in the witness chair under oath was quietly echoed by Ben and the six jurors. "You just testified under oath. You just testified that the only reason you didn't inform Mr. Bishop about Coach BB's crime against these female students was you knew the superintendent would fire him immediately!" The "Coach is my friend and a great coach" reply to the judge resulted with a directive to the district attorney to file charges against the three no-sayers as accessories in this case. Coach's firing by Mr. B. was unanimously upheld by the jury.

The state Department of Education refused to remove his teaching license. The charges against the three school committee members were subsequently dropped as a result of private negotiations between the judge and several "connected" lawyer friends. According to the "insiders" the local jail wasn't large enough to hold three committee members, several teachers, the varsity team members, plus a few other suspects." The "connected" lawyers didn't want the three committee members to name everyone who knew "Because it would destroy the town. Too many of our good citizens would be destroyed." Ben's "Ugh" said it all.

Ten Percent

"Good morning, Mr. Bishop," chanted the 26 fourth-graders in Sally Strict's classroom. "Good morning, boys and girls," responded Mr. B. as he was welcomed into Mrs. Strict's class. Ben usually scheduled one day per work week to begin with a classroom visitation. Sometimes this pleasant start of his day was not available to him as a result of the weight of his work load. Happily, this day he was able to enjoy a lighter moment before the challenges of his office caught up with him.

Sally had just finished her disciplinary talk with her mischievous student, Bernhart, and the class had just finished a story on frogs, etc., and of their living habits when Mrs. Strict asked "Bernie" to be quiet and to participate with his classmates. Bernhart responded by saying, "Sal, my name is Bernhart."

Mrs. Strict had just completed her "correcting" lecture to Bernhart when Mr. Bishop entered the room. Mrs. Strict attempted to return her students' minds back to the differences between frogs and toads. She called on Bernhart to tell the class and their guest what the differences were between a frog and a toad. Bernhart stood up and said, "Mrs. Strict, *you just toad us.*"

The class laughed at Bernhart's fresh remark. The room was quickly silenced when Mrs. Strict instructed Bernhart to, "Go to the principal's office now!" As Bernhart left the room, Mrs. Strict took a deep breath, calmed herself and continued with her class discussion of frogs, etc.

Twenty minutes later Ben left the class and headed back to his office so that he'd be on time for his meeting with the union president. He enjoyed repeating the story of Bernhart's response as to the differences between frogs and toads to Naomi. He entered his conference room chuckling as he repeated Bernhart's, "I just *toad* you."

The meeting began with the union president informing the city school superintendent that Hartland's teacher of the year was about to be named the state teacher of the year. Ben reminded his guest of his objections to having Maria Chestra named as the local teacher of the year. He asked the union president if she remembered the public hearing six months ago.

Ben continued by stating that Maria's complete lack of ethics was just the tip of the iceberg. The uproar resulting from Maria's comments during the hearing had been made by 26 teachers standing and shouting, "Maria, you know that is not true! Tell the truth," they shouted.

The union president completed Ben's story for him. "Maria didn't change her story that evening. The teachers had to correct the issues with the school committee. Afterward the teachers had forced Maria to step down as union president."

"Yes," said Ben, "You became the union president as a result of her deceitful actions. You kept that embarrassing incident out of the press. You own the press. I don't understand why you are using your political strength to name Maria as the state teacher of the year! Please be assured that when the state press asks for a statement from this superintendent about the teacher of the year my response will be as follows. Hartland has 446 teachers. Maria Chestra is ranked as teacher number 447. All 445 are better teachers than Maria. I would be pleased to accept her resignation anytime."

Ben picked up the phone and asked Naomi to get the commissioner on the line so that he could forewarn the commish about his finalist for the state teacher of the year award. Ben repeated his story to the Commissioner of Education about the state's finalist while his guest sat across the table from him. The next day Maria was listed as the first runner up and another teacher was named as the state's best teacher,

In spite of the difficulties Maria Chestra had generated during the past few years, she remained a school committee favorite. Maria was a federal grant writer/supervisor in the Middle school. Every year her project showed great results. The academic growth of her project students was always higher than any other group in the state. Because of the success of her project parents fought to have their children registered in one of her classes.

As the union president was leaving Mr. Bishop's office she said, "Good morning" to the superintendent's next visitor. She had no idea as to the name or occupation of the well-dressed gentleman awaiting his scheduled appointment.

Mr. Sleuth was a federal investigator from Washington, DC. Mr. Sleuth informed his host that the statistics of success by Maria Chestra's students were 99 percent impossible to achieve. The purpose of his visit was to examine her project records.

Ben phoned the middle school principal and told him that the federal auditor, Mr. Sleuth, was on his way to the school to review the federal project records. Mr. Sleuth was to be shown every courtesy and he was to be introduced to Maria before he started his research.

Maria happily gave Mr. Sleuth a tour of her work area and of her classroom. She introduced her staff to her guest. All proclaimed her program and their leader as *just the best!* As the coffee cups were being refilled, Mr. Sleuth asked to see the records of the previous three years. Maria proudly went over her program records, personally highlighting the statistics which illustrated the outstanding achievement of the students in her program. Mr. Sleuth retired to the conference room to study the documents given to him by Ms. Chestra.

Two hours later he asked Mr. Bishop to examine six pages he had removed from the heavy file he had been studying. The two men readily agreed that the papers in question looked like they had been tampered with. Each page appeared to have different numbers in the academic growth column than the adjacent test scores merited. The two reviewers also noticed that the signatures on each page had been changed as well!

At this point both Mr. Sleuth and the superintendent assumed someone other than Maria had doctored the records. When Mr. Sleuth asked Maria about the "erasures" she charmingly assured the federal auditor that she had made the corrections. She further informed her guest that she had also erased the signatures of her teachers on the six pages of statistics because, "Those teachers made too many mistakes." Maria went on at length in an attempt to prove her point. Mr. Sleuth became convinced Maria had "corrected" the reports to hide the projects' failure rates in order to continue receiving federal monies.

Mr. Sleuth asked Ben to schedule a meeting with Maria Chestra to discuss the reported program irregularities. Ben invited Maria and the union president to meet with the federal auditor and himself the next day after the school day had ended. The meeting concluded with Mr. Bishop giving Ms. Chestra 48 hours to resign. Maria clearly heard Mr. Bishop's, "Absent a letter of resignation on my desk at some time during the next two days, then you will be handed a letter of dismissal in the 49th hour."

Mr. Sleuth informed the group present that he was canceling the federal grant as of the 30th of the month. Since he had concluded the theft of the federal monies was solely due to the actions of Maria, he declared that the government would not ask for a return of the monies spent illegally to date.

During the 48-hour grace period Maria called her school committee friends and tearfully lied to them about the actions of Mr. Bishop in the issue at hand. The committee called an emergency meeting for the next evening. The chairman challenged Mr. Bishop to apologize to Maria and to direct the federal government to reinstate her program. Mr. Sleuth stood up and suggested an executive session might save the committee from "being charged with aiding and abetting a criminal in a federal matter."

The executive session ended with Maria's resignation being accepted with deep regret. Ben told the committee they were a disgrace to the city and its taxpayers and suggested that they should resign their school committee seats immediately. Not one resignation was submitted. In fact they all ran for re-election the following year.

Political Wrath

Ben reported to his office for a few minutes before he left for three days to serve as chairperson of a high school accreditation team. Naomi assured her boss that she would carefully take care of all the tasks he had left on her desk while he was away. She also was cognizant of his enjoyment assisting another group of teachers improve their working conditions and abilities to serve the students in their care. This was to be Mr. B.'s ninth visitation committee service for the New England Association. Ben was about to leave to travel the 150-plus miles to work with a team of 17 secondary educators who would examine the curriculum, staffing, finances and school facilities of the host high school, when the phone rang.

Naomi told Mr. Bishop a former student just wanted to say hello. Ben picked up the phone and happily heard that a math student of his was an ear, nose and throat surgeon. Reminiscing with Dr. Zane Owen about his enjoyable math classes of 18 years (maybe 23 years) ago gave Ben a bright and pleasant start to his day. Zane's farewell story was repeated in the office as with Ben's evaluation team in district X. Zane reminded his math teacher of one of his 'crummy' jokes he recalled from his algebra class.

Dr. Owen had been in the operating room working with a team of doctors and nurses removing a 35-year-old's cancerous tongue and throat tissue when he decided to lighten the atmosphere of his hospital's surgical suite.

Ben asked Zane if the poor patient had joined in the laughter with the hysterical surgeons working on him. Zane assured Mr. B. that the operation had been a success. Zane had asked his work team what it meant when someone states that his feet "smell" and that his nose "runs"! Their silent stares were rewarded with Dr. Zane commenting, "He must have been born upside down!!"

Ben began the meeting of his evaluation team with a reminder of their responsibilities to "X" High School, its staff, students and to the community. By the end of the second day every member of the visiting evaluation team reported to their section leaders about the 'Family" problems they had encountered.

Each visitor had to spend a minimum of twenty minutes in an average of seven classes and had met with the "X" High School teachers in a department meeting or two during their first two days on the job. They also were expected to research with the assistance of the local academic dept. chairpersons the strength of the curriculum, and the staff's professional readiness to present the approved academic program to the district's students. The third day was dedicated to the development of a rough draft for their final report as to 'X' High School meeting state standards and identifying the relative strengths and weaknesses of the curriculum, staffing, facilities etc. Visiting chairman Bishop's perusal of the district's records verified the research and concerns as expressed by his team.

At first the realization that 97 percent of the high school staff were all native "X" townies was enough to raise a few eyebrows. The discovery that the principal's wife was the guidance director generated a "Wow!" from several visiting team members. After Ben and his accreditation team assistant had finished reviewing the personnel files, the "X" High School staff became the focus point of the evaluation team's final day in "X" Town.

A careful listing of the staff and of their relationship to other teachers in the system along with the methods used to appoint new teachers over the previous 12 years clearly illustrated the obvious academic weak spots in the high school. When the central office was turned over to a new superintendent 12 years earlier, he decided to hire locals only. The few non-resident teachers hired during this period were to fill vacancies which could not be filled by a friend or relative from "X" Town. The "X" Town Super had appointed the Mayor's son as his assistant superintendent. The assistant super's daughter served as the high school assistant principal. Most of the high school staff were related by blood or marriage. All but one of the school committee's spouses worked in the district school system. At least one half of the staff had never been interviewed for their teaching assignments. They had received a phone call offering them the vacant job. In many cases no applications were on file for the employee. Two of the high school teachers had failed college courses in their major area of study. That fact startled the team members. "Teachers teaching the subject to high school students which they themselves hadn't passed in college!"

One teacher was listed as a permanent substitute because he couldn't get certified. He had been teaching in "X" Town for seven years. The "X" Town super informed Mr. Bishop when he was questioned about the sub that he expected him to get certified by the end of the next school year.

The three worst cases unearthed by the evaluation team during their staff visitations, conversations with the community representatives and with selected students generated a call for legal assistance.

The high school band instructor during his first ten years in " X" Town always selected a Junior girl to serve as his unit coordinator. By January of each of these ten years the coordinator and the teacher would be playing private sexual games in the instructor's office. After the fourth student became "involved" with him, his wife divorced him. The band leader was denied all visitation rights with his children as a result of his estranged wife's divorce filings. The band leader shortly thereafter married his 4th band coordinator. Two years later he was back to his old routine sexually "educating" his newest band coordinator, a Junior in the high school. No charges had ever been filed against the band director although federal and state laws very clearly dictated against such teacher/student relations.

The second teacher had been asked to stop giving her students the answers to the state's annual assessment test of eleventh graders. Yet every year a majority of her students received perfect test score awards from the state department of education. She was praised by her principal, the school superintendent and the school committee as an exemplary teacher. She was never asked a second time to cease and to desist.

The final staff rumor presented to several of Ben's visiting team members had been given only after each visitor promised not to identify his/her source(s). The source(s) had reported that the assistant superintendent of schools purchased drugs from a known student drug dealer. The story as told to the visitor(s) was that the assistant super would visit with his selected student pals in an empty room in the high school guidance suite. A member of the evaluation team had made an appointment to visit with the "X" Town police chief. She reported her findings to the chief. The chief s response to her, "No, I personally didn't observe a transaction," was a simple, "Then there isn't any case against him and I do not intend to hunt for one. Have a good day."

Ben and his team visited with two lawyers about their findings at "X" Town High School. The visitor's reaction(s) resulting from the attorney's legal advice was, "I now know what the 'X' In 'X' Town stands for—Xcuse, Xcuse, Xcuse." The evaluation team sent a report to the state attorney general's office. They also filed the original report with the high school accreditation offices. 'X' Town High School lost its national ranking as a result of a state review based upon the thorough work of Ben's visitation team.

While the team members were saying "goodbye" to each other, just before they headed out for their respective homes the "X" Town High School secretary entered the room to tell Mr.

Bishop he had an urgent phone call, Ben heard the final assessment of 'X' Town as he hurried to the principal's office to receive the important call. "The 'X' ers were truly born upside down. They were born with their brains in their feet. They are constantly walking on them!"

Mrs. Goodnotes' call to Ben was devastating. The Hartland School Committee had held an unscheduled, non-publicized school committee meeting at a friend's house in a neighboring town. Mrs. Goodnotes had attended in order to know what was happening. The assistant school superintendent and the seven school committee members met while their superintendent, Mr. Bishop, was out of town. The alleged purpose of the illegal meeting was to discuss, "the problems created in Hartland as a result of Mr. Bishop's services as school superintendent."

The committee agreed by a 4 "Yes" and a 3 "No" vote not to extend his contract for the next three years. The committee had also agreed to meet with Mr. Bishop the day after he returned home from 'X' Town. Ben thanked Mrs. Goodnotes for her call and positive support and agreed to meet with the full committee at 7:00 P.M. the following evening. With a saddened heart Ben drove home to tell his family of the new crisis in their lives.

The school committee voted at 7:10 P.M. to enter into executive session to discuss their illegal meeting with Mr. Bishop. Ben had argued pointedly about the wording of the resolution to enter into an executive session.

Behind closed doors the proverbial gloves came off. The angry three had talked one of the honest four into joining them to vote not to renew Ben's contract for another three years.

Three of the four who had voted to not renew reminded Mr. B. of his "wrongful deeds" during the previous nine years. Their complaints included the new high school (not stated—we lost the chance to make at least a million dollars on the land), the basketball coach (he was our friend and he frequently won the state championship game), the computer operations director (he was our friend and he shared his extra earnings with us), the payroll clerk (the extra names on the payroll were related to important people), the dismissal of the governor's nephew (so what if he used a secret peephole to watch boys in the restrooms) and not hiring the city's favorite architect (we lost our chance to make more money) etc. All of these issues were cited as the reason Mr. Bishop was being told to leave Hartland.

Ben told the full committee they were malicious and dishonest and that he would be proud to have his contract end if the committee had the guts to publicly cite their reasons for conducting an illegal meeting two days earlier, and the reasons they had just recited to him.

Ben finished his statement and walked out of the private session. He seated himself in the audience with the "good citizens" of Hartland. The citizens loudly applauded when the committee reassembled and asked Mr. Bishop to join them on the stage. Ben's "I'd rather sit with the honest citizenry of Hartland than be on the stage with dishonest school committee members."

The applause resulting from his refusal to sit with the committee was enough to quiet his pounding heart. The chair called for the vote not to renew the superintendent's contract beyond the first of July, The motion was defeated with 3 "Yes" votes and 4 "No" votes. The odd man who had changed his vote was wildly applauded by the audience. (Two years later there were four new school committee members and Mrs. Goodnotes was the chairperson. Hartland also had a new council president as well as a new city solicitor.)

Mr. Bishop stood up and recited to the audience the reasons the committee used to illustrate their unhappiness with his services. The facts listed noted his refusal to knowingly allow the committee to accept bribes or to use tax-raised money to fatten their friend's pockets. He also commented on the fact that the teacher dismissal cases he had won had improved the character of the school system. The committee apparently had no interest in the over 5 percent improvement of the system's achievement scores over the previous few years! The chairman called for a vote to extend Mr. Bishop's contract for another three years. The motion passed with 4 "Yes" votes and 3 "No" votes. The audience cheered. The ugly and painful meeting ended. An exhausted Mr. B. headed home.

The headlines of the morning edition of the *State Times* told a different story than the one as recorded by the school committee secretary during the previous evening. BISHOP OF HARTLAND IS FIRED sold many extra papers the following morning. The editor refused to print a correction for the next day's news. He pointedly stated, "The story behind the headline reported the facts of the two meetings and of the final outcome. Besides I (the editor) enjoyed writing that headline!"

Four months later Ben accepted an invitation to serve in a larger school district as their superintendent of schools.

Retired

On occasion Mr. B.'s services in his new school district were peppered with political weights for and/or against his initiatives. Two school committee members during an eleven-year period lost a considerable number of business accounts due to their personal support of school budget growth. One committee member actually voted against the politicians' directives, he voted for the approval of the education budget during the town meeting. The next morning he resigned from the school committee and he quit his job. One week later he and his family sold their home and headed West for a new beginning.

As the years passed, Ben and his family realized (knew) that the city and its elected representatives on the city council and the school committee were there to provide a good education for the city children albeit with limited budget growth.

During Ben's fourth month in his new job, he was surprised when his secretary told him a couple of old friends had dropped in to say "hello." (Ben's secretary had actually scheduled the appointment and had agreed not to list the names of his visitors on his appointment calendar.) When the Hartland School District union president, along with two other union reps, entered his office, Mr. Bishop was clearly speechless.

The guests from Hartland enjoyed reminiscing with their old boss. They reported on their new strength as teachers and proudly thanked Ben for turning their city around. The union president candidly told Mr. B. how the union had organized the public to support him (Ben) during his contract renewal meeting of a year ago.

The union president and his two friends proudly cited their leadership activities in organizing the school parents' organization to speak up during the subsequent city elections. The three men bragged about the new pride in Hartland now that the "what's in it for me" Politicians had been voted out of office. Ben's guests left after thanking him for his sacrifices on behalf of Hartland's students.

Two years later Mrs. Goodnotes called Ben and asked him to return to Hartland. Ben and Mrs. Goodnotes had a happy reunion over the phone. After Ben hung up his phone he sat and thought about her call and everything she had told him. He finally felt the pain ease from his spirit. During the evening dinner conversation with his family Ben said he believed Mrs. Goodnotes knew how much appreciated her call had been.

Mr. Bishop announced his retirement date on the first day of his tenth and final year in Great Hills. This year was to be his last year as an educator/businessman. He quietly watched as the "wanna be's" pushed and shoved to get the job. Fortunately for the Great Hills students and their families the committee found a candidate who believed in honesty, had educational foresight and was capable of functioning with the job pressures.

Mr. Bishop's retirement speech was a brief synopsis of his academic journey as he had lived it and, as he had shared his work life with his family at their dinner table. He proudly reported the percentages of increased achievement levels attained by the hard work of the city's professional staff during his years in town.

He concluded his remarks by noting the quiet strength he had been gifted with by his wife and children.

As he was leaving the stage Mr. B. announced that he intended to end his career as he had started it. He planned to take on the most important task in the universe. "I'm going to complete my career as a teacher—a MATH teacher, of course."

Author's Comment
Classroom Visits

As a first-year junior high principal in 1965 I was directed to visit at least twenty classes per month.

This was neither my idea nor plan as I contemplated my Ed-Ventures as a school principal. The decision had been made for the district by the school committee several years earlier. My boss, the superintendent of schools, let me know early on that I was expected to honor the teacher visitation mandate. I admit that as a former high school math teacher I had been observed only annually by my principal.

During my three years of twenty mandatory classroom visits per month I frequently began the fourth week finding it necessary to visit four or five classes per day. This last minute routine of mine created a hardship not only on the last minute principal (me) but also on my secretary. JB had to prepare two copies of my teacher commendations, one for the super and the other for the classroom professional.

In my fourth year as a school administrator, I had the privilege of serving as a high school principal. During these years, I continued to visit classrooms and to write a commendatory line or two to each staff member.

Ultimately as a school superintendent, I strongly encouraged the building principals I worked with to visit one classroom per school day. After thirty years as an educational administrator I continue to believe such classroom visits are one of the most beneficial services a building principal can add to his/her supportive role.

From my perspective the job of a school superintendent and that of a school principal is to be a knowledgeable academic leader dedicated to assisting his/her professional staff to teach in the best circumstances possible. I continue to believe teachers have the most important job on planet earth. Thus the educational administrator's task is to provide the district's teacher with the equipment, safety, training and professional/personal support necessary for them to succeed.

A school administrator who rarely enters a classroom or only visits to do the mandatory once a year or every other year evaluation is missing the opportunity to improve the learning for which he/she is responsible.

Further, a school administrator should retain his/her stature as an educator and refuse to allow the administrative title of principal or superintendent to convert him/her into a full time business person.

Most school administrators know what is happening in their schools and accept professional responsibility for same. But to truly *know*, rather than to function with hearsay opinions, one must visit every classroom more than once or twice a year.

I firmly believe a twenty-minute time period can be regularly scheduled into most of the headmasters' busy day(s) for the singular purpose of improving the learning curve in his/her school. Personally observed teaching provides the school administrator with strength of opinion necessary to improve the staff's services to the children in their care. Hearsay evidence does not provide the essential confidence to champion educational growth.